The Reiver's Cub

by

Laura Strickland

The Reiver's Cub

Cover Art by *Diana Carlile*

The Wild Rose Press, Inc.
PO Box 708
Adams Basin, NY 14410-0708
Visit us at www.thewildrosepress.com

Publishing History
First Tea Rose Edition, 2020
Trade Paperback ISBN 978-1-5092-3305-2
Digital ISBN 978-1-5092-3306-9

Published in the United States of America

Maxwell gave Callum no chance to reply. With a rattle, he set his helmet on the wooden settle that flanked the fireplace and quite deliberately laid his sword beside it.

"Surely, mistress, we can discuss this in a civilized fashion. Are we no' civilized folk, after all?"

She shifted her stance, the better to face him. Many were the stories she'd heard of this man over the years. On that day, the day she'd fled through those dark passageways with Dexter, she'd not seen his face. But she had an eyeful now, right enough.

Merciless, folk called him. Any account of his past deeds would also brand him so. But he did not look it.

He had a strong face with high, slanted cheekbones and a jaw clean of beard. He held his lips now in a half smile and kept his expression pleasant. But the dark brows hovered in an incipient scowl. A face like a rainy day, she decided—sunshine one moment and storm the next. His dark hair, very nearly black, surprisingly held a few threads of silver. And his eyes—

Ah, but he could not disguise the expression that lay there, and she beheld the truth of his reputation and, quite possibly, the origin of the name he'd been given. The eyes of a wolf they were, tawny gold and brimming with unfettered threat.

"Civilized?" she echoed incredulously, and her hand moved unpreventably to her dirk. "Both you and I, Master Maxwell, know that is not true."

Praise for Laura Strickland and...

***DEVIL BLACK*:**

"The setting is vivid. The characters are three dimensional. The plot takes so many turns it'll make you dizzy. The danger and intrigue in this story will have you biting your nails to the last page."

~*Sandra Dailey, Author*

~*~

"Laura Strickland is an excellent writer. She really brings the setting and the characters alive, and I'd like to read more about these characters or her next books. Laura Strickland is an author to watch. *DEVIL BLACK* is definitely a 5-star read."

~*Marilyn Baron, Author*

~*~

***HIS WICKED HIGHLAND WAYS*:**

"The historical detail and storyline meshed well. The characters resonated with me, and I felt what they felt. This one definitely goes in the 'will read again' pile."

~*Cocktails and Books Review*

Words and Dreams (sequel to *Forged by Love*)
Stars in the Morning
Awake on Garland Street
Christmastime on Donner's Mountain
Devil's Food Ripple with a Cherry on Top
Ask Me
A Walk on the Wylder Side
Guardians of Sherwood, Books 1-3
Daughter of Sherwood
Champion of Sherwood
Lord of Sherwood

Prologue

The Scottish Marches, Summer 1587

The battle in the hall could be heard all the way up in the highest bedchamber, where a woman lay in the bloodstained, rumpled sheets with a babe, new born, in her arms. Raised voices and a clatter of arms, wild shouts and sharp demand—it sounded as if an army of savages had breached the keep.

The woman had labored a day and night to deliver the child, her first. Weak and spent, she might lack the strength to stand, but she understood the meaning of that commotion all too well.

She drew in a sharp breath. "He is come."

"Impossible," whispered her companion, a younger woman who, alone, had shared the long vigil and helped bring the infant boy into the world. "It will be your brothers, returning from hunting."

The face of the woman in the bed twisted with distress and outrage. "Nay, Bess; it will be my brothers trying to repel him and his vile crew." Her eyes slid to her companion's face. "He will try and take from me what he bestowed by force."

As if to emphasize her words, the sounds from below grew still louder. Grunts and curses, the unmistakable clang of sword on sword—muffled thuds and footsteps.

The woman in the bed gathered herself. For an instant, she looked at the child in her arms before, with an almost violent gesture, she held him out to her companion.

"Here, take him."

"But—"

"Bess, you must do this for me. You must keep him from his father. It is no fate, for a boy to be raised by the likes of that. Hide yourself, hide him."

The second woman froze in dismay. "Hide? Where? How?"

"Use the door concealed behind the draperies. Go down the passage there and get the bairn away. Quickly! I can hear him already on the stairs."

Indeed, the sound of footsteps grew closer, cracking echoes from the stone. Through the stout, oaken door came sounds of fighting, much louder now, as if the intruders battled their way up step by step.

Bess took the infant into her arms even as she protested, "If he should search the room, find the passage, and come after—"

The woman in the bed met her terrified gaze. "You must keep him hidden, keep him safe. His father must no' be permitted to find him. Not ever, understand? Promise me, Bess."

"I do so promise."

Bess looked down at the child and cradled him more protectively. She ducked behind the curtains that screened one wall—no window there, but the door leading to a passage, cleverly concealed, that led through the stone walls of the keep and away.

She opened the door just wide enough so that she and the child could slip through. It gave way with a loud, rusty screech, fortunately lost when the door of the chamber also flew open.

A voice bellowed, wild and thick with rage, "Where is he?"

Bess, caught behind the draperies and afraid to close the door of the passageway, stiffened where she stood. The child in her arms chose that moment to mew weakly, the sound also lost when his mother spoke from the bed.

"Get out of my chamber."

"I think no'." Instead, the intruder came farther in; the woman holding the infant heard his step and the rattle of the weapons he wore. She laid her fingers lightly over the infant's mouth, and terror seized her by the throat.

She knew all too well who this man was—what he was. Reiver, rapist, enemy to the family of her dearest friend and of her own. Father of this child in her arms.

He spoke again, in a roar. "Where is my son?"

The woman's voice came in response, wondrously stronger. "There is no child."

"Lying bitch! The stink o' the birth is still on ye. Where is my son? Would ye hide him fro' me?"

Behind the draperies, Bess trembled, afraid to move and draw the intruder's attention. What might he do, if he heard the creak of the door? Follow her and the child down the dark passageways beyond?

Half paralyzed by fear, she peered out through a narrow gap in the draperies.

She'd seen him before, if only from a distance— Aleck Maxwell, he whom they called the Reiver Wolf. She'd heard much more of him, stories of raids he'd led across the border at the head of his band of savages.

Every English household within miles had reason to fear him. He stole all that could not be tied down—cattle, horses, plate, and coin.

He'd stolen something more as well, according to the woman in the bed—waylaid her, and plucked her maidenhead. The result lay even now in Bess's arms.

He looked much larger, and more frightening, up close. Surely topping six feet in height, he possessed a mane of wild, black hair and held a naked, bloodstained blade in his hand.

He moved like the creature after which he'd been named, lightly and with deliberation. He circled the bed where the helpless woman now sat, the bedclothes clutched to her breast.

Bess could not see his face, but she could see that of her friend, bright with courage and defiance. What did the reiver mean to do to her? And why did no one rush up the stairs to her rescue? Had he slain everyone in the hall? Nay, for she could still hear the sound of fighting from below. Did his men detain any likely rescuers?

"Where is my son?" the reiver bellowed again.

Something flickered in the woman's eyes. "Dead. He did no' survive the birth."

"Again, ye lie. 'Tis what ye do best."

"I swear it. 'Twas a hard birth. He came out still, and never breathed."

"Where, then, is his body? Show me."

"Gone. The midwife took it awa' so as not to distress me."

Midwife. There had been none—just the two of them, struggling and sweating, and praying.

The babe in the woman's arms stirred feebly. She

jiggled him and prayed much harder than she had that afternoon.

Do not let this monster find us, please.

"I do no' believe ye. Your tongue's as crooked as your soul. He is hidden here, somewhere."

"You are wrong! And what made you think 'twas a son?"

"We heard so, below." He gestured with the bloodied blade. "No one denied it, while I battled them."

The hidden woman bit her lip till it bled. Aye, she'd sent word below, as soon as the babe finally entered the world. The master here, father to the woman in the bed, and cousin to her own mother, had anxiously awaited news that his grandchild was born and his daughter survived. The Reiver Wolf must have arrived soon after.

The eyes of the woman in the bed narrowed to vicious slits. "If you ha' injured my father—"

"Aye, mistress?" He leaned over the bed. "What if I have?"

"I will make you pay."

He laughed, a harsh sound that contained genuine amusement, and started the hidden woman's heart to racing so hard, it made her feel sick.

What would he do, if he found the child? Steal him away? Keep him?

"The babe's still here. I ken it fine."

He caught the bedclothes with the bloody blade and cast them aside, revealing the woman's near-naked and equally bloody legs, along with the stained linen. Not satisfied with that, and apparently enraged, he moved about the room, looking behind the hangings at the head of the bed, opening chests and knocking over fixtures.

Soon—all too soon—he would look behind the draperies where the woman with the child hid. She breathed another prayer and stepped back into the passageway. Under cover of another crash from the chamber, she shoved the door shut. It closed with a protesting squeak.

The child in her arms whimpered. She murmured softly to him and, moving like a hare before the wolf, groped her way through the dark of the passageway, in full flight.

Chapter One

The Scottish borders, ten years later

The clamor from the forecourt rose all the way to the window of the solar and caught Bess Mowatt's attention. For an instant she froze, taken back through time, as if hearing the echo of an ill wind. Violently, she shook herself. She was not the woman she had been ten years ago.

She strode to the window, which stood open to the early summer afternoon. What she saw below made her smile. The lads—her lads—contested once again in mock battle. Indeed, she could scarce keep them from it, no matter how she tried. Now they clashed and tumbled together, very like a litter of puppies who'd just learned their sharp teeth had been made for biting. The blades in their hands might be blunted, but still they could inflict welts and bruises.

She'd better get down there before blood was drawn.

"Are they at it again?" asked Anne, who stood behind Bess holding a book of household accounts. The woman ran the keep, nestled in the Scottish borderland, like a well-ordered ship at sea. But gentle Anne had not been made for upheaval or strife, and she fretted over what Bess considered unimportant details.

What matter how many sacks of flour and casks of

dried fish they had in the cellar? Winter was a long way off, and Bess would far rather be down below with the lads, perhaps knocking a few heads together.

She glanced at Anne and encountered a pair of blue eyes as sharp as her own. Anne MacGregor might appear a demure widow, a woman of breeding with the fine manners Bess herself had shed. But steel lay beneath her soft exterior, along with a razor wit.

"Bess," she said now, "please do concentrate. Can you not afford me ten minutes of your attention?"

"They will slaughter one another if I do not go down."

"I trust they are merely playing. Anyway, is William not below?"

Bess stole another look out the window. The aged bailiff stood at one side of the melee, with his beefy arms crossed, grinning.

"Aye."

"He will surely stop them before things get out of hand."

"'Tis I am responsible for them." Especially for one of them. Bess's eyes isolated a dark head among the other shaggy ones. As she should have expected, he was at the center of things, quite likely having perpetrated the fray.

The blood of a wolf ran through that boy's veins, after all. That did not matter; over the past ten years he'd become Bess's lad, and love bade her guard him, even if duty did not.

Truth be told, all her lads came from warlike border families. Only one of them, though, was the reiver's cub.

"When is Callum due back?" Anne asked. "He can

show them some discipline."

"Callum's arrival is overdue." And in the back of Bess's mind, worry niggled at her because of it. The border marches lay in deep unrest. And Callum MacFee, brown-haired, even-tempered, and loyal to the heart, ran this school for boys along with Bess. He it was who undertook to board and train other men's sons, a foster system as old as Scotland itself. He it was who had taught Bess to fight.

Since Bess had moved here, the two of them had become close—like brother and sister, in truth. He was her rock, and her best friend.

The furor in the forecourt rose to a crescendo. One of the boys had got another down on his back, the thin blade to his throat.

Holy God, Bess thought. What would they tell the parent of a lad murdered by another while in her care? She did not wish to find out.

She hurried past the still-protesting Anne and flew down the stairs before she could think further on it. She burst into dazzling sunlight and the howls of the lads filled her ears. They sounded very like a pack of hounds that had trapped its prey, demanding blood.

She did not need to ask whom she'd see at the center of the throng. One dark head and one fair. 'Twas only a matter of which, this time, had got the upper hand.

William—the old rascal—started forward when he saw Bess, a look of mock concern coming to his face. She did not know how many times he'd told her they must let the dislike that existed between these two play out. They'd settle it eventually, the way pups in a litter did. One would emerge as leader, the other would accept it.

Trouble was, so far as Bess could see, they both carried the pack leader instinct. And much injury could occur before one of them won.

The watching lads parted to her hearty shoves. By that time, William had hauled both lads to their feet—one fair, as she'd guessed, and one dark.

Dexter—her Dexter—and Ronson MacNab. Ronson, who had a head of yellow curls that would do any lass proud and the narrow eyes of a feral cat, also had blood trickling down his face. Superficial wounds, she decided—at least his throat still appeared whole.

She turned her gaze on Dexter, who returned the stare with one of bland innocence. Oh, he was a rascal, sure enough, but she loved him right down to his bones.

He had his mother's blue eyes, the color of the sea on a summer's day, and her clear brow. Anyone who knew Mary as well as Bess once had would see her in him, even though his mother had but rarely seen the lad for more years than Bess could easily count.

Nay—ever since the day he'd been born, the day Bess took him in her arms and fled, he'd been hers.

None but a few knew his true identity—herself, Callum, and Mary's uncle Robert Lithgow, patriarch of the family. Not even William knew more than that the boy had been here forever.

All his life.

Now she inspected Dexter swiftly for injuries—a scrape to one cheek and a graze on each knee below the hem of his ragged kilt—and sighed with relief.

She addressed him, rather than Ronson. "What ha' I told you about fighting?"

Light filled the blue eyes and a grin parted his lips.

He tossed his wild, black head before he replied, "That 'tis my fate in life. I will be a mercenary, and earn my bread wi' my blade. So I'd damn sure better get good at it."

"I told you no such thing." Bess turned an accusing look on William, who had the grace to look abashed. William it was who filled the lad's head with ideas about hiring his sword.

"Bastard," whispered Ronson under his breath. Bess barely heard the word, but she knew then what had started the scuffle. And from the look in Dexter's sea-change eyes, it might well all break out again.

Bess interposed herself physically between the two lads. A tall woman, and well able to take care of herself, she realized with shock both lads had very nearly reached her height.

They grew like bracken in the spring.

She glared at each of them in turn. "What ha' I said about name-calling here among us? We are supposed to be comrades and friends."

She didn't need to hear William's snort to know that was a daft thing to say. She corrected herself hastily, "We are like family, are we not, if no' friends?"

A far better comparison. Family sniped at and argued with each other, but when trouble came, they stood together like a wall of stones. And heaven knew, in these border marches, there was always trouble enough.

Ronson jerked his tumbled, blond head at Dexter. "He is no kin o' mine."

Aye, and therein lay the problem. Upon arrival here at the keep, Bess had extended to Dexter her own last name, Mowatt, which implied he belonged to her family. Which he did, in a manner of speaking. But rumors, and some truth, got around. The lads who came here to train at arms asked questions, and very often made up their own answers.

She stared Ronson in the eyes, fiercely. "He is kin of mine. Do you ha' issue wi' that, Ronson MacNab?"

He dropped his gaze, just slowly enough to hint at insolence. "Nay, mistress." All of these lads, so she would have said, held her in some esteem. None of them yet wanted to take her on at arms. She'd trained hard with Callum and William both, since before some of them were born. She supposed the time would come when the lads would be able to best her in a contest at arms; not yet.

"Come," she urged. "Clasp hands like brothers."

Dexter hissed, precisely like a snake. Ronson's gaze came up once more and speared his opponent.

"Come," Bess repeated. "I will have none of this animosity between you. We stand together here, aye?"

Before either lad could reply, an interruption occurred. A clatter of hooves came from beyond the gate, which stood open on this fine afternoon, and a call to the guards echoed in a voice Bess recognized. *Ah, relief!* Callum had returned, if overdue. Let him help her school these two imps.

The knot of lads opened, and Bess looked up with a greeting on her lips. The words swiftly died. Callum had returned, aye, but not alone. A second man rode at his side, on a tall roan horse—someone Bess did not recognize. He sat his mount easily and held his head— one covered by a steel bonnet—with confidence. Ah, was this what had delayed Callum? Had he met someone along the road? A father, perhaps, looking for a place to send his son where he might train, safe out of the constant border warring?

For this place had long been off limits from attack, by tacit agreement of the lowland chiefs all round.

Quite likely this stranger had come to view the training center and decide whether he would pay to have his lad schooled here. From what little Bess could see, the man appeared the right age to have a fledgling lad.

And yet...Callum's eyes met hers across the forecourt in a look so grave it set her every instinct on edge.

And...what was this? Another rider entered the gates behind Callum and his guest...and another.

No ordinary visit, then.

Bess's hand flew to the dirk she wore at her side. Few in the borders ever went unarmed, and surely not she. Yet the riders continued to enter the yard behind one another, a strong company. How could this be?

She stepped forward from among the lads and stood braced to meet the new arrivals. The bright sunlight, suddenly merciless, made her squint as she sought Callum's face.

"Well come," she called to him, striving mightily to hide her alarm. "You are overdue. And who is this?"

The stranger at the head of the company gave Callum no chance to reply. Instead, he sketched a rough bow from horseback and said in a voice that rang through the yard, "Greetings, Mistress Mowatt. 'Tis pleased I am to make the acquaintance o' the famed warrior maiden of the marches."

He hauled off his helm, revealing a wealth of rough, tumbled black hair and a face that gleamed with glee, or perhaps victory. "I am Aleck Maxwell, the new owner of this keep."

Chapter Two

Bess wanted to fall through the stones of the forecourt. Moreover, she wanted to throw an arm around Dexter and draw him to her side in a gesture of pure protection. That, though, would be the worst thing she could do.

For the Reiver Wolf had come. Here. Now. The absolutely worst thing that could happen.

Hide my son, so Mary had said. Hide him in plain sight, so her uncle, Robert Lithgow, had agreed—secret the child like a needle in a haymow, among a crowd of other boys. Never, never let his father find him.

But now his father rode in through the gate with a party of one, two—six men behind him, and the devil himself could not look more terrifying.

"Impossible," she breathed. She switched her gaze to Callum's face and turned sick inside.

Callum had a calm, if handsome, countenance. When first she'd come to the keep with her charge, he'd been in residence with a young wife, awaiting the birth of his first child. His wife, Ellyn, had died not long after, in childbirth, and the bairn with her. Since then, he'd devoted himself to the lads here, even as did Bess. And, working together with a common cause, he and Bess had bonded.

Closely enough that now, despite his guarded expression, she could read his emotions—rueful and stricken. She saw, also, a hint of warning in his eyes that made her wonder how many more men might wait outside.

Aleck Maxwell, a Scottish border lord and a reiver of wide fame, might command a small army, if he so chose. The scion of a powerful family, he'd spent the years since Dexter's birth building both wealth and a fearsome reputation.

That didn't mean he could gain possession of Kellsbrough Keep. That belonged to Mary's family. They would never give it up.

William, the old soldier, had started forward with a naked blade in his hand. The last thing they needed, Bess decided, was bloodshed here in the forecourt with Bess's charges at risk.

She lifted a palm to William, effectively halting him, and addressed Callum rather than Maxwell.

"What is the meaning of this?"

Callum parted his lips to speak, but before he could, Maxwell swung down from his horse and engaged Bess's eyes. "Just wha' I say, mistress. I am the new owner, and I've come to tak' possession."

****

They withdrew to the hall, Bess shepherding the lads ahead of her in a messy flock. Most of them had been struck dumb—fortunately, for she knew how their tongues could wag.

Unfortunately, she also knew the size of their ears and did not particularly want them to hear the conversation to come. So when Anne swept down the stairs, a concerned look in her eyes, Bess bade her, "Pray, take the lads to the kitchen. They will need something to eat. William…" She turned to the old bailiff. "Please go with them." Guard them, she begged silently.

But William had his own ideas. He braced his feet and said, "Nay, mistress, I will stay here and learn the meaning o' this."

"William, please."

"I ha' overseen this keep since I were eighteen years old. All that while, it's belonged to the Mowatt family." He shot a barbed look at the tall man who walked by Callum's side. "Do you no' ken who he is?" He lowered his voice, without much effect. "The Reiver Wolf."

Maxwell smiled, a disconcerting action that managed to encompass both satisfaction and threat. "So they do call me. But be no' concerned. I intend ye no harm."

That, so Bess decided, staring at him hard, must be a lie not even a fool would believe.

Anne, taking over the role of sheepdog, swiftly hurried the boys—including Dexter—away. The lad shot Bess a look of concern over his shoulder. She strove to return it with one of reassurance, despite her own uneasiness.

William trailed the lads reluctantly. Likely he'd not go farther than the kitchen door.

She turned to face Callum and his companion.

Aleck Maxwell. Here. The last time she'd shared a space with the man, it had been at the stronghold of Mary's father, and he'd not known she was there. What awful twist of fate had brought him now?

"Callum?" she questioned.

But Maxwell gave Callum no chance to reply. With a rattle, he set his helmet on the wooden settle that flanked the fireplace and quite deliberately laid his sword beside it.

"Surely, mistress, we can discuss this in a civilized fashion. Are we no' civilized folk, after all?"

She shifted her stance, the better to face him. Many were the stories she'd heard of this man over the years. On that day, the day she'd fled through those dark passageways with Dexter, she'd not seen his face. But she had an eyeful now, right enough.

Merciless, folk called him. Any account of his past deeds would also brand him so. But he did not look it.

He had a strong face with high, slanted cheekbones and a jaw clean of beard. He held his lips now in a half smile and kept his expression pleasant. But the dark brows hovered in an incipient scowl. A face like a rainy day, she decided—sunshine one moment and storm the next. His dark hair, very nearly black, surprisingly held a few threads of silver. And his eyes—

Ah, but he could not disguise the expression that lay there, and she beheld the truth of his reputation and, quite possibly, the origin of the name he'd been given. The eyes of a wolf they were, tawny gold and brimming with unfettered threat.

"Civilized?" she echoed incredulously, and her hand moved unpreventably to her dirk. "Both you and I, Master Maxwell, know that is not true."

****

So she meant to draw a weapon on him, did she, this woman of whom he'd heard so much? Aye, and him having laid his sword aside in a show of good faith.

Aleck Maxwell eyed her carefully from the top of her head all the way down to her toes. Hair the color of dark honey, now braided and tightly confined, a brow turned tan by the sun—that made a change from all the women who seemed to want their skin white as that of a corpse—and a pair of militant eyes gray as a winter sky. Cold as one, also. A set of strong shoulders and a lithe, if spare, body clad in men's clothing. Ah, but no man with any red blood in his veins would stand fooled by that.

Indeed, he had heard much of her—the woman who trained lads at Kellsbrough Keep. Legendary she was. He hadn't expected her to be quite so young, or so beautiful.

"Bess," Callum MacFee said in warning. No fool, MacFee. He'd assessed the situation immediately when Aleck met up with him, carrying the writ that conveyed upon him ownership of this holding. Not a drop of blood spilt. He eyed the dirk in the woman's hand and silently corrected himself. At least, not yet.

Her nostrils flared. She demanded of Callum, "What is he doing here?"

MacFee said, "He has a paper signed by Robert Lithgow."

"Impossible," she breathed again.

Aleck drew the paper in question from within his leather jack. He had no idea whether or not she could read. Most women, in his experience, could not. Then again, most women could not fight with a sword, either.

He held the parchment out toward her, and she snatched it as if it might bite her. She unfolded and looked at it, but Aleck still could not tell whether she read what lay thereon.

MacFee said baldly, "Your uncle, Robert Lithgow, has died."

"What?" That made her eyes fly to MacFee's face.

"When?"

"A fortnight ago," Aleck replied.

"But no one sent word to us. And the last we heard he was hale and strong."

"An unfortunate occurrence. He took a sudden injury that poisoned. He died after only a few days."

Bess Mowatt raised her eyes to Aleck's face and echoed, "A sudden injury?"

"Aye. Before he died, he signed that paper to me."

"Why would he do such a thing? Your family and his have been enemies for time out o' mind."

Aleck shrugged. "Things change, mistress. New pressures come to play. Danhal Thomson and his cousins have banded together."

Bess gasped, as well she might. The Thomson clan, as notorious on the English side of the border as the Maxwells on the Scottish side, had long feuded among themselves. Now, though, if they had laid their private quarrels aside in order to better attack their enemies, without regard for which side of the border they occupied, it boded well for no one.

Aleck smiled at her. "Master Lithgow was convinced I am the man to keep this place safe. Thus he placed it in my hands before he died. Many men have much invested here—namely their offspring." He added blandly, "There is naught a man values more than his son."

Bess Mowatt stared at him. A dull flush rose to her face, and for an instant, an unnamed emotion flared in her eyes. Aleck smiled again, grimly this time.

Wildly she looked at MacFee. "Is this true?" she rattled the paper. "Can such a thing be?"

Deliberately misunderstanding her, Aleck said, "I

assure ye, mistress, I can defend Kellsbrough Keep, whatever the Thomsons throw at us. I ha' come wi' a small army at my back, and I am here to stay."

She swallowed down whatever words rested in her mouth. To misunderstand, she would need to be far less clever than Aleck judged her.

Chapter Three

"Callum, tell me this cannot possibly be true." Bess growled the words in a fierce undertone, so the intruder—now giving orders to his men in the forecourt—would not hear. She and Callum stood with their heads close together in front of the fireplace in the great hall, having retreated there in haste.

Without conscious thought, Bess seized Callum's sleeve, anchoring herself to this man who for so long had represented security in her world. She stared into his troubled brown eyes.

"'Twill need to be verified," Callum said. "I will have to travel to Linlith Castle and speak wi' Lithgow's people there. But, lass, the paper looks legitimate to me. It bears Lithgow's own seal. And when I met wi' him, Maxwell had a lawyer in attendance."

"How did you meet wi' him?"

Callum grimaced. "He waylaid me on my road back here." Callum had been away speaking with a man who'd asked them to accept his son for training. "After he intercepted me, he explained the situation, and insisted on the legality o' the paper."

Callum could read, if not well. Bess could read a few words, and scribe her name.

"This paper, it bears Lithgow's true seal and signature?"

"So far as I can tell, it does. It shall, as I say, need

to be verified."

"Why would Robert Lithgow do such a thing? Hand the keep over to one of his sworn enemies? Especially when he knows—knew—what lies here."

"Hush. It may be as Maxwell claims. The Thomsons are fearful, taken one after the other. Who might stand against them, do they come together?"

Who, indeed?

"Besides, was it not Lithgow who always said to hide our treasure in plain sight? Maxwell has no reason to believe it is here."

"If he sees De—"

"Do not. Do not even speak his name."

"He will surely know. They are enough alike."

"Not so much."

"The hair—"

"There are at least three lads here with black hair, and several more with fair, like—like *hers*. The greatest danger lies in one of us letting something slip."

"I will not," Bess vowed devoutly. "Yet having Maxwell here—"

"Is unsettling, aye, I ken. I like it no more than you. But he has come in a train, half a score strong. We are responsible for these lads. Were it to come to bloodshed, 'twould be on our heads."

"You are right, Callum. We must put the safety of the lads first."

"Always."

"But if Maxwell does not know the—the treasure is here, why would he agree to help his enemy, Lithgow?"

"For gain, of course. This is a valuable property, a plum, and thought never to change hands. 'Tis the opportunity of a lifetime for Maxwell."

Bess contemplated that. "Do you think he will toss us all out?"

Callum shrugged. "I do no' ken."

"We will need to send word to the lads' families. Some may wish to withdraw them. If they do, then—well, our cover will go with them."

"Aye. Let us worry about that when it happens. Our first task, as I see it, is to verify the endowment be true, and not some ruse on Maxwell's part."

Bess contemplated that also, and turned sick inside. It would mean Callum leaving her here, in charge, while he once more rode off. Ordinarily, that would not trouble her. Now it did.

"Did I hear my name?" with a clatter of boot soles on flagstone, the man himself strode into the hall with a second man at his side. Bess released Callum's sleeve and turned to meet Maxwell's stare.

He eyed her the way a fox might eye a plump grouse. "I hope, mistress, I do no' interrupt an important discussion. But I wanted to introduce ye to my cousin and right-hand man, who will be staying here along wi' us."

Cousin? Bess almost snorted aloud. Indeed, it might be said many who lived along the border marches could claim that connection. Relationships were old and complicated, and extended clear across the border. Was she not Mary's cousin, and hence Dexter's? And since Callum was also connected to Mary by blood, Bess shared a distant relationship with him. A virtual stew pot of kin, welcome or otherwise.

The man at Maxwell's side looked nothing like him. Instead, he appeared the very worst kind of reiver, rough and reckless. Lacking Maxwell's height, he made up for it in bulk of sheer muscle, and had a broad, ugly face, a bald head, and pale gray eyes. He fair bristled with weapons.

"Anald Robertson," Maxwell went on calmly, as if he did not introduce a feral beast into their civilized hall. "This is Mistress Bess Mowatt, and Callum MacFee, both o' whom do, to my understanding, run this fine school o' which we've all heard so much."

Robertson subjected Bess to an inspection that began at the crown of her head and moved downward, lingering at significant places along the way. A wide grin split his face. "Mistress Mowatt, an unforeseen pleasure. I do no' think I ha' ever seen a lass in trousers before. Be ye able to fight, or do ye merely dress the part?"

Bess returned his look with one of disdain. "Perhaps you would like to find out, Master Robertson."

"Ah, now, Anald," Maxwell spoke soothingly, "if the rumors be true, 'tis hersel' helps to train the lads. Had ye no' heard?"

"I had not." Anald eyed Bess anew and wetted his lips. "Though I confess, I would no' mind taking her on."

Bess's fingers once more flew to her dirk. "Any time you choose," she told him. "And just so you know, if you—if any of your men—harm as much as a freckle on any of those lads, you shall answer to me."

Anald pulled a face of mock injury. "And why should we be wanting to harm those fine lads? I ha' three boys of my own."

All fast learning to be reivers, no doubt, Bess thought. Though to be fair, did they not more or less school their own charges toward that same occupation?

Robertson took a step closer. "So, lass, how did ye learn to fight?"

"He taught me." Bess jerked her head at Callum. "So you might want to keep that in mind."

"The legendary Callum MacFee," Maxwell mused. "A man, so 'tis said, among a thousand."

"Ten thousand," Bess declared.

Maxwell said, "I wish Anald to meet everyone within the household. He will act as liaison between them and the rest of my men, if I am awa'."

Callum spoke quickly, "We cannot accommodate so many. Wi' all the boys in residence, we ha' no room."

"My men do no' require fancy accommodations. Do ye, Anald?"

Robertson grinned again. "A bivouac outside will suit me very well."

Maxwell appeared to muse. "We will need to meet all the lads also, to be on the safe side."

Bess's gaze flew to his. Did he know? Did he suspect? Callum might believe not, but she felt less certain, and the very idea turned her sick inside. If ever she lost Dexter, she could not go on.

But nay, she would not even allow that thought room in her mind.

Maxwell suddenly switched his gaze to something behind her and nodded. "Mistress."

Anne had come down the stairs that led from the solar, and entered the hall. Bess saw how pale she looked, her gentle face carefully blank and her hands clenched into tight fists.

Anne's beloved husband, Geoffrey, had been

murdered by ruffians just like these when their holding, on the English side of the border, came under attack. In hiding at the time, Anne had listened while he lost his life in her defense.

Bess could only imagine what it cost her to walk in among such men now.

Yet she noted how Anne's appearance and demeanor struck both men. A gentlewoman to her bones, she wore a dress of black and had confined her soft brown hair in a plain knot at the nape of her neck, yet her beauty shone.

She appeared, to every inch, the direct opposite of Bess with her dirty leathers and well-worn boots.

"Mistress Anne," Callum said, "is one of those in residence here." His voice softened. Bess knew full well Callum had feelings for Anne. But Anne had declared she would never risk her heart on another man after losing Geoffrey. "She plays mother to the lads, mends their hurts, and keeps us civilized."

"Ah, Mistress Anne," Maxwell acknowledged her. "Shall ye attempt to keep us civilized also?"

Anne answered in a voice that trembled but slightly. "Some things, I suspect, lie beyond my reach."

Anald Robertson snapped to attention, captured Anne's hand, and sketched a surprisingly gallant bow over it. "Mistress Anne, if anyone might tame me, I do no' doubt 'twould be a lady such as ye."

Anne's pale complexion flushed deep pink. She snatched her fingers away as if singed and looked at Maxwell. "How long do you expect to billet all these men here? It's just that we are used to our own ways, and the boys do not need the distraction."

Maxwell's face went carefully blank. "As to that,

mistress, I canna' say. I will need time enough to view my new holding, learn what is here, and secure it against marauders."

"Marauders?" Anne paled again, and dread flooded her eyes.

"Not to worry, mistress," Robertson said gallantly. "The Thomsons are, aye, on the rampage, having joined forces in an effort to spill more blood. But wi' us here, ye stand in no danger."

"Oh, sweet Jesu," Anne breathed. "Is that why you have come?"

"To secure the place," Maxwell reiterated. "And I do assure ye, mistress, we will do all we can, while here, to keep out o' your way and disrupt your life as little as possible."

Anne failed to look reassured, and Bess could not blame her. How should a gaggle of wild men escape notice? Their lives had all changed inexorably, and it turned her sick inside.

But that did not matter. Only keeping Dexter from the Reiver Wolf's notice truly mattered.

She'd do whatever she must to assure that.

Chapter Four

"I want no trouble, mind," Aleck told Anald over his breakfast the next morning. "Tell the men so, and mak' sure 'tis understood. None o' their usual shenanigans and no bloodshed, if we can help it."

"No bloodshed?" Anald repeated, like a child being told there would be no sweets. "Ah, Alexander, I do no' ken about that. They are a wild lot and enjoy their fun."

Aleck knew all too well the nature of a reiver's amusements. He narrowed his eyes at Anald, who sat bathed, very like an ugly cherub, in the dusty morning sunlight coming in the windows of the hall.

For the moment, they sat alone, most of the men having bivouacked and fed outside and the members of the household unsurprisingly absent.

His men liked to drink. They liked to steal, and they enjoyed breaking what they could not steal. They weren't above terrorizing a woman or two.

He said firmly, "I do no' want the lads here frightened."

"Why no'? 'Twould be good for them, help 'em grow a thick skin. Were we no' picked on when we were weans?"

"Mercilessly."

Anald regarded Aleck from gleaming, pale eyes. "Made ye strong, did it no'? Made ye ready to fight. Turned ye into the wolf y'are."

"Aye," Aleck acknowledged softly. "But these are other men's sons, entrusted here. Ye do no' harm a man's son, lest ye want a war the like o' which these marches have never seen."

Anald grunted his agreement, though he did not appear pleased. "They will be terrible soft, being raised up by yon MacFee and a woman."

"Do no' underestimate MacFee. He is one o' the best warriors in Scotland."

"What's he doin' here, then, training up pups instead o' out raiding?"

"There's a good living in it, plus a measure o' honor."

"Honor!" Anald laughed till he choked on his oatcake. "Who are ye to chase that?"

"I did no' say I chased it, merely that MacFee owns it. As for the woman—" Aleck stopped speaking abruptly as an image of Bess Mowatt flooded his mind. Hair the color of dark honey, a pair of stormy eyes, and a body that promised a battle royal between the sheets. By God, he'd never seen such a woman.

But he was not here for that.

To Anald he said, "Ye ken how good my instincts are."

Anald grunted again. "Uncanny, so they be."

Indeed, Aleck's gut feelings rarely steered him wrong. And ever since he'd walked into this keep, they'd clamored aloud. Nay, even before then, he'd known he should talk to old Lithgow, even as he'd known—or suspected—all these years what that bitch Mary told him in the tower room had been a lie.

His son might not be dead. Even though he'd searched for the last ten years and been unable to locate any stray lad who might be his own blood.

A flock of boys lived here, most of them the appropriate age—other men's sons, aye. And, perhaps, his own?

Impossible to tell yet. He'd never laid eyes on his lad—if, indeed, the boy lived. His son might look like him, or like his wretched, lying mother. Or like neither of them.

Aleck had to hope his instinct would tell him the truth of it, when he got closer to the lads, which he fully intended to do. Not even Anald, though, knew about his search. His longtime companion believed this effort all about the property, a right prize unto itself.

"That Mistress Anne, now," Anald mused. "There's a woman worth knowing."

Aleck eyed him sternly. "Ye must leave her alone, mind."

"Leave her alone? Why should I do that? She will be lonely, aye? In need of a bit o' gentle company."

Now Aleck snorted. "Ye ha' not qualified for the name 'gentle' since ye were a two-year wean."

Anald pressed his hand to his heart. "Ye wound me, so ye do. I could play at the gallant, for a woman like that."

"Let her be. She wants none o' us."

"And if the Thomsons come? She'll throw hersel' on my protection then, right enough."

"No doubt." Not that the Thomsons worried Aleck. Well, mayhap they worried him a bit. That Danhal Thomson was a murderous bastard even by border reiver standards, and his cousins not much better. The very thought of them joining forces made him wince.

As did the idea of those women being here with no

one but MacFee and the old soldier he'd seen, and all those lads to guard, should the Thomsons show up.

Forcefully, he told Anald, "We are here as guardians, naught more."

Anald emitted a rude sound, very like a fart. "Since when ha' we taken that role, guarding other men's sons?"

"Since I said so." Aleck jerked his head toward the door, now flooded with sunshine. "If ye do no' like it, ye are free to go. The same for any o' the men. Pass the word among them."

When Anald's gaze cooled, Aleck leaned toward him and said, "I ken fine there are no grand rewards here, such as the men are accustomed to earning. No plunder, no real chance for wealth, though they are still in my pay."

"And what o' loyalty?" Anald demanded indignantly. "I canna' believe ye would say that to me, and us friends from the age o' these lads."

Aleck relaxed a hair and smiled. "Loyalty among reivers, who'd as soon slit each other's throats as blink?"

"Loyalty between ye and me."

"Aye, so, and 'tis grateful to ye I am. Never doubt it."

The two men fell more peaceably silent. "I just hope," Anald said then, "ye ken what ye be doing, me lad."

****

"'Tis intolerable, entirely," said Bess, looking around the bailey—her bailey, by right if not by ownership. For ten years had she lived here and developed a proprietorship.

32

She could not believe Robert Lithgow had betrayed them this way, after offering a refuge to his niece's son for so long. It had been his idea to hide Dexter here, on the Scottish side of the border where his father would not expect to find him. Why would he now turn around and pass their keeping into the hands of that very man?

Had he gone mad at the time of his death?

Callum grunted in agreement and followed Bess's gaze. Maxwell's men appeared to be everywhere, guarding the gates, as might be expected, but also on the stairs that led into the keep proper, in a knot near the stable block, talking and sharing their breakfast on the walls. Two of them had even engaged some of the lads, reporting here for drilling, in conversation.

She asked Callum, "How am I to keep the lads away from them?" The boys led rather dull and isolated lives. The advent of a lot of well-versed and well-armed warriors drew them like hornets to a honey pot, or perhaps more accurately like flies to a midden.

"I do not think you can. Bess—"

She interrupted him by calling across the forecourt, "Geordie, Ronald—get to your drills!"

The boys moved away from the reivers reluctantly, and raised their practice weapons, facing one another.

Bess muttered a word no lady should speak. "The worst of it is, I will now have an audience while training them. These reivers will soon grow bored, with naught much to do."

With a touch on her arm, Callum turned her to face him. "I am sorry to abandon you wi' all this. But I must go to verify the details of Lithgow's passing—learn if what Maxwell says is true. I much mislike leaving you and Anne and the lads here as hostages, if he is lying through his teeth."

"Do you think he is?"

"To be honest wi' you, lass, I do no' ken. Men like Maxwell lie as readily as they breathe, and just look what his claim has already accomplished for him—he's ridden in here and taken possession o' this place without spilling a drop of blood."

"I know." Bess had not slept last night for thinking about it. Just the idea of so many strangers within the walls—her walls—made her skin crawl.

"Will you be all right," Callum asked unhappily, "with me gone?"

"I have William." A dubious comfort. The old campaigner might be tough as old boots, yet he was only one man, and, in fact, much aged.

"I am sorry, lass. This place has been off limits to raiders so long, given Robert Lithgow's reputation, I'd grown complacent. I should have been on guard."

"And should you have kept an army, to stave off so many?" Again, Bess eyed the men lounging around the forecourt. "When will you go to Linlith?"

"I should leave today."

Her gaze returned to him. Her heart sank so fast it turned her stomach. "Och, today?"

"Aye, lass. There's naught to be gained by waiting. If Maxwell's claim proves false, I will try to return wi' an army to rout him out."

"Where will you get an army?"

"Among the fathers o' these lads, if nowhere else."

Bess swallowed back her panic. "Aye. How long will you be gone?"

"Who can say? It may be as quick as a ride to Linlith and back. Longer, if I need to raise a troop of men."

But if he came back with a troop of men, he'd be attacking his own walls. Aye, and he'd have her, William, and all the lads aiding him from within.

She nodded.

"Will you be all right?" he asked yet again. "And Anne—given what she's endured, it sickens me, leaving her here with these savages in residence."

Bess lifted her chin. "You need not worry for my virtue, if that is what you are asking. And I will defend Anne with my life."

"That Robertson—"

"He is a scoundrel, and no mistake. I worry more, though, for the guarding of our treasure."

As if her thoughts had summoned him, Dexter came running up to them, with Jamie Hume in tow.

"Mistress Bess," Dexter began, "I was just talking to those men, who said—"

An immediate wave of dismay rose up and swamped Bess. "I do not want you speaking with them."

"But who are they? Why are they here? They say they will be staying." His eyes widened. "No one stays."

No one, save him. The lad's entire life had consisted of other folk coming and going, including others of the boys who finished their training and went back to their families.

Never had he asked why he alone stayed. Ah, well, Bess had been with him. And the bond between them just deepened.

"Listen to me, lads," Callum addressed both boys. "You are to keep awa' from these men as much as possible. They are here to exert a claim, and naught we can do about it unless I can prove it untrue. To that end, I maun leave to go speak wi' others, who will know the truth.

"You and the other lads must help keep the fortress safe while I am gone. That means doing all Mistress Bess and Mistress Anne and Master William say, eh? And no fighting amongst yourselves."

Both boys straightened their spines, and nodded solemnly.

But the gleam that appeared in Dexter's eyes frightened Bess to the bone.

Chapter Five

"I wish to speak to you. Come, Dexter, sit with me."

"Ah, Bess, we ha' already had a lecture before Master Callum rode out. Must I ha' another?" The lad called her "Bess" rather than "Mistress Bess" when they were alone. She didn't mind, since she stood in lieu of his mother.

"I am not going to lecture you." Warn him, perhaps, though aye, Callum had already tried to warn all the lads. In truth, she didn't know if she had the words for what she needed to say.

They sat on the ledge that fronted the keep. The sun had now moved and, it being afternoon, the stones of the building afforded some welcome shade. Most of Maxwell's men lounged about, having watched Callum ride off on his journey. They played at dice or, as best she could tell, gossiped.

Where Maxwell himself might be, she did not know. Indoors, she thought, with his particular crony, Robertson.

She told the lad, "I want to warn you about how dangerous these men be."

"So Master Callum said." Callum's lecture had been stern. He'd reiterated the lads should not associate in any way with the reivers.

But when it came to Dexter, Bess's heart remained

unsatisfied. The very idea of the man discovering Dexter's true identity rendered her breathless.

"I wanted to let you know their leader, Alexander Maxwell, is particularly dangerous."

"I ken. He is the Reiver Wolf. Everyone's heard of him. Geordie says there's no man in the marches can fight like him, and Ronson says—" He broke off abruptly. He would not echo his enemy even for the sake of good gossip.

"The man is a snake and not to be trusted. I do not want you speaking with him, understand?"

"Aye." Some of the fierce light faded from Dexter's eyes. "So Master Callum did say. But if Master Maxwell speaks to me directly, would it no' be rude to keep from answering him? You ha' taught me never to be rude."

Scamp, Bess thought. But she replied, "In this case, 'twould not be rude. You just say to him, 'Mistress Mowatt has forbidden me speaking with you.' If he has a quarrel with that, let him come to me."

Dexter inspected her carefully. "And if he challenges you to fight?"

"Then I will fight him."

The gleam returned to the lad's blue eyes. "But he is the finest fighter in the marches."

"Do you doubt me, lad?"

"Nay," he returned with flattering promptness. "But—"

"It is not your worry," she assured him, "but mine. I am here to stand for you, Dexter, as I always have."

He digested that in silence before he blurted, "But I do no' wish to see you injured."

"I will not be."

Dexter did not appear quite so convinced on this point.

"Should he press you, all you need to say is your name is Dexter Mowatt and you are son of my cousin, Edmund, being brought up here after his death." She had once had a cousin called Edmund, who'd been slain without leaving a son behind. The Mowatts were many—and included several branches, including that which had produced Dexter's mother. Maxwell should not question the assertion now.

"The truth, then," Dexter said. He'd been told he was Edmund Mowatt's son, even though Bess doubted he believed it entirely. The other lads called him bastard, more often than not, and he'd engaged in endless scuffles over it.

Dexter did not need to believe the tale. Just so long as Maxwell did.

"That is what you tell him." She nodded. "Understand?"

"To be sure. I am no' stupid."

Indeed, he was not. Sharp enough to cut himself sometimes, was Dexter—and that worried Bess.

"Just keep away from him if you can."

"Master William says the keep might come under attack."

She was going to throttle William.

"He says that is why these men ha' come—to defend us." Dexter's blue eyes engaged Bess's. "What do you think?"

"I am not certain. 'Tis what Maxwell claims. But he is not a truthful man. He may claim any number of things. That is why Master Callum has left us, to go learn what is true."

"Aye, so. I vow to ye, Bess, if that Reiver Wolf threatens you wi' any harm, I will see him straight."

She lifted her brows. "Will you, then?"

"Aye." He tossed his wild head. "Are you no' like a mother to me?"

Bess's heart promptly melted. An imp and a rascal, this lad might often be too impetuous and undisciplined for his own good, but she loved him to the very heart. And the bond they shared went deep.

She wanted desperately to hug him. But a number of the lads and Maxwell's men thronged the forecourt, and Dexter, liking to feel more man than lad, hated such displays.

Instead, she told him gravely, "Master Mowatt, your loyalty honors me."

He grinned, a boy's grin after all. Please God, she thought, keep Maxwell away from him. Above all, keep him safe.

****

Ah, Aleck thought as he exited the keep and paused on the stone steps that led down to the forecourt. He might indeed have trouble on his hands. He let his gaze rove over the heavily armed raiders lounging about, most of them already looking bored. How would he ever keep them occupied until the Thomsons came?

If they came. The keep did make a tempting reward, now Lithgow lay dead. And if he knew Danhal Thomson, the man would make a bid to seize the place just for the hell of it. To see if he could.

Aleck smiled ruefully. He could not say but he would do the same, in Thomson's place. Good thing he'd got here first.

Good thing Robert Lithgow had seen fit to set the

place in his hands.

Aleck thought of him lying on his death bed, sweating and groaning.

"Why ha' ye called for me?" Aleck had asked the man.

"Because I am dyin'. And you be the only man, the only man…"

Aleck had to wait for the pain to pass before Lithgow spoke again. He nearly sweated himself, in sympathy.

"You can defend them," Lithgow forced out.

"Who?"

"Those there, so dear to me. At Kellsbrough."

"Ye mean the lads? At the school?" The keep had achieved fame all through the borders—families on both sides vied to send their sons. Callum MacFee, a warrior without equal, trained them. Aye, and rumor said his assistant, a young woman, fought nearly as well as he.

"I ha' been thinking a lot, knowing I would die," Lithgow said, his gaze agonized. "Mayhap I ha' done wrong. There are bonds should no' be broken. Understand?"

Not sure he did, Aleck had said nothing.

"To men such as us, kin is everything."

"Aye."

"Besides, I would rather see the place in your hands than that bastard Danhal Thomson's. He will rape the women and the lads also. Promise…" Lithgow's hand came out and clasped Aleck's with unexpected strength. "Vow you will protect them. If you promise, I will deed the keep over to you—now, while still I draw breath. But you maun protect my niece, Bess, and all she holds dear."

Aleck had agreed. What else could he do? He wanted the keep, aye, and wanted even more what just might be hidden here. He'd also wanted to afford an agonized man a measure of peace.

Robert Lithgow had summoned his lawyer on the spot and signed the paper. Not an hour later, he passed.

Aleck drew a breath and narrowed his gaze on the forecourt. No room for sympathy and no time for regret. He must keep this place safe, and his men occupied.

"Seumas, Nelson—" he began, calling orders even as he descended the stairs, "get ye up off your arses and ride out. I want a patrol 'round this place day and night. The rest o' ye—form a hunting detail and finish setting up camp. This is no holiday."

The men gave him insolent looks and obeyed. As they began clearing off, Aleck noticed the woman and lad seated together over to one side, their heads—one honey-colored, one black—bent close to one another.

A spear of emotion passed through him, part curiosity and part longing. He swore even as he directed his feet toward them.

Nay, but 'twas not likely to be so easy as that. Fate would not simply present him with the prize.

Still, he eyed the lad with interest as he paused beside the pair.

A typical lad, some might say, with a grubby, angular face browned by the sun, and a tangle of dark hair that wanted to curl. Naught typical, though, in the warlike blue stare that met Aleck like a shield, flashing bright.

Are ye mine? Aleck asked silently, even before the

lad surged to his feet.

"I ken fine who you are," the boy said in a growl like that of a hound pup. "And you'll no' harm a hair on her head, lest you go through me."

Aleck's eyes, still searching for a resemblance, narrowed. *He does not look like me, save for that hair, and any number of lads might have dark, unruly hair. Does he look like her?*

Aloud, he asked, "Who am I, then?"

"The Reiver Wolf." The lad's expression wavered almost comically between fierce protectiveness and admiration. "You raid, pillage, and kill wi'out mercy. But you shall no' harm Mistress Mowatt."

"Dexter…" Bess Mowatt also got to her feet.

Dexter? What sort of name was that for a lad?

"I assure ye, pup, I ha' no intention of harming your Mistress Mowatt. How might I do so if I would, given ye as her defender?"

That made the boy's gaze narrow. "You mock me." His hand flew to the small dirk he wore, and the woman seized his arm.

"Dexter, pray go find William. Bring him here to me."

The lad looked torn. He wanted to obey the woman's request, but wanted also to maintain his fierce defensive stand.

"Peace," Aleck told him, as one warrior to another. "No harm will befall her whilst ye are awa'."

Dexter tossed his head. "To believe that, I would ha' to believe in your word."

"Believe it," bade the Reiver Wolf.

Chapter Six

"Dexter," Bess repeated sharply, her voice so choked with apprehension it didn't sound like her own. Her worst nightmare come to life, this. She had looked after this lad—guarded him with her every thought and action—from the moment he'd entered this world. She'd made sacrifices, aye. No family of her own, no real life to speak of, other than here at Kellsbrough Keep. But she loved this lad, and would not trade time spent with him for any number of riches.

Now, the Reiver Wolf stood there, danger in every particle of him, looking as if he wanted to eat her boy up. She reminded herself Alexander Maxwell had no reason to suppose his son was alive, much less residing here. By all that was holy, he had no cause to believe other than that his son had died at birth, as Mary Johnstone told him.

The greater part of the danger lay in her mind.

"Dexter," she spoke it in demand this time, and the lad looked at her. "Please go fetch William to me."

Dexter ran off, shooting one doubtful look back at the Reiver Wolf, and Bess strove mightily to disguise her relief.

"No need to chase the lad awa'," Maxwell said. "I will no' challenge him."

Did he look amused? Difficult to tell. He disguised his emotions far better than she suspected she managed to do, but Bess caught a flash of light in his odd, tawny eyes. He had a well-carved, canny face, handsome as that of the Devil, she had to allow. Strong cheekbones, an angular jaw, fierce dark brows, and a proud nose. A scruff of beard now covered his cheeks.

The sort to seduce a woman, he was, and treacherous with it. Though he'd not seduced poor Mary but raped her.

Still, a good thing Dexter had not inherited those eyes. There would be no hiding him then.

"It is my duty to keep these lads safe," she told Maxwell, "no matter the peril."

"Ye think me the sort o' man to harm a litter of young lads?" he returned evenly. His deep voice flowed like music, yet threatened like a honed dirk.

"Oh, aye. I think—know—you capable of all sorts."

Rather than take offense, he stared after Dexter, and asked the question that frightened her most of all. "Who is he?"

"Dexter Mowatt." She had to swallow the fear and unclench her fists before she went on. "The son of my cousin. Him being my blood, I feel protective."

"No need. Whatever ye believe o' me, I do no' attack children. But I will need to know the identities of their families."

"Why?"

"Because I am now as responsible as ye are for their safety." He gave her a grim smile.

"I would prefer their identities remain with Callum and me."

"Why?" he asked in turn.

"Because some, like Dexter, come from the

English side of the border and are the sons of your enemies. This, Master Maxwell, is a curious place, one like no other. The lads train here together. They may even form friendships. Later, they will return to their respective homes along the marches and perhaps, one day, be called upon to slit one another's throats."

"Using the skills ye and MacFee teach them."

"Aye."

His bright gaze searched her face. "Does that no' trouble ye, mistress, given your profound sense o' protectiveness?"

"At times, it does. But I like to think we turn out lads with a sense of moral responsibility, as well as skill at arms."

He laughed, a booming sound that brought heat to her cheeks and turned heads in the forecourt. "Would ye teach honor to the sons of reivers?"

"Why not?" She tossed her head. "Someone has to."

"Do ye no' suppose, mistress, such a sense might prove inconvenient to the men they shall become?"

"I do not, and neither should you. Would you not have me accept it is your honor has brought you here to help defend us?"

"And ye should be glad of it."

Bess did not feel glad. She would much rather take her chances against the dreaded Thomsons than allow this wolf within the gate.

William came hurrying up then with steel in his eyes and not one but three lads at his back. If the boys thought something interesting happened, there would be no keeping them away.

"You sent for me, mistress?" William raked

Maxwell with a look. "What is it?"

"Set the lads to drilling. They are not to expect an off day just because their world is turned upside down."

"Aye." William turned on his followers. "You heard your mistress. Run and fetch the others. And bring your weapons."

Maxwell smiled his ironic smile. "Shall ye, mistress, work wi' them also?"

"William will put them through their paces. Then I will take some of them on for individual training."

"Now, that," he rumbled, "I would like to see."

****

Aleck, with Anald for company, stood to one side of the courtyard, well out of the way, when the exercises began. He did not know what to expect. A lot of shouting and some wild hacking and flailing, maybe. Instead, the lads fell swiftly into order and put on an impressive display.

Aleck told himself he wanted an opportunity to lay eyes on all the boys, examine their faces, and determine if one of them could possibly be of his blood, his son. This made a better chance than he could have hoped. But he quickly became distracted by the skills he beheld.

Others of his men, those to which he had not given specific orders, drifted up to watch also. They soon fell silent.

All but Anald, who whistled between his teeth. "No wonder men vie to send their sons here."

Aleck nodded. And no wonder Robert Lithgow's dying concern had been to protect this place. Some magic lay here. A place where, as Mistress Mowatt said, these lads did not war against each other, at least

47

for a time.

The presence of the intruders distracted the boys, though. A few got right smart knocks because they watched the men instead of paying attention to their opponents, and blood started to flow.

Then Aleck became distracted in turn when, the common drills over, Bess Mowatt stepped into the fray.

He didn't know what he'd expected. Rumor had it she was almost as skilled as Callum MacFee, though he had trouble believing that of a woman. He'd thought she must play at being a warrior.

This, though, revealed no play. As soon as she stepped up to face the first of the lads, she changed, her body becoming as taut and deadly as the short sword in her hands. She feinted, she whirled, she stepped with precision—and grace. Her feet danced, and her hair, confined in a plait, swung out behind her.

The lads, no fools, faced her with caution. Some, near as tall as she and well-versed in their drills, seemed at first able to take her on. But possessing more speed, and being far more lithe, she touched them all.

Once touched, even lightly by her blade, each immediately fell back, allowing her time with another. With the youngest, she proved gentle yet unsparing.

Watching the display had an unwanted and unexpected effect on Aleck. He first felt a rush of admiration that swiftly transformed into something more. He imagined that taut, supple body beneath his own, all strength and heat, the passion that fueled her directed at him. And he grew hard where he stood.

When she faced Dexter, her young cousin, he fancied he saw the resemblance between them. Their movements, near mirrors of each other, proved pretty enough to prompt a smattering of cheers when they finished.

Mistress Mowatt gazed around as if surprised to see her audience. Aye, she'd lost herself in the artfulness of it, right enough.

Anald shot a knowing look at Aleck. "Now, there be a woman and a half, right enough. Might e'en be strong enough to tak' on the likes o' ye."

"I ha' no time for women." Aleck wished he dared adjust himself; he felt hard enough to split wood.

"True." Anald grinned. "But if ye did—"

The sky chose that moment to burst open and fling down rain, sharp as knives. Everyone hurried to the entrance of the keep, the lads scurrying ahead of Mistress Mowatt.

Just what I need, Aleck thought, to cool my unwanted heat. But as he and Anald also followed Mistress Mowatt, he could not keep from admiring the view.

Chapter Seven

"How long will Master Callum be gone?" Dexter repeated the question plaintively as he sat down by Bess's side.

"I am not certain," Bess told him, and sighed. Indeed, she wished she knew. Two days had passed since Callum's departure.

It seemed longer.

An impossible situation, and no mistake. The rain that interrupted their practice session out in the forecourt had moved in to stay. Wet darkened the stones of the keep, and banks of cloud cloaked every rise. When Bess looked out from the walls, she could see little beyond mist.

Thomson's whole raggedy crew might lurk out there, and she would not be able to tell.

Of course, Maxwell's men still patrolled despite the weather. Those she'd observed coming in to the hall while others went out appeared impervious to the wet.

She'd half expected Maxwell to ask if he might billet his men in the hall for the duration, but they continued to bivouac outside, coming in only for their meals, ale, and a turn by the fire.

Still, the lads suffered from the confinement and could not but run into the men who did come in. She'd tried drilling them there in the hall this morning, but found little enough room, given so many extra occupants.

Now she eyed Dexter severely. He must, indeed, be bored. He did not usually whine, nor did he follow her to the solar where she'd retreated to share Anne's company.

"Can you not keep yourself occupied?" she suggested.

"How?" he asked with justifiable annoyance. "You've forbidden me talk wi' Maxwell. And he's there—speaking wi' all the other lads."

"Is he?" Bess asked worriedly.

"Aye."

"He is teaching them some game at dice," Anne put in, not ceasing with her fine needlework. "Trying to keep them occupied, I suspect."

Bess narrowed her eyes. This whole situation worried her, aye, and Alexander Maxwell worried her most of all. Despite the many times she'd requested him not to, he did speak to the lads. She'd herself caught him at it, chatting in a casual way that drew them in. He and that rascal Anald Robertson, so often at his side— she trusted neither of them.

"Why did you not tell me?" she asked Anne, who shrugged.

"I thought you knew. It is difficult enough to miss aught that goes on, given we are like rats trapped all together in a sack. There is precious little privacy."

True enough. Robertson, on an apparent campaign to capture Anne's attention, had even followed her here to this sanctuary once or twice. The only places they had now to retreat were their bedchambers, and no one spent time there during the day.

Bess fixed Dexter with another stare. "Has Master

Maxwell attempted to speak with you?"

Dexter returned her look with one of blatant innocence. "I ha' been trying to keep awa' from him as you asked. But 'tis difficult. And"—a new gleam entered his eyes—"the men tell braw stories. Of battles and combats, and murder and blood."

Bess just bet they did.

"Why can I no' speak to them? Why can I no' sit and listen?"

Because I dare not risk letting him discover who you are. But Bess did not say that aloud.

Anne, bless her, answered the lad. "Such men, Dexter, are a poor influence. Mistress Bess does right to keep you away from them."

"But while I keep awa', the other lads are learning things I will never know."

Aye, and he misliked that, no question.

"To be fair, they do not speak only of blood and murder," Anne put in. "I also overheard part of a conversation about the troubles here at the borders, and the English Queen. Robertson has, supposedly, set eyes on her."

Dexter burst out, "He was telling us how very ugly she is."

"Ugly?" Bess repeated. "She is a queen."

"But he tells that she wears a vile white paste on her face that makes her look like she's been dead a fortnight. And her mind, so he says, is going—"

"Master Robertson spins a wealth of stories, so I perceive. And, my lad, how did you hear it all if you were not there?"

"I stood behind the door," Dexter confessed. "'Tis cruel to tell me I canna' listen."

Perhaps it was, but better than allowing Maxwell to become so well acquainted with this boy he started to wonder about him.

Still, something must be done. She needed to speak with Maxwell—again—and she had to find a better way to keep her boys occupied.

Aye, some if not all of their fathers would be livid if they knew she'd allowed them to sit about chatting with the likes of Alexander Maxwell and his men. Of course, some of their fathers were little different and certainly no better than Alexander Maxwell.

"Come, Dexter." She got to her feet. "We shall see about this."

The lad's eyes lit up. "We are going down to the hall?"

"We are."

****

Aleck's whole body came to attention when Bess and her young cousin entered the hall. Aleck liked the lad well enough—scrappy and bold, he was—but the boy's presence did not make every fiber of his body respond. He fixed his gaze on the woman with the honey-colored hair, and his heartbeat immediately elevated.

He did not understand what it was about her, just. Ah, well, he understood. After that display she'd put on in the forecourt the other day, none of the men could stop talking about her. A woman in a thousand, aye, but not the sort who usually made Aleck sit up and take notice.

He was standing now, however—every part of him. She had only to enter the room to achieve that.

And, most astounding of all, she did not even try.

The women of his past acquaintance—and granted, they had been surprisingly few—tended to make much of their appearances. They sought out fine fabrics for their gowns, they dressed their hair, whitened their already pale skin, and rouged their cheeks.

Not Bess Mowatt. She dressed in men's—or more precisely, lad's—clothing. She braided her hair, for the most part, or when not drilling, like today, let it hang down her back, undressed. She possessed few airs and graces. She did not simper but looked a man in the eye like—well, like an honest man.

And she had the power to wring him out like an old rag.

Was she beautiful? Cursed if he could say. Anald never stopped going on about the fair Anne, who even Aleck had to admit was bonny, though in a way that did not require artifice. Perhaps, he thought as he watched Bess cross the room, her strength and grace merely fascinated him.

Or perhaps 'twas that small, rounded bottom of hers, so well displayed in her trews. A glimpse of it never failed to make his hands tingle.

Ye fool, he chastised himself. She wants naught to do with ye, or ye with her. Have ye no' learned your lesson?

Aye, so he had. Mary Johnstone had taught him well that attraction made for a fine trap, and a beautiful woman—for Mary had been the most beautiful he'd ever seen—might disguise a cursed, lying bitch.

That reminder allowed him to fix a wry smile on his face before Bess Mowatt glanced at him. Her gaze slid over his face and on down his body where he lounged with his ankles crossed beside the hearth.

What was this, then? Had he captured her attention in turn? Or was that still distrust he saw in her eyes?

"Sit here beside me, mistress," called one of the men.

"Nay, here by me." Another, that rascal Charlie, patted his knee.

Bess gave him the kind of stare a queen might afford a peasant.

Unoffended, Charlie grinned. The other men all began clamoring together, making a game of it. Aleck saw the boy light up with indignation. Aye, the lad would fight to the death for her, if required.

His heart ached for a moment over the beauty of that. Did his son live, still? Had Mary Johnstone told him the truth of it, that terrible day up in the tower room? What would he not give for a bond with his own son such as Mistress Bess shared with her young cousin?

The trouble was, Mary had taught him all too well the cost of a liaison without benefit of marriage, and he'd not yet found a woman worth wedding. Difficult to do, while he avoided the breed.

But he could not avoid Mistress Bess, could he? They found themselves effectively tossed together here, and his body told him ignoring her would not be possible.

He unpropped himself from the wall. "Mistress Mowatt, I pray ye disregard these mannerless heathens. They would no' ken how to treat a lady were she borne in on a white mare."

Her stormy blue eyes returned to him in a glare. "And am I to suppose you do?"

The men hooted, ready for any diversion.

Before Aleck could speak, she dismissed him and called to the lads.

"Gather 'round me, now. I will not have you sitting about, engaging in idle gossip, hear?"

"No' gossip, mistress," protested one of the older lads. "Master Anald Robertson was telling us stories o' past battles."

"Was he, so?" Nostrils pinched, she treated Anald to one of her stares.

"Aye," spoke up another of the boys. "So we will be well prepared when the Thomsons storm the gates."

Anald lumbered to his feet, somewhat in the manner of a mountain stirring. "Think of me, mistress, as the voice o' experience for these lads."

"I am more likely to think of you as a right pest," she spat. "An uninvited guest who will not keep his opinions to himself."

Some of the men laughed. A few of the younger lads looked shocked.

Anald lifted conciliatory hands. "Ah, now, are we no' here for your benefit?"

"So you keep insisting. I have only your word for it." She jerked her head at Aleck. "And his, that the Thomsons have joined forces and have us in their sights. They have been warring among themselves as long as I can remember."

"That they have," Aleck rumbled. "But things change. Men, even angry ones, die, and distant cousins form new alliances."

"Meanwhile, I have you idling about here, disturbing my students."

Several of the men had the grace to look abashed at that. One or two got to their feet.

"But, lady," said Tommy Ogilvie, "we ha' men out on patrol despite the rain—"

She sneered at him. "Oh, and am I to suppose you frightened of a wee bit of rain? Great, stout warriors you must be."

Aleck cleared his throat, summoning her attention, and her anger. "If ye ha' a quarrel wi' the men, mistress, ye will talk to me. What would ye ha' them do, that they do not?"

"I would have them clear out from underfoot and return to their own homes."

He told her starkly, "This is my home."

Rage flowered in her eyes. "We shall see about that, will we not, when Callum returns?"

"Aye, so we will. Meanwhile, my men patrol the hills all round to keep ye and these lads safe. We hunt for food to feed ourselves so we will no' deplete your stores. If ye object to Anald's tales—"

"I do."

"Then he will stop telling them."

"Eh?" Anald croaked.

Several of the boys murmured protests, and Mistress Bess's nostrils flared.

She gazed around at them. "You are meant to be working, improving your skills so you may take your swords home to your fathers' service. Instead, I find you learning bad habits from the worst kind of men."

"Hey!" Even Aleck had to protest that.

"The sort," she went on inexorably, "who mistake derision for wit, and have no notion how to respect a woman if she carries a sword in her hand."

"Seems to me," Tommy spoke up again, a gleam in his eye, "'twould be the very best reason to respect her."

Bess turned on him. "Yet you hoot and you grin, and you show these lads the worst possible example." Suddenly, her short sword appeared in her hand. "Do you fear me?"

"Nay, mistress."

"Perhaps you should."

With those words, she had at him. Indeed, Tommy barely had time to come up out of his lounge and get his own weapon in his hand before she attacked.

A cry of protest rose to Aleck's lips. Tommy Ogilvie, a hulk of a man, would make two of Bess in weight and towered over her in height. One of Aleck's best warriors, he had a temper that matched his flaming red hair, and he did not know how to back down.

Indeed, Mistress Bess looked like a wasp taking on a bear. Yet after pushing Dexter out of the way, she did just that, and Aleck's protest died a swift death.

Tommy might be twice her size, but she was ten times quicker, light on her feet, and an ever-moving target. She darted, she danced, she made Tommy look the clumsy oaf, and drew blood three times while yet he stood looking confused.

The men hooted again, but with admiration this time. When Tommy stood looking like a steer beset by a particularly dangerous wolf, Aleck called a halt to it.

"Enough!"

Bess turned on him and waved her blade in his face. "Keep your men occupied and out of my hall," she warned, "or next time it will be you."

Chapter Eight

"A word, mistress, if ye do no' mind."

Bess Mowatt turned when Aleck spoke behind her, and her hair—a tumble of honeyed curls spilling down her narrow back, gleamed in the low light of the stone chamber.

A vixen she was, right enough, Aleck told himself—and one with dangerous claws, as proven by the way she'd handled poor Tommy. Knowing that, how could he let her make him feel this way?

Hot and cold by turns, tongue-tied—him, tongue-tied!—and with his fingers tingling to plunge into that hair, slew her around, bend her to his desire.

Desire? He must have gone mad if he thought he wanted this. Trouble was, he did not think. His mind warned him, and loudly, away from her. His body, though, responded to her helplessly.

What was he, a green lad to be overcome at a lass's presence?

"What is it you want?" she asked impatiently. *I am a busy woman*, her attitude declared. Indeed, he'd tracked her down in the armory—a cavernous place— where she sorted weapons.

He wondered that he dared approach her at all, in the vicinity of so many blades.

"I wished to speak wi' ye about what happened in the hall earlier."

She turned to face him fully and propped her hands on her hips. "What did happen, just?"

"Ye humiliated my man in front o' his companions."

She snorted. "I silenced a bully, more like—one who does not know how to pay respect, unless it comes armed."

She had done that, aye. But he could not let her see he agreed.

"He meant no harm. My men are rough around the edges. Ye, above anyone, should understand that."

She tipped her head, looking at him again in that way which both heated and chilled his blood. "Why do you say that, I wonder? Because I am, also, rough around the edges?"

"Nay, I did no' mean that."

"Especially for a woman?"

"Peace! God's teeth, ye be prickly. I meant only that your lads, as ye call them, come of men such as mine. And I imagine ye are trying to smooth some o' those edges, nay?"

She calmed a whit. "It is no use turning them out of here knowing how to use a blade and a pike yet thinking they can ride o'er everyone they meet and wrest by force what will not be given—especially," she repeated, "when it comes to women."

Before he could answer, she leaned toward him and lowered her voice to a growl. "Oh, aye, Alexander Maxwell, I know very well what you are."

"What am I?" he asked, in defiance of all wisdom.

"A reiver. A bully like the rest of your men. One who will take a woman against her will if she refuses to give in to you."

Aleck went cold. "Where did ye hear that of me?"

"Where do you suppose?"

His thoughts raced. He'd heard the stories—lies—Mary Johnstone had put about, stories of him. Did Bess listen to those lies? His mind, well-versed in the tangled relationships of the borders, sorted it out for him.

"Ye maun be her cousin, aye?"

"Whose cousin, pray?"

"Mary Johnstone. I will ha' ye know, all she said o' me was a lie. We encountered each other when out riding, see. 'Twas she who later sought me out, said we should arrange a tryst."

"Liar."

Aleck blinked at her. "I do no' lie, mistress."

"So you would have me believe she lied? She told me all, Master Maxwell. How you held her down, tore her clothing. How she wept when you hurt her, and you showed no mercy."

Aleck spoke an oath that should reach no lady's ears. "Not true. We met for weeks in secret, because her father would ha' had her whipped if he found out."

"Liar!" she cried again, and bared her teeth. "Mary was my closest friend when we were young. She has her faults, aye, but she would not lie about such a thing. And you, sir, have a reputation."

Aye, he did, and he'd worked hard to earn it—a fierce reiver, merciless with his enemies but not with those weaker than himself. Especially women.

It crossed his mind this woman might not be weaker than him. He'd never met anyone like her, and he did not begin to know how to deal with her.

"Whatever Mary told ye," he stated in a tone like flint, "I did no' force her. I ha' ne'er forced a woman and ne'er will."

Her gaze flicked over him, weighing and assessing in a manner that had his cold blood sizzling once again. She tossed her head. "I suppose you'd claim to have no need? That women just fall into your hands. Even Mary, one of the bonniest women ever to grace the marches."

"Mary may be bonny, aye." As well as a deceitful shrew with a temper that sought its outlet in spite rather than honest anger. Anyway, gazing into Bess Mowatt's face, he wondered how he'd ever thought Mary, with her rouged cheeks and simpering smiles, attractive.

"She wed wi' Michael Cunningham after," he went on, "and happy enough, so I heard."

"'Twas an alliance arranged by her father and not for love." Bess added, "And that was two marriages ago."

Aleck shrugged. In his experience, few enough folk wed for love. Marriage solidified bonds; it was an advantageous agreement. Love came in stolen moments, fleeting as desire itself—like to those he'd shared with Mary some ten years ago. Though, if he'd ever thought he loved Mary, he was sadly mistaken.

Bess admitted, "I have not seen her in years. Following the grief you did cause her, and the end of her first marriage, we lost touch, for the most part."

"The grief I caused her?"

"The rape," Bess insisted starkly, still not convinced. Something kindled in her eyes. "The death of her babe."

Aleck felt a rush of disappointment. "He did die, then, at birth? I had it in my mind she might ha' lied about that also."

"What woman would lie about such a thing?"

Aye, indeed. Even Mary Johnstone would not prove so heartless.

"I hear she has other children."

"Aye. Two daughters and a son."

Aleck supposed it would become easier to dismiss one child when you had others. He had no such other issue. But if Bess said his son had died at birth, none of the boys here could be his, after all.

A cruel fancy, that had been. Then why did his heart refuse to leave go of it? 'Twas as if something inside him knew his son still existed, somewhere in the world.

He drew a breath. "Mistress Mowatt, I sought ye out to ask whether we might no' strike a manner of truce. I and my men are here for the foreseeable future. We are here to the benefit o' ye and those lads. Embarrassing my men in contests and with displays of temper will accomplish naught."

"Display of temper?" she repeated indignantly.

"Aye, such as we had earlier today. I understand our arrival has turned your life upside down."

"It is not my life that concerns me but those of my lads."

Aleck resumed patiently, "We ha' disrupted their lives and their lessons, aye. Henceforth I will do my best to keep the men occupied and out o' your way. Yet ye might consider us a valuable resource, an opportunity for those lads to see how real men fight."

"Real men? Are you suggesting Callum MacFee is not that?"

"Never. MacFee is legendary. But the men would also work wi' the lads, if you'd permit. Many o' them have sons—"

"I will not permit that."

"—and would find it no hardship—"

"I will not permit it. Now excuse me, Master Maxwell. You are taking up my time."

Royally slapped down, Aleck stepped back a step. "Ah, I ha' no wish to do that."

"Then, pray, keep out of my way. And aye, keep your men away from my lads. They are naught but a bad influence."

Aleck gave her a polite bow and took himself off, his only available course of action. Back in the hall, he gathered up those of his men who still lingered and bade them, "Come. We will ride out."

"But," one of them protested, "the patrol has already gone."

"We will double the patrols, henceforth. I want naught to move in this country but we know about it."

They grumbled but came with him. Outside, great rafts of gray cloud lowered overhead, and the rain still pissed down, persistent and penetrating.

It felt almost good to Aleck when he mounted up, though he fancied steam rose from his heated flesh as it cooled.

That woman—as aggravating as she was attractive. Was there naught he could say would placate her? Naught he could do to make her look at him favorably? He feared not, and why did he even care? She believed the worst of him and looked to hold fast to her conviction that he'd forced Mary. His lip curled as he recalled how Mary had thrown herself at him, crawled all over him, practiced wiles unnecessary at the time. He'd been ready for her, aye—he'd been eighteen years old and went through life pre-primed. But the babe he'd put in her belly had been conceived by her desire as much as his.

Anald nudged his horse up beside Aleck's and peered into his face. "Now, what does that great frown warrant, I wonder. Ye maun be thinking about a woman."

"I am thinking what a curse they be upon this world." And a delight. It had been far too long since he'd run his hands over a woman's velvet skin, fused his lips to hers, and buried himself in her heat. That and nothing else explained his attraction to Bess Mowatt. He needed to get her out of his head, cease thinking about her.

"Can ye believe how that wee lass served Tommy, right and proper?" Anald chuckled, raising the one topic Aleck wanted left alone. "The look on his face was worth a gold sovereign."

"I do no' want to talk about her."

Anald slanted an interested look at him. "I fancy ye do no' want the rest o' the men talking of her, either. Ah, lad, I see the way ye come to attention when she enters the room."

Aleck swore, a curse ripe with bitterness. "We are no' here for that. And I do no' need the distraction."

"None o' us needs it. But who can say when or where love will strike?"

"Love." Aleck snorted. "I'll ha' no truck wi' that. I am no' certain I even believe in it."

"No' believe in love?" Anald pretended at outrage. "What manner o' man are ye?"

"'Tis but a by-blow of desire, nothing more. It fools a man into thinking an act o' lust is something more. It will trip him up, in the end."

Anald laughed again. "There speaks the sage."

"There speaks experience. By any road, can ye imagine making the braw mistake of loving a woman such as yon Bess Mowatt?"

"I do no' ken. Can ye?"

Aleck considered. He imagined her turning to him with gladness rather than affront in her eyes when he entered a room. Imagined catching a smile from her, seeing her face light up just for him. He imagined stealing a kiss and feeling her melt against him, kindling heat instead of anger.

He swore again, an ugly oath indeed. "Nay," he told Anald firmly. Nay, I cannot."

Chapter Nine

"The situation is intolerable," Bess bemoaned as she paced in front of the bench where Anne sat, in the solar. "That man is intolerable. How dare he come into my own hall and lie to me?"

Anne glanced up from her stitching—her seemingly eternal stitching—and weighed her companion's mood. "His hall now, if that paper of his can be trusted."

Bess's angry step faltered. "I do wish Callum would return with an answer. I believe every word which passes that rascal's lips to be a lie."

"They are nice lips, though," Anne said unexpectedly and tipped her head to one side. "He is a handsome man, withal."

"He is not." Bess stumbled to a halt, staring at her friend. "Never say you are falling under his spell?"

"His spell?"

"Aye. 'Tis said countless women followed after him, in his day. Despite what he is." She hunkered down at Anne's side. "I confided in you what he did to Mary. If other women believed that of him, as do I, they would stop admiring him soon enough."

"Indeed, and so they would," Anne agreed mildly.

"A woman would have to be mad to so much as look at a man like that."

"Though," Anne insisted, "he is a fine-looking

man—quite apart from his character, that is."

Perhaps, though Bess certainly did not want to admit it. Maxwell had a strong, tall body, aye, but so did many other men. Callum, for example, was much finer. Even old William…

Well, no.

And Maxwell's face did have a certain pleasing quality, something in the way the bones fit together, well proportioned without being pretty. Nay, no one could ever call Alexander Maxwell pretty. That wild head of hair, all black waves with the threads of silver through it, might please many a woman. Other women than Bess, certainly. He had nice hands, long-fingered and supple. But a woman did not succumb to a man merely because of his hands.

His eyes—now, those might well bring a woman to her knees. Extraordinary enough in color and expression, the fact that they regarded the world through fringes of thick, black lashes made them all the more beguiling.

"A strange thing," Anne mused, drawing her thread through the fabric inside her hoop. "I always thought Mary had an eye for a fine-looking man. Of course, I never knew her as well as you do. But does it seem to you a man who looks like Alexander Maxwell would need to force her into his arms?"

"What are you suggesting?"

"I do not know that I am suggesting anything."

"Are you calling Mary a liar, rather than Maxwell?"

"I am not. Just musing over possibilities."

"Mary might tell a fib here or there, but she would never lie about such a thing, not to me. We were close as sisters, and she entrusted all her secrets to me." *Especially the greatest of them.*

"Aye, then," Anne said peaceably. "You are best keeping away from him."

"I would keep away from him, and gladly, were we not all crammed here together like fish in a cask."

"An apt description."

"I have asked him to keep his foul-mouthed, foul-tempered beasts of men away from my lads."

"Did you phrase it thus?"

Bess made a face. "I have a responsibility to those lads." *And to one in particular.* "More than ever, with Callum away." She added with some impatience, "How can you sit there sewing while the world crumbles around our ears?"

"Sewing calms me, and brings me comfort. It got me through my grief when Geoffrey died. I embroidered an entire coverlet. And then set fire to it."

Their eyes met. In Anne's normally mild gaze, Bess beheld a veritable storm.

"Why?" she breathed.

"'Twas symbolic. Something I treasured went up in flames, destroyed. 'Twas either that or cut off my hair."

"A rash step, indeed."

"I wish I had, now. It might keep that Anald Robertson from looking at me as he does." Anne laughed softly. "I suppose I still could—lop it off and toss it at his feet in a gesture of disdain."

Bess laughed also. "I would like to see his expression if you did."

Anne gave a mischievous smile. "Men are such odd creatures. They focus always on a woman's physical attributes. That man has had his eyes all over my hair and my bosom. And I swear he's measured the length of my legs beneath my gown. But has he looked me once in the eyes and wondered what I may be thinking? Nay."

"They are coarse and crude. Not like Callum," Bess reflected. She sighed. "How I wish he would return."

Anne shot her another look. "You know, my dear, from time to time I have wondered if you are not a wee bit in love with our Callum."

"Just as I have wondered if he is not a wee bit in love with you."

Anne blushed. "He is still in love with his wife." Callum's dreams of a son had died with Ellyn. Now, Bess reflected, he cared for other men's sons.

Just like her.

"Have you ever noted," Bess asked softly, "we have all three chosen a solitary path? At least, our hearts have done."

"Aye." Anne sighed, and her needle stilled at last. "I am none too certain 'tis a healthy way to live."

"No matter. We need only concentrate on weathering this particular storm."

****

The lads stood all in a gaggle when Aleck entered the forecourt next morning. He'd fully intended to keep away from them, if only to please Bess Mowatt. He needed no more of her strident complaints echoing in his ears. But the snares set by the men had caught two fat rabbits overnight, and he wanted to bring them for the cook pot. He did not wish to admit, even to himself, he did so as a peace offering.

Yet the sight of the lads stopped him in his tracks.

The plaguing rain had at last moved off, rolling across the broad hills to the east, and watery sunlight lit the scene.

As always when he beheld lads of a certain age, Aleck's heart clenched hard in his chest. If only one of them were his. Or if only he could make himself believe his boy had truly died…something he had good reason to believe. For as Bess Mowatt told him, even that bitch Mary would not lie about such a thing. Instinct continued to insist something else again.

If his boy lived, why not here?

He returned in thought to that terrible afternoon some ten years past. A loyal servant had brought him word Mary had gone into labor, running all the way on foot to find him. Aleck knew there would be a fight, given the lies Mary had told her father of him, and had gathered a knot of warriors before riding thence with all speed. He did not intend to snatch the child, not for all his thieving. What devil would snatch a newborn bairn from its mother? But he wanted to lay eyes on it, behold his own flesh and blood, be it lad or lass.

No sooner had he arrived and made his demand— and, aye, he had to admit it had been a demand—than word came down the child had been born, a lad.

His son.

But the birth had not been easy. The child might not live.

Mary's father sought to turn him away then, and it had come to battle. No one—not even the lad's mother—would keep him from seeing his son.

He barely recalled the fight, but he did remember climbing the stairs to her chamber and crashing his way in. He recalled the heat of the place, filled with the raw, coppery smell of blood.

And death? Had he smelled death there?

No. But perhaps such a tiny scrap of humanity, so soon come and gone, did not leave a scent or much other trace behind.

Grief touched his heart, the same that had overwhelmed him that afternoon ten years gone.

He should wed some woman and get a brood of sons on her. Everyone told him that—his own father, and his brother Kenneth, who had four sons and two daughters of his own. Even Anald advised it. But the thought of it, after Mary, turned Aleck's stomach.

Upon that thought, one of the lads turned his head, engaged Aleck's eyes and gave him a grin. Mistress Bess's cousin it was. Young Dexter. The lad gestured with his blunted short sword. With the sun out, they prepared for practice.

He, Aleck, needed to get out of the way before Mistress Bess came on the scene and caught him.

Too late. Upon the thought, she strode down the stairs and out into the low sunlight, which struck a dull gleam from her hair. She wore hide boots laced to the knees, which seemed to emphasize the length of her legs, and moved with a supple, almost feral grace.

Aleck experienced the now-familiar tightening of his body that occurred whenever he laid eyes on her. What the hell was it about this woman? He'd not known the like in years.

Trust him to feel attracted to a woman who detested him.

As if to prove his point, she gave him a glare scathing enough to blister skin.

He held up the hares by the ears, one in either fist,

and gestured toward the kitchens. She planted her nose in the air.

Curse it all, the mare might show some gratitude. He filled her cooking pots and defended her walls.

No pleasing some women. Though, by God, he'd like to try.

Chapter Ten

"Here, lad," Aleck said, against his wiser instincts. "Let me show ye."

Dexter Mowatt turned, as if startled when Aleck spoke, and lowered the blade he held in his hand. The forecourt lay empty for once, except for the two of them. With the better weather, Aleck's men had moved their camp outside the walls, and the rest of the inhabitants were at their dinner. Aleck had just given Mistress Bess and that old rascal William a report on the state of the country all around, and he'd paused on his way out when he saw the lad.

"What am I doing wrong?" Dexter asked.

"Naught. Ye do naught wrong, lad. But I might show ye a thing or two, to make ye do even better."

Dexter's face lit. "I would like that."

Aleck sauntered over to him and laid a hand on his shoulder. "First point—never work wi' weapons in low light, if ye can help it."

"I already knew that one. Master Callum told me."

"Then why are ye here, swinging a blade in the shadows?"

"I did no' want anyone to see me."

"Why?"

Dexter thought about it and corrected, "Well, I do no' want Ronson MacNab to see me. I want to get better than him, see. He never ceases with plaguing me,

74

and I need to thump him hard enough to make him let up."

"Which one's Ronson MacNab?"

"A bit taller than me, blond curls and pretty as a lass."

Aleck grinned. "I think I know the one. And how does he plague ye?"

"He calls me 'bastard' because I do no' ken for sure who my father was."

Aleck's heart froze in his chest. His fingers, still resting on the lad's shoulder, tingled. He strove mightily to disguise his reaction. The shadows no doubt helped.

"How is that? Mistress Mowatt says you are her cousin's son."

"So she says, aye. But I never knew him. And I do no' think he was married to my ma. At least, that is what folk whisper. The Mowatts are a big clan. Mistress Bess's mother had a lot o' sisters, and her father a lot o' brothers. I ha' a lot of aunties and uncles."

"Aye so, don't we all?"

"Some get along. Some don't. My own mother came from a branch no longer on speaking terms wi' my grandfather. And she—well, she did ha' me out o' wedlock, like, so was shamed. I am shamed also." For an instant, the lad looked terribly crestfallen. "Master Callum says 'tis a terrible mountain to climb, yet one that is before me in my life so I maun climb it."

"Aye." Once again, Aleck wracked his brain trying to remember the ins and outs of the Mowatt family. One so old, and with so many branches, might indeed hide any number of such indiscretions. Aye, and Mary

75

Johnstone had Mowatt connections.

"It happens," he told the lad in an effort to alleviate his chagrin. "Do no' let it color your life. Many a good man came up not knowing his father." Or his son.

"That is just what Master Callum says. But the others brag about their fathers, always. I wish I could."

"Brag on your uncles, instead."

"Aye, but 'tis no' the same. That MacNab never ceases wi' mocking me. Says my father was a coward who would no' own me."

"Does he, so?"

Dexter gritted his teeth. "I wish I could shove his words down his throat."

"Well, keep up wi' your practice. Ye might do just that." As the rascal no doubt deserved. "Can ye no' brag on your mother?"

"I do no' see her."

Aleck's heart skipped another beat. "Why not?"

"I think 'tis because I cause her too much shame. So her family sent me here to train. Anyway"—Dexter tossed his head—"no one brags on their ma."

"Well, they should. A good ma is a matter o' great pride."

"Do you ha' a good ma?"

"I did, indeed, growing up. She's dead now." And his father still grieving inconsolably. Aleck had wanted to find her grandson and bring him to her, when she fell so ill. Quite likely they were both dead.

Unless this lad with the stubborn chin and warlike eyes might be his. Indeed, Aleck could see no great resemblance to either himself or Mary. And the lad's story might be all too true. But Aleck did feel drawn to Dexter, in a way he could not explain. Perhaps 'twas just because he felt hungry for a son and Dexter for a father.

"Will you show me those tricks?" the lad asked. He stole a look at the doorway of the keep. "But we will ha' to hurry. Bess will no' like it, and she'll come looking for me soon enough."

"Aye, so." Miraculously, the forecourt remained empty. No sooner had the thought crossed Aleck's mind than a shadow stirred. Anald came strolling down the stone stairs.

"Hie," Aleck told him. "Keep watch, will ye? Let us know if anyone comes."

Anald glanced into the lighted doorway behind him. Then, with a nod, he leaned against the stonework, blocking the way.

"Here," Aleck told Dexter. "Adjust your grip, so." He guided the lad's fingers a bit higher on the hilt of his weapon. "When ye swing, do no' hold back. A man maun commit to a strike, ye ken? Each and every strike. And step forward wi' your leading foot, shift all your weight into it. Like this, and this and this."

They mock battled their way all around the forecourt, bobbing in and out of shadows while Anald half watched them and half guarded the hallway beyond.

At last he whistled, "Hup—hie. She comes."

Aleck melted into the shadows, up against the rough stone wall, even as a voice could be heard floating through the semi-darkness.

"Dexter? Are you here? Ah, Master Robertson." The tone changed when Bess spied Anald. "Have you seen my young cousin?"

"Indeed, I ha' just been watching him at practice,

there."

Aleck held his breath as Bess stepped outside. Dexter had given him a good workout. He'd enjoyed it full well. But he could not let her hear him.

"What are you doing?" Bess demanded.

For an instant, Aleck thought she'd spotted him. But Dexter replied.

"Practicing so I might best Ronson."

"Alone? In the dark?"

"I was keeping an eye on the lad," Anald rumbled. "So he was nae quite alone, was he?"

In his concealment, Aleck smiled.

"You are meant to be at your supper, Dexter."

Again, Anald spoke. "But ye canna' fault the lad for lack o' ambition, can ye?"

"No. Dexter, please go inside. What have I told you about being on your own?"

"I am no' on my own, Bess. As Master Robertson says—"

She snorted, a clear indicator of her opinion. "If you wish for extra practice henceforth, come to me. I will drill with you, understand?"

The lad nodded, ducked between her and Anald, and disappeared into the light. Bess promptly treated Anald to a tongue-lashing, denouncing him for usurping her authority, to which Anald, in his inimitable fashion, raised his hands.

"What ha' I done, save keep a weather eye on the lad?"

"I do not want my boys alone with any of you."

Anald grumbled and went inside. Aleck expected Bess to follow, but she came out into the now dusky courtyard and glanced about, almost as if she could sense him.

Or smell him.

Aleck did not doubt it. The sweat had dried on his skin, and the wind pricked cold. His lungs felt ready to burst as she stepped close.

But she did not see him. She made a sound, very like a hiss, from between her teeth before, hand on her dirk, she turned and went inside.

Curse it all, Aleck thought as he detached himself from the wall. The woman was a harridan, for sure. He needed to keep away from her.

If he could.

****

The next morning, Bess banished everyone from the courtyard, forbidding any of Maxwell's men who entered the gate, and set the lads to work. They'd been too much off their routine and far too distracted. A score of reivers, so she concluded, made a bad diversion, and with Callum away, the lads grew disobedient.

There had been a spate of quarrels among them, physical encounters as well as verbal altercations. Not only had Dexter and Ronson been at one another more than usual, the others seemed to have lost all patience with their fellows.

Anne said it was to be expected, with Callum away. Bess felt the lads should obey her as well as they did Callum, and that the reivers had brought a cantankerous humor into the keep with them.

What else might be expected of such men?

She decided she would work her lads so hard this day they would have no energy left to fault one another. However, rain once more threatened, and with a wary eye on the sky, she chased them out right after breakfast.

Not a man to be seen in the forecourt. She huffed her satisfaction and set to work.

As so often, when she exercised the lads, she lost herself in the activity. It muted her own worry and feelings of intrusion as well as occupied them.

As if obedient to her will, the rain held off, though clouds boiled over the courtyard, and a cool wind kissed the sweat from her skin. She and William worked the lads hard, allowed them a short break for their dinner, and set them to drilling again.

At nightfall, she sent them to their suppers, and they went off groaning. Bess smiled to herself as she patrolled the forecourt, picking up discarded weapons. Let them claim they wanted extra practice now. They would likely fall asleep over their suppers, or—

She froze both in movement and thought when a voice spoke behind her.

"That was a fine day's work, and no mistake."

She whirled, her paralysis breaking, and raised the sword in her hand.

Aleck Maxwell eyed her up and down in the dim light.

"Ye ha' no need to defend yoursel' from me."

"This? 'Tis but a blunted sword."

"Regardless, I ha' no doubt ye could take my head off wi' it."

Bess fumed. "Were you watching us?"

"Me, and half my men, from time to time. We could hear, see, from the other side o' the wall, and took turns climbing up. 'Tis as hard keeping reivers frae the sound of a swordfight as bees frae honey." He took a step closer, abandoning his position at the gate. "Besides, I think some o' them are missing their own lads."

"You said that before—that they have sons."

"Aye, many o' them. Why do ye think they work so hard?"

"Killing and thieving, you mean. Setting a fine example."

He frowned. "Why are ye set so hard against them?" He took yet another step, and Bess felt a thrill of alarm.

She did not need to be alone with this man, just as she did not need to fall victim to the attraction he exuded. She, above all women, knew how treacherous that might prove.

But, curse it, he made a braw picture standing there in the evening light—beautiful as any seductive demon.

She needed to get out of the courtyard.

"Let me help ye," he offered and bent to retrieve a dirk abandoned on the stones. When next he approached her, he had any number of weapons in his hands.

"Put them here," she told him hastily, indicating a pile already started against the wall. "I will send the lads out to retrieve them before bed."

He did not demur and placed the weapons down carefully but did not move away. When he turned his gaze upon her again, it felt like a physical touch—on Bess's hair, on her cheek, and moving down her body to probe places no man had seen.

Alarm flooded through her in the wake of that stare, crying danger. This man had forced Mary. What might he try to do to her, here? She must remove herself immediately.

Yet for all that, she remained where she stood, up against the wall while those feral, golden eyes of his had their way with her.

"I ha' never met a woman to match ye, Bess Mowatt. Ye worked those lads as might any man, sparing nothing o' yourself. But ye are all woman beneath those leathers, eh?"

At the moment, with him gazing at her thus, Bess had to admit she felt all woman. An unusual sensation for her, who gave little thought, ever, to being aught but an instructor, and a good one.

She gave a wry smile. "I assure you, there is naught to remark beneath these leathers but aching muscles and a few bruises."

"Och, I assure ye there is."

He took still another step closer and lifted one hand to her cheek. Backed up against the wall, Bess stiffened in every limb. She did not want him to touch her.

Except—except she did.

The tips of his fingers brushed the curve of her cheek, and he dropped his voice to a silky purr. "Bess Mowatt, ye be gey lovely."

She nearly spat in derision. But for the sake of the sensations slamming through her, stealing the ability for speech and making her throat go dry, she could not.

Her, lovely? Aye, now she knew he lied.

But oh, what had happened to her heartbeat? It hammered through her chest like some blacksmith gone mad, bashing the iron.

She raised her hand and placed the flat of it against his chest, intending to push him away.

Bad idea. The heat of him, even through his leather

jack, penetrated her palm and seemed to flow into her, a second bombardment upon her senses.

Get away from me.

She spoke only in her mind. And her disobedient fingers, acting entirely on their own, closed upon his jack and drew him closer and closer still, till their mouths met.

She'd been kissed before, once or twice, but not like this. Quick, furtive actions those had been, stolen at her father's house by young warriors, as soon ended as they began.

Aleck Maxwell hurried nothing. Slowly, inevitably, his mouth claimed hers. Softly and almost gently, his lips abraded her lips—once, twice, thrice—before adhering to them in a rush of heat so bright it stole what little breath remained in Bess's body. His mouth felt incredibly hot there in the evening dark, and tasted like nothing she'd ever known—a wild, sweet flavor that flowed into her and ignited every nerve.

His fingers cupped her ear, and her knees promptly went weak. He touched her nowhere else—only with his mouth and his fingers. But he might as well have made a full-body assault.

Bess's fingers, on his jacket, dug deeper. His lips wooed hers apart, and his tongue invaded her mouth in a glorious, languorous act that seemed to melt all her resistance.

Or almost all.

Nay.

The word, like those others, sounded first in her head and then aloud, when she tore her mouth from his. "Nay."

He did not move away. To be fair, he couldn't

while still she had her fingers latched onto him.

Horrified at herself, she released him with alacrity.

For an instant, he seemed as stunned as she. Neither of them moved, and Bess's dismay warred with her desire to kiss him again.

She made herself say, "Get away from me."

"Here, now," he whispered, the way a man might seek to calm a fractious horse. "Do no' come over all angry."

She drew a breath. "How dare you—"

"Ye wanted that as much as I did."

Faith, and she could not deny it. But she did not *want* to want him. By heaven, what did a woman do with such feelings?

She tossed her head. "And now I suppose your men are once more watching over the wall."

He shot a startled look over his shoulder. "I hope not. Nay, too dark. They will no' see much."

"Not much to see." She slid out from between his body and the wall with more haste than grace. "Please do not come near me again. Your advances are not welcome."

"Are they no'?"

She shook her head. "Keep away from me, understand? Clean away."

He gave her a tight smile. "I will, Mistress Mowatt, if ye will."

Chapter Eleven

Callum returned the next day, riding in right around noontime, splashed with mud, weary and grim.

It had started raining, soon after Bess parted from Aleck in the forecourt, and continued all night. She'd listened to it while tossing in her bed, weary to the bone yet unable to sleep.

Perfectly natural, she assured herself, for her to be attracted to a man like Aleck Maxwell. A man who looked, moved, and smiled the way he did, who possessed a potent masculine magic—why should she suppose herself unsusceptible? Women did fall victim to such men. And as he'd said—and even though she often forgot it—beneath her male clothing lay a woman.

He made her feel it, the way no man ever had. She hadn't expected the power of it, the delectable pleasure of his mouth and his touch. How, once having tasted that, might a woman resist?

Through discipline, she assured herself as she dressed.

The same way she'd learned to fight. Sheer, dogged determination. But she did not want to encounter him, and lingered long before she descended to breakfast in the hall, where she found only William, overseeing the lads.

"Where are Maxwell and his men?" she asked

William, not looking him in the eye. She half fancied the old rascal might see what had happened in the courtyard last night.

William waved a hand toward the door. "Maxwell's out beyond the gate, where ye want him."

Was that where she wanted him? Bess snorted. "I am surprised they are not coddling themselves here out of the rain."

"No' men for coddling, are they?" William returned.

No, indeed.

She'd seldom been so glad to see anyone as Callum, when he came riding in drenched and weary. She met him in the courtyard, and one look into his eyes informed her he brought ill news.

He dismounted and handed the reins to one of the lads who ran out to meet him. No one could deny how fond the lads were of Callum. He greeted them all and remarked he hoped they'd tended to their lessons and minded Mistress Bess while he was away, before shooing them off.

"Look after Hector." His mount. "He's ridden far and needs a good feed, and grooming."

To Bess he said, "In the solar, lass. Give me but a few moments to change into dry clothing."

Bess used the time to order mulled ale and a plate from cook; when she arrived in the solar, Anne put her sewing aside with a look of concern.

"Callum has returned," Bess said.

"Aye, I saw him from the window. The news is not good?"

"I fear not. Oh, Anne, what shall we do if we lose this place to him—Maxwell?" Just speaking his name brought a wave of heat to flush Bess's body and redden her cheeks.

"Let us not jump to conclusions before we hear what Callum has to say. And I imagine we will transfer household elsewhere, if necessary, school and all."

"Aye, but this has been my home for ten years. I raised Dexter here."

"Indeed, but take it from one who knows, home may be anywhere. 'Tis the company that matters."

Callum came in, hair still wetted but wearing dry clothing. He embraced Anne gently, gave Bess a nod, and fell upon the food and ale like a starving man.

"Bless you for this. It has been a long journey and not a pleasant one. I was forced to follow kinsfolk from house to house. Everywhere I went, men were raising their defenses. It does seem clan Thomson has united and are on the raid."

He directed a dark stare into Bess's eyes. "Aleck Maxwell has not lied to us."

"But what of the keep? Did my uncle, Lithgow, indeed sign it over to him?"

Callum answered unhappily, "I said, Maxwell has not lied to us."

Curse it all! Anger and trepidation washed over Bess in equal measures. "What are we to do? We cannot stay here—not under his dominion."

Callum shrugged. "I will need to talk with the man. He has said he comes here to defend rather than chase us out." Again, he leveled a stare at Bess. "Or has he decided different while I was awa'?"

"If so, he has said naught to me."

"Believe me, Robert Lithgow's offspring, and the rest o' your Mowatt relations to whom I spoke, are as outraged as you are. They canna' imagine what the old man was thinking when he signed that document on his deathbed. They would love to think Maxwell pressed him—he's that much hated. But there's no proof, and the paper was duly signed. 'Twas Lithgow sent for Maxwell, and his lawyer will speak to it."

Bess began to sweat. "What are we to do?"

Callum looked grave. "There is talk among your relations of coming here and mounting a rescue, taking the keep back by force. If they banded together, your kin, it's they could protect this place frae the Thomsons."

Bess thought of last night's scene, in the shadows of the courtyard. Aloud she said, "Right now it seems the accursed Thomsons are the least of our troubles."

"What will you do?" Anne asked Callum in turn.

He drank deep from his cup of ale. "Talk to the man, as I say. Ask him about his intentions. Above all else, I ha' a duty to keep the lads beneath this roof safe. I mean to send William out to inform all their families o' our situation, give them a chance to withdraw their sons home if they wish. The last thing we need is a war. Bad enough if it comes to a battle wi' the Thomsons—imagine a load o' angry fathers on top of it."

"At least," Bess stated, "that might get Maxwell out."

"I do no' think so." Callum shook his head. "The man's well dug in now. And how would I keep those lads from getting hurt? As it is, if we come under attack, the oldest among them will want to fight."

"Aye," Anne put in softly. "And 'twould give Maxwell any number of hostages to hand."

"Just so." Callum laid aside his mug and scrubbed

his hands over his face. "I am tired and spent."

"You need your bed," Anne told him.

"In daylight? Nay, there's too much to be done. I want that word wi' Maxwell, first of all."

"At least rest here by the fire a wee while," Anne cajoled.

"I will. But not before Bess tells me what is gnawing at her."

"Me?" Bess strove to appear bland and unconcerned.

Callum gave her another hard stare. "I know you, lass, and I can tell when you are troubled over something."

"Who would not be troubled? With Maxwell here, disrupting our peace and our training—"

"Are you certain that is all of it? He has no' offended you or threatened you in any way?"

Bess contemplated it. Maxwell threatened her peace of mind, and no mistake. Having him here felt like an assault on her self-control. But she could scarcely describe that scene in the shadowy courtyard to Callum, or admit the truth even she wished she could deny—that her fingers had, indeed, curled into his jack and pulled him closer.

She shook her head. The hard stare Callum gave her let her know she'd not convinced him.

Anne rose gracefully. "Let me, Callum, get you another cup of ale."

"Aye. And pray you ask William to come speak wi' me."

But Callum did not take his gaze from Bess, and she knew their discussion, if postponed, had not come to an end.

****

The rain let up before nightfall, great rafts of deep gray cloud moving off to the east, and Callum MacFee came out to speak with Aleck soon after.

The man looked troubled and not well rested. He paused beside Aleck with a nod and directed his gaze at the sky.

"Damned, fickle weather," he remarked.

"Fickle as a woman," Aleck had to agree. The climate of the borders put a man through any amount of suffering, as a woman might. In the past, given the bitterness lodged near his heart, he might have remarked that of Mary Johnstone.

Now, though, he could think only of Bess Mowatt and of touching her in the courtyard last night. How she'd tasted, like wild honey. How she'd made him feel, and the heat of her that went straight to his head.

What had the woman been about, denying she wanted him even while she hauled him closer? Had she now fed MacFee some story about him trying to force her, just like Mary?

But nay. MacFee did not look angry enough for that. Worried, aye.

"Maxwell, we need to speak together."

"Aye, to be sure." Aleck fought to keep his expression bland. "I expect ye heard the truth frae Lithgow's lawyer? Ye believe me now."

MacFee grimaced. "Is there somewhere we might sit down together?"

"Aye," Aleck said again. "Come."

He led MacFee to his skin tent, one among the many in the bivouac just outside the walls. Dark inside, and malodorous, it stood empty at this time of day and would afford them a measure of privacy.

They sat down together. Aleck offered MacFee a jug, but he shook his head.

"I do no' ken how you persuaded him," he began, "but it seems true Robert Lithgow signed this place over to you before he died."

"I did no' persuade him. As I told ye, he sent for me. I was no less surprised than ye be now."

"But you accepted the gift. Robbed his kin. This keep should ha' been theirs." MacFee fired up. "It should ha' come to Bess Mowatt. She's earned it."

"Was I to tell a dying man where to bestow his property?"

"You might have tried."

"I tell ye, man, when I got there he was already determined on it. Had his man, and the letter, standing by. He was on his last—weak and near gone—but if there was any strength in him, it reached to that."

MacFee looked Aleck in the eye. "Why would he leave wealth to you—his enemy and the man who raped his granddaughter?"

"I did no' rape Mary Johnstone."

"So you say. She said differently."

"O' course she did. D'ye think she wanted to admit she'd spent that summer tumbling the enemy? 'Tis an old story, that, a woman wanting one thing and saying another." He thought again of Bess. "They are far more deceitful than we."

"Some of them."

A hard man for morality, MacFee looked implacable. Aleck doubted he could convince him.

"Look," he said, "the only reason I can conceive for Lithgow granting me this property is to mak' up for the past. I believe he came to doubt Mary, in the end."

MacFee snorted in derision. "His family and kin are no' happy. They feel the place has been stolen out from under them, and they're all for sharpening their swords."

"When ha' their weapons ever been aught but sharp?"

"The only thing keeping them from it is the safety o' the lads here. No one wants them caught in the middle o' a fight."

"Including mysel'."

"What are your plans, then?"

"As I told ye when we met on the road, I wish to stake my claim and defend this keep from Danhal Thomson and his wild lot, when they come."

"You seem very certain Danhal will come."

"He and I go way back and contested wi' one another when barely older than the lads ye ha' here. Danhal looks always for the chink in the armor—the weak place. He thinks Lithgow's death provides that. Trust me, he will come."

"Trust you?"

Aleck shrugged, trying not to show the words stung.

Callum rubbed at his chin. "D'you think that is truly why he deeded the place to you, so you might defend it? For I tell you, I do no' quite believe he granted such a gift to make up for his past bad opinion o' you."

"I do no' ken."

"Why not just call up the Mowatt clan and have them defend it? Especially wi' Bess here."

Bess. Even her name had Aleck at attention.

He gave a tight smile. "Mayhap he did no' wish to risk his own blood for the place. I canna' say."

"Aye, well." Callum planted the palms of his hands on his thighs. "It is so, no matter why. You ha' the paper. The place is yorn. Will you chase us out?"

"Have I no' said I came here to defend ye? Why, then, would I send ye and that lot awa'? If families wish to come and collect their lads, I will no' prevent them."

In truth, it might be to Aleck's advantage if some of the lads went home. He could better examine those left with an eye to one of them being his son.

But nay—he had to accept his son had died in infancy.

As that bitch Mary Johnstone had said.

Chapter Twelve

Another lad gone.

Bess stood at the gate that fronted the keep watching young Jacob Grant ride away with his father and uncle, all under heavy guard, and fought down her feeling of melancholy.

That made three just this past week, since Callum had returned. Faith, she hadn't realized how attached she'd grown to some of the boys until they departed.

Now if only some of the intruders would leave also. Especially one among them.

She'd done her best to avoid Aleck Maxwell since their encounter in the forecourt, but it proved difficult in the extreme. He and his men spent much of their time outside the walls, true enough, patrolling and hunting, but the keep was not so large that, when he came in for any reason—to speak with Callum or to bring game for the kitchen pot—she could miss him.

She usually spent her own time in the forecourt, working with the lads, and Maxwell always seemed to look for her when he made his way through.

Or perhaps she but fancied so, because she looked for him.

God's teeth, she could not prevent it. When she heard his voice or his step—for, Heaven help her, she recognized even that—she preached at herself sternly to keep her gaze locked upon whatever task she performed, for she kept always busy. But it seemed as if his presence pulled at her, and for all her best efforts she must look. Then his eyes would snag hers before dropping to her lips like a promise.

Or a memory, stirred.

Damned handsome man! Why did he have to look like that? Why must he possess such eyes, bright as burnished gold between those black lashes?

What woman could help but think about him? So far, she'd avoided speaking with him, though she could not help hearing that deep voice when he spoke to someone else. However, she should talk to him—she truly should—about that friend of his, Robertson. Otherwise, there would be trouble, and soon.

Callum rarely lost his temper. A calm and very patient man, his anger came slow and righteous. But the stresses of their situation, as well she knew, would try anyone.

Callum had ridden out so soon after Maxwell's arrival with his entourage, she doubted he'd had time to take full stock of Anald Robertson. But he'd had time now. He'd seen the way Robertson behaved around Anne, the attention he paid her, not all of it welcome.

He did not like it and, unless Bess missed her guess, wanted to thrash Robertson soundly.

And he could accomplish it. Callum was as good with his fists as with his sword, and that was very good indeed. Robertson might be the bigger man, aye, strong and burly, but in a contest with Callum, Bess did not think much of his chances.

As she turned away from seeing young Jacob off, she knew she must address the situation. But with whom? Callum? Robertson himself? Anne?

Not Robertson, she decided. And Anne could do little, though Bess had to admit to a measure of surprise. Anne accepted Robertson's compliments, it seemed, more readily than Bess might have expected.

Surely she did not begin to like the man?

The choice, then, seemed to be speaking with Callum or Maxwell.

She found Callum sorting weapons in a storeroom. He turned and gave her a sympathetic smile.

"Another o' your chicks gone, eh? 'Tis difficult, aye, to see them go. But," he straightened and reflected, "who would no' leave this madhouse, given the chance?"

This too seemed out of character, coming from Callum.

Bess returned his smile. "Oh, I thought it was but me feeling the strain."

"Nay, lass, the strain fair permeates these walls."

"But, Callum, you would not flee from us? You are the very spirit of this place."

"As you are its heart." He sighed. "Nay, I would no' leave. I ha' made a commitment, and I will no' flinch in my duty."

Bess parked her hip on a work bench. "Yet 'twas not duty so much as a joy, was it? Before they arrived."

Callum nodded.

"Now," Bess went on, "the place no longer feels like our own."

"'Tis no longer our own—but his. I think I could deal wi' the man, did I no' ken what he did to Mary Johnstone. Other than denying that deed to my very face, he seems honest and straightforward. He has no' threatened to disband the school and turn us out."

96

"I know. He must be practiced, indeed, at deception."

Callum's gaze met hers. "He does no' suspect the identity o' his—cub?"

"Nay, though I did catch them together once or twice. Callum, 'tis not of Maxwell I would speak to you, but his companion, Robertson."

Callum swore and returned to his task, tossing weapons onto the stone floor. "The man's a pillock."

"He is a crude and offensive boor. But I pray you do not fall out with him."

"Why not? He needs taking down a few pegs. Two broken arms and a cracked head should wipe the smile frae his face."

"It would. But what about after? 'Twould make things even more intolerable than they already are. We are all trapped here together. And as you always say, we must think first of the lads. You and Robertson at loggerheads will not help them."

"Ah, bah! Where did you learn such sense?"

"From you, along with everything else. God knows, I had little enough before."

A lass of seventeen with any sense would never have accepted a newborn babe to raise, when she knew little of infants. She wouldn't have gone off to the land of her enemies, a keep in Scotland, to rear the boy in secret.

Of course, she'd believed then that Mary would soon call for her son, when she felt it safe for him to return. That had never happened. Indeed, despite every message Bess had sent, Mary hadn't seen her son more than thrice or so since the day Bess took him away out of Maxwell's reach.

Back then, Bess had never met Callum MacFee, the man Robert Lithgow had installed here as custodian, not till she arrived with Dexter. But she'd come so swiftly to rely on him, and now counted him among her dearest friends.

Him, and Anne who'd arrived looking for refuge after her husband's death. Bess knew Callum had a fondness for the gentle Anne. She hadn't suspected one of her friends had fallen so deeply for the other, till now.

Callum said, "If you want my promise to keep frae killing Robertson, I will no' give it."

"Callum—"

"Nay, Bess. I will no' make a promise I canna' keep. Ha' you seen the way the man treats Anne? As if she was a plaything wi' which he might trifle and amuse himsel'."

"I have seen, and I've seen how Anne is handling it."

Callum glared. "How is that, then?"

"In her own gentle, implacable way. Let her deal with it, for now. To interfere would only give the matter more weight."

"You think so, do you?"

"I do."

"Ha' you heard the absurd compliments he pays her? 'Lady, yer skin is like the snow atop Ben Nevis.' "

"So it is."

"But what man says such a thing? And she laps it up, Bess."

"She does not. I have seen her turn him away time after time."

"With blushes. With a flattered smile. No wonder

the man feels encouraged."

"I believe she blushes from embarrassment."

"Then Robertson should no longer be permitted to embarrass her. I warrant he could no', wi' all his teeth knocked out."

"Callum," Bess lowered her voice, "do you have feelings for Anne?"

"Of course I ha' feelings for her. She is a lady of dignity and grace who should not be subjected to the attentions o' a cur like Anald Robertson."

"Aye, but—"

"I ha' grown fond of her since she arrived here, and I would defend her honor."

"No more?"

"What more could there be?"

"I have been thinking about that. I suspect there may be love."

The word caused Callum to freeze where he stood. "I ha' said I hold her in affection, as I do you, and the lads—even old William, truth be told."

"'Tis not mere affection of which I speak. Are you in love with her?"

"Of course not." He tossed another weapon aside. "I ha' no time for women, no—no capacity. My life is full, and after Ellyn died…" He stared away into the air, as if beholding his beloved wife once more. "I killed her, Bess, with my love. You think I would inflict that on anyone else?"

"Women die in childbed," Bess said softly. "And their babes with them."

"'Twould not have happened, if I'd never touched her." Before Bess could object further, he hurried on. "Besides, Anne would no sooner welcome my suit than

Robertson's."

"You think not?"

"I do. She has never let me know by word or look that she regards me as—"

"As you do her?"

"As more than friend and protector."

"You know Anne. She lets on very little about her feelings. Her heart might be breaking, and you would not be able to tell."

"I fancy I can tell. All her thoughts are visible in her eyes."

"Would you like me to speak with her on your behalf? Sound her out as to her feelings toward you?"

"I would not."

"But Callum—"

"Do you no' dare, Bess. 'Tis no' as if I will ever take a chance, loving another woman or taking another wife. It hurts far too much."

"And if she should care for you, as you do for her?"

"She will ne'er love anyone but her dear Geoffrey."

Bess snorted. "Then you need not fret over Robertson, aye?"

"Robertson is a damned thorn in my side."

"So I am to sit and watch you come to blows, am I?"

"Perhaps I will challenge him to a contest at arms." Callum grinned suddenly. "As you did wi' another of Maxwell's fellows, so I hear, while I was awa'."

"And if you kill him?"

"Then," said Callum blithely, "the world will be that much better a place."

Chapter Thirteen

Aleck heard Bess's step even before she emerged from the door of the keep and came down the stone stairs into the forecourt. It seemed his ear remained tuned continually to the sound, but he'd certainly not expected to see her here. Indeed, this—scene of the blisteringly hot kiss they'd exchanged—must be the last place he supposed she'd dare face him.

Maybe the lass liked playing with fire. Maybe she felt as hungry and desperate as he for another taste. Just one brush of the lips, the heat of contact, the delectable, delicious surge of feeling.

For evening fell and, once more, they found themselves alone. He'd taken dinner with her, MacFee, and the gentle Mistress Anne at MacFee's invitation. Bess must have followed him out.

He'd sensed MacFee wanted to speak to him about something, yet the moment had passed with no more than common talk. MacFee hadn't even broached the subject of how soon he thought the Thomsons might appear over the horizon. But at the end of the meal, he'd given Aleck an implacable dark stare and asked him to keep his men in line.

An interesting man, Callum MacFee. Who knew exactly what such a request meant? 'Twas a difficult enough task, at any rate. Even now, he could hear his men out beyond the wall, taking their own supper while telling tales, laughing, and joking.

Did MacFee not realize a loosely gathered band of reivers lay nearly beyond anyone's control?

If not, he should.

Aleck turned toward Bess Mowatt and desire flooded over him. She stood outlined by the light from within, slim and muscular with a body like a whip. She wore leggings not unlike his own, and a leather jack.

Fine, that, he thought. 'Twould make it easy, getting her out of those, since he was so familiar with the fastenings.

"Master Maxwell, if I might have a word?"

The last time she'd asked that, it had ended far beyond conversation. The tension between them had been building for days. Every time he saw her, when their gazes snagged and held across a room or the yard, it raged still higher. Now she spoke, and his heart began thundering in his ears as if he'd run over the brae.

"Aye?" he managed. He'd faced harder things than this—mobs of angry Englishmen and agents of the crown. She was but one lone Englishwoman.

She stepped down from the last stair and approached him. Brave lass.

"I do not wish anyone to overhear us."

"Sit, then." He patted the stone curb where once she'd sat with Dexter. "And speak softly. No doubt Anald will soon come looking for me."

She sat on the curb, and he joined her—not too close.

"It is of Master Robertson I would speak. Have you any influence over him?"

"Influence? Over Anald?" Clearly she did not know the man. "God himself has little influence over

Anald Robertson."

"Yet he is your friend."

"I ha' the good fortune, aye, to call him such."

"Good fortune?" She sounded both surprised and derisive.

"Anald Robertson might be a verbose trickster wi' a gob too big for his own good, he may be a tremendous pain in my rear, but he has a mighty heart. And he is a loyal friend."

"It is of his gob I wish to speak." She laced her fingers together on her knee. "He is far too outspoken and needs to keep his thoughts to himself."

"Anald?" Aleck would have scoffed, were the lass not so earnest. "He is a man who feels he has earned the right to speak his mind and will battle anyone who tells him differently. For the most part, he says whatever comes into his head."

"There will be trouble, then. And us all shut in here together like rats."

Aleck gusted a sigh. "What has he done?"

"He has been busy complimenting Mistress Anne, ever since his arrival."

"The scoundrel!" Aleck lifted a brow. "Might a man no' compliment a woman?" Might he not himself spill words into this woman's ear? Tell her that her skin looked like new milk in the starlight, or that her eyes shone like two of those stars, fallen from the sky? Ah, bah—he did poorly at compliments and always had.

"'Tis the way he compliments her. It is—"

"Offensive?"

"Lewd."

"Oh." Aleck thought about that. He could plainly see Mistress Anne was a lady, right down to her littlest toe; he did not want her distressed. "That is just Anald's way. He can mak' a comment about the weather seem lewd. Pray tell Mistress Anne not to tak' him seriously."

"'Tis no' Mistress Anne about whom you should worry."

"Whom, then?"

"Callum, now that he is back and listening to such nonsense. He will not tolerate it. I warn you, it will come to blows. And your friend will not get the better of that fight."

"Ah." Aleck contemplated that with dismay. "I did no' realize Callum had staked his claim upon Mistress Anne."

"Staked his claim?" Bess repeated, not so quietly. She leaped to her feet. "Is that how you regard women, Master Maxwell? As goods a man might claim? I should have known, since in that regard you feel you can take what you want."

Aleck answered roundly, "If I took what I wanted, I'd ha' ye—here and now." The words were out of his mouth before he could catch them back.

She stared. He watched her eyes widen and even in the dim light could see her cheeks grow red.

"How dare you? How can you speak so to me? Neither you nor your friend has any respect. I was a fool to try to reason with you. Let Callum settle your friend—it is what he deserves."

"Hush."

"I will not have you telling me what to—"

"Do ye want everyone to come running? Foolish lass, hush."

He pulled her back down onto the bench, but this

time she landed on his knees. He closed his arms hard around her, crushing her body to his. His mouth found hers with a hunger that could not be denied.

And oh, sweet Jesu, it felt like heaven, even better than he recalled from before, and he'd relived that a hundred times over in his mind. He might have expected her to fight him, hauled down against her will, as she would likely say. She did not. Instead she melted, her body easing into his even as her mouth clung to his avidly.

No room in this for sense, for wisdom or reason.

It felt primal, like surviving a battle, like drawing his next breath. Need poured through him, pure and simple, and desire that reached from his toes all the way to his shattered brain.

She made a sound in her throat—not protest, nay—and wound her arms around his neck. Strong arms they were, and left no doubt she wanted more of him.

Obligingly, he deepened the kiss, parted her lips with burning deliberation and dove inside. She did not bar him, and he searched out her tongue, captured and stroked it just as he wanted to stroke her everywhere.

She moaned again.

Did she wish to speak? If she thought he meant to release her mouth, she was mad. He wanted only more of her. A bottomless pit was this desire.

He bent her back across his arm and set up a rhythm with his tongue, in and out the sweet cavern of her mouth. She must be able to feel what she did to him. He felt like iron beneath her buttocks, yet she began to participate still more intoxicatingly, stroking his tongue in return and digging her fingers deep into his hair.

He should break this off, truly he should. Someone might come—

Instead, his fingers moved without his permission, slid up under the jacket so like his own. Nothing beneath, though, was like. He felt a smooth expanse of belly before he found a breast, soft and full to his hand. His mind, which had only begun regaining itself, blanked again.

She gasped, and he took advantage to plunge deeper. They now sat connected as closely as any man and woman might be who did not engage in that most intimate of acts. He caressed her breast, thumbed the nipple with awed delight, and she arched into him.

Just as he wanted to arch into her. Because he'd never felt anything the like of this, never—

Someone cleared his throat.

At first, Bess did not seem to hear. She'd set up a steady moan as soon as he touched her breast—or maybe it was a purr—and that turned to a sound of decided protest when Aleck broke the kiss and looked up.

Into Anald's grinning face.

The big lout leaned against the stone wall, ankles crossed as if he'd been there some considerable length of time.

"I wondered where ye'd gotten," he said.

Bess stiffened in Aleck's arms as if a whip had been laid on. She fought her way free of his grip and surged to her feet, trembling.

Aleck felt the loss like the sudden coming of winter. By God, what was wrong with him?

"I confess," Anald went on, "I expected to find ye detained inside, not out here."

Aleck rose, pretending at nonchalance. "This is no' how it appears." His voice sounded rough in his own ears.

"Nay? It appears," Anald said the words thoughtfully, "ye indulge yersel' with fierce Mistress Bess. I'm that surprised she did not knife ye instead."

So was Aleck. He stole a look at Bess and found bright consternation on her face—consternation and embarrassment. She stood on the balls of her feet with her hands curled into fists and looked like she meant to fly at Anald.

"If I draw on anyone," she told Anald stridently, "'twill be you. I was just telling Master Maxwell he should keep you harnessed and away from Mistress Anne."

"Was that what ye were doin'? Communication without words, was it?"

Bess ignored that. "Either keep away from her or I'll settle you myself, understand?"

"Perhaps ye should first be asking the lovely Mistress Anne if she enjoys my company."

"I have. She is repelled by you. Understand? Repelled!"

"Just as ye be repelled by our Aleck, here?"

She flew at him. The suddenness and violence of it shocked Aleck. Before he could blink, she'd drawn her dirk and held it to Anald's throat.

"Another word," she invited. "Just one."

Anald went immediately silent.

Aleck seized Bess from behind. The mere feel of her body up against his threatened to sear his brain all over again.

"Enough," he growled. "I will no' ha' bloodshed

amongst us."

Bess fought her way free of his grasp, the dirk still in her hand. "Talk to him," she spat. "Keep him away from my friend."

Without awaiting a reply, she spun on her heel and disappeared back up the stone steps, soon swallowed by the light.

Anald and Aleck remained, staring at one another.

"Jesu," said Anald, putting two fingers to his throat.

"Did she cut you?"

"No worse than I might, shaving." Anald reflected on it. "If I did shave. But merciful heavens, Aleck, what a bundle o' aggression!"

Aleck smiled slowly. "Isn't she, just?"

"She's as touchy as any drunken reiver, and possesses no sense o' humor. Are ye certain ye want to get involved in that?"

"I'm no' involved."

Anald swept him with a look. "That's no' how it looked to me."

"Och, my head says one thing, argued by my—"

"Cock?"

Aleck nodded.

"Ye keep the path ye're on, ye'll ha' more trouble than ye can likely handle. Me, I like trouble. But even I would keep clear o' that."

"I am not on any path." Aleck waved a hand. "That merely—happened."

Anald snorted.

"And while I think on it, ye keep clear o' Mistress Anne, eh? Mistress Bess insists your attentions are unwelcome."

"Are they, then?"

"Aye, and MacFee will ha' something to say about it, if ye keep buzzing around her."

"I didn't ken she belonged to MacFee."

"I do no' say she does, merely that he's feeling protective. So keep awa' from the woman, will ye not?"

Anald grinned nastily. "I will agree to keep awa' from Anne, if ye agree to keep awa' from Bess."

Chapter Fourteen

William returned late the next day from his rounds, having delivered warnings to the families of the lads at the keep, and bringing one lad's father back with him.

"I wish to see the set o' the place," Mordock Callander told Callum after greeting his son, Jock. "The borders are afire, and I'm thinking the lad might prove safer here than at home for the duration."

He turned a bright blue stare on Aleck and Anald, who both stood by, and added to Callum, "Christ's blood, but this is an unholy alliance."

"It is," Callum agreed. "But my main concern is for the lads. Come, sit with us. Tell us what you mean by saying the borders are afire."

They all repaired to Aleck's camp, where he called for ale. Callander seemed a verbose man, or perhaps worry made him talk so much.

"Tensions ha' been building all summer," he began, having taken a grateful draught of his ale. "But old Lithgow's death appears to ha' set something off— fire, as I say, to dry tinder." He ran his troubled gaze over them. "There ha' been more raids over the past weeks than in the last year. And alliances as unholy as yours formed."

MacFee said thoughtfully, "Is it true the Thomson clan has come together?"

"Aye, and behind most the raiding. My nearest

neighbor, Keith, has had his barns burned to the ground and his cattle stolen. His young son, Elliot, is sore injured and may no' survive."

That sobered all four men.

"I thought," MacFee put out, "the new laws enacted by the Crown were to cut back on the raiding, if no' eliminate it."

Callander and Anald both snorted.

"Naught will e'er stop the raiding," Callander said before Anald could. "Not if Queen Bess hersel' came to pass the word, wi' all her glittering court in attendance."

Aleck had to smile. He liked Callander. But he nodded. "Ye be right. Raiding is in our blood. I doubt aught so fragile as laws will e'er prevent it."

Callander gave him a frank stare. "Indeed, it surprises me, you ha' left off reiving and taken on the protection o' those here, Aleck Maxwell."

"Robert Lithgow deeded me this place," Aleck informed him.

"Ah." Callander shot Callum a look. "I should ha' thought he'd given it to you, long since."

"Nay. He merely installed me here, for a time."

"A long while," Callander added. "And why you, Aleck Maxwell, of all men?"

Aleck shrugged. "Who kens wha' goes through the head of a dying man?"

"Aye, well." Callander glanced about the greensward fronting the keep. "You ha' a strong company o' men at your back, I will say that. Given your reputation and the strength o' Master MacFee's sword, I may be better leaving Jockie here."

"Aye, but if ye do," Aleck warned, "'tis but a

matter o' time before Danhal Thomson turns his attention to us."

Callander looked at MacFee. "Come, let us put my Jock through his paces and see how well you ha' trained him. Then I will decide."

The session that followed proved lively in the extreme. MacFee called for all the lads to fetch their weapons and provide for Mordock Callander a demonstration. This gave Aleck a chance to observe Mistress Bess, who joined in, directing and guiding them. Indeed, he missed most everything but the way she moved, the strong lunge of her arm, the grace of her legs.

Those arms had been twined around his neck while he plundered her sweet mouth, the heat of her body pressed to his. He wanted her legs wrapped around him also, in wild abandon.

For if ever they did come together in that way, 'twould be abandoned. He knew that to his very soul.

Anald nudged him with an elbow and gusted into his ear, "Ye might try watching the lads."

So he might. Aleck scowled and hoped no one else had noticed his interest. But Bess might well have done, for she looked at him now, one long, stolen stare from those stormy blue eyes.

In the end, Callander decided to take Jock away with him, but not before spending the night. Aleck did not feel sure about what that said about the man's opinion of their defenses. Perhaps he, Aleck, should send for yet more men to strengthen them.

Trouble was, he had no idea when Danhal Thomson might attack. And sending for more men meant losing the sword of whomever he sent as courier.

"The lad's mother will want him close," Callander said when he and Jock left the next morning. "'Tis only that, you ken."

Aleck shook the man's hand, but felt unconvinced. Not long after, he put the question to Anald.

"I do no' like the picture Mordock Callander draws for us. Do ye think I should send for more men?" If he sent Anald, that would put paid to the tension between him and MacFee. Trouble was, if attack did come, he wanted Anald at his side.

"Ah, now, there's a question. I maun admit, it's been in my own mind."

"Has it?" They stared at one another, struck. They did not often think alike; when it happened, it scared Aleck a bit.

"But who would come?" Aleck speculated. "'Tis a pile o' trouble, this, and little reward in it."

Anald advised, "Send for your wild Kennedy cousins. They'll come just for the sake o' lifting their swords."

Aleck contemplated that prospect with misgiving. The Kennedy clan, related on his mother's side, were undisciplined as a pack of wolves. They'd once waylaid a train of travelers including the Queen's own courier, and Elizabeth had placed prices on all their heads.

"Aye, so," he allowed, "and that would be a last resort."

"But ye've vowed to keep this place safe, so ye have, and all in it."

"And who would keep everyone here safe from the Kennedys? That tribe are as hard to control as rabid hounds."

Anald grinned in appreciation. "They're your

blood, lad."

"Do no' remind me."

"I can see several similarities."

"Och, hell." Aleck might send for his cousin, Dunston Kennedy, the oldest and tamest of the lot. "If Dunston would come with just a troop of his own men and leave the others out of it, that might serve."

"So it might."

Impulsively, Aleck said, "Ride to Dunsyre Castle now while ye can, and ask him. But get him alone, mind."

"I will try. But ye ken what that lot are like—what one knows, they all seem to know."

"Then ye will ha' to be discreet." What was he saying? A bloodied axe was more discreet than Anald Robertson.

****

Bess heard raised voices when she passed by the solar on her way to fetch a new strap for her boot. The other, well frayed, had broken during practice. She paused in surprise.

At this time of day, late afternoon, no one inhabited the solar but Anne. And, aye, though Bess recognized one of the voices as hers, Anne rarely shouted and would not be doing so at herself.

"I suppose you think you own me?" Anne threw the words out with a passion Bess had never heard from her. "You think you may tell me what to do?"

"The man's a boor." The identity of the other voice, equally slow to shouting, shocked Bess into complete motionlessness. "He's dangerous, and I do no' want him near you."

"Och!" Anne sounded choked with ire. "And is it

about what you want? Or what I want?"

"Tell me you do no' welcome the attentions o' a lout like Anald Robertson. I believed you to be a lady wi' far more self-worth."

Ah, so that was it. Callum had brought the matter that ate at him so fiercely not to Robertson but to Anne herself.

"Trust a man!" Anne spat.

"Eh?"

"Trust a man to deem it a woman's responsibility, how another man may speak to her. How dare you suppose I welcome his advances? Or that I do not?"

"I ha' yet to see you slap his hand, either by word or action."

"You were not here to see it, but off on your eternal, sacred duties." Anne hurled the final word, which hid Bess's gasp.

She knew Anne well, or so she should have said. She'd believed her friend fully occupied by her stitching and her grief for her dead husband. She'd had no inkling that under the composed exterior lay a woman seething with resentments.

And quite possibly other emotions.

"What else should I do?" Callum wondered aloud.

"What, indeed? 'Tis not as if you have ever looked at me with anything more than courtesy. Who would blame a woman starved for enjoying a bit of interest?"

Oh, ho, Bess thought, now pressing herself against the side of the passage so she might not be seen, and listening shamelessly. It was wrong to listen, aye, but how could she tear herself away?

Callum's voice trembled when he said, "You ken, Anne, I regard you wi' far more than courtesy."

"I ken no such thing. When have you ever told me so?"

"A man should no' have to say."

Anne made a sound far too rude to come from her refined lips.

"Besides," Callum went on in a rush, "you were always far too occupied wi' your grief, as I was wi' my duty. I wanted to respect that. I respect you, Anne. I would no more subject you to the sort o' insulting suggestions Robertson has than allow him to continue doing so."

"Then, if you are prepared to stake no claim, Callum MacFee, I am not yours to guard."

"Of course you are."

"I am not your wife, your ward, or your possession."

"All beneath this roof are mine to guard."

"You have no claim on my heart."

The solar went suddenly silent.

Fool, Bess thought at Callum. *Tell her she's wrong, that your heart claims hers. Take her in your arms and show her what words cannot say.*

Indeed, the silence within the chamber became so complete, Bess thought he had done just that.

Then she heard Callum step to the door. "You are right, Mistress Anne. I ha' no right."

Bess tiptoed off down the passage as swiftly as she could, the strap for her boot forgotten.

Chapter Fifteen

"That great, loud man called Anald Robertson has gone," Dexter confided while eating his breakfast. "He rode out this morning."

Bess felt surprise and also a twinge of sympathy for Robertson. It had started raining hard some time during the night and showed no signs of letting up.

"Truly?"

"Aye. Henry and I saw him go. The Reiver Wolf sent him."

"Do not call him that." The name reminded Bess all too strongly of what she did not want to recall. That Aleck Maxwell, a thief and rapist, could not be trusted. That he'd lied to her about his behavior toward Mary and might well lie about any number of other things.

She could not trust the man, no matter how her body might crave the sensation of touching him.

"What is it, Bess? What is amiss?"

"Naught, Dexter." She did not permit this lad, so like a son, to call her Bess unless they were alone. Since he'd lingered at his breakfast, however, they were as good as that.

"'Tis just, for a moment, you looked ill."

"I am wondering where Anald Robertson has gone, and why." At least it should defuse the situation between Robertson and Callum, if not that between Callum and Anne.

"Would you like me to ask Master Maxwell?" Dexter offered brightly. "He and I are on gey good terms."

Alarm raced through Bess like fire through thatch. "Are you, then?"

"Oh, aye," Dexter said comfortably.

"Did I not ask you to keep away from him?"

"Aye, but 'twas no' a reasonable request, nor a rational one."

Bess's eyebrows flew up. "Eh?"

"Quarters are too close to allow folk here to keep awa' from one another. If 'twas otherwise, I would keep clear o' Ronson, would I no'?" Dexter reflected upon it. "Why could Ronson MacNab no' be recalled home?"

"I do not know. But—"

"By any road, Master Maxwell has much of value to impart to a lad like me."

Not Dexter's own words, plainly. Bess began to grow angry. "Och, and I suppose he told you that."

"Nay, though well he might. I take him for an honest man."

Honest!

"He is a reiver," Bess said carefully.

"As are many of our kin. That does no' mean he will no' deal honestly with me, Bess." Dexter fixed her with a compelling blue stare. "I like him. And I feel—I canna' explain it, truly—comfortable wi' him, like no one else."

A second wave of surprise passed through Bess, stronger than the first. Even as she wondered where and how Dexter had found opportunity to grow comfortable with Maxwell, her heart cried with alarm. Here—here did it become dangerous. Through Dexter did not know it, though neither of them knew it, Maxwell was related to him by closest blood.

Had she the right to deny them contact?

But Maxwell—a deceiver, and a liar, a man who'd forced Mary—did not deserve a son like Dexter, and could only prove a bad influence on him. Or could he? A lad needed contact with a man who cared about him. She and Callum both believed that, and it formed the very basis of this place.

Carefully, while striving to hide her dismay, she asked, "What is it you so like about Maxwell?"

Dexter's face lit. "He is clever and amusing, and—and I canna' truly say, but he thinks the way I do, and he understands the things I tell him, even as Master Callum often does no'."

"Master Callum loves you very much."

"I ken. But he is so serious. And he never knows when I am fooling. Master Maxwell always does."

Always? "How much time have you spent with Master Maxwell?"

"Not so much. As I say, 'tis difficult to avoid him. But," Dexter stole a look at her, "I thought you should ken."

"I see." So, even though she'd told Dexter to keep away from the man, he'd gone behind her back. And even though she'd asked Maxwell the same, so had he.

And she did not know whether to holler or weep. The two of them had found each other, come together despite her ban. Did that mean blood would out?

If God had brought them together in this unexpected way, by Lithgow granting the keep to Maxwell, had she a right to keep them apart?

Aye, for had she not promised Mary to hide the lad from his father?

Maybe she should place the matter in Mary's hands, go see her or send a letter describing the situation. Trouble was, Bess did not know where Mary might be at the moment. In the last ten years, she'd married thrice and been widowed twice. She'd borne three more children and had not been in touch with Bess.

She seemed to have dismissed Dexter from her life and her mind.

Bess could not imagine it. Looking at the lad stuffing oatcakes into his face, dark hair tousled—as always—and clever eyes alight, she tried to conceive of never having known him. Not as a babe who alternated between wailing and gazing at her with an intensity that seemed to claim her. Not as a sturdy toddler, learning to climb almost before he learned to walk. Not as the boy he was now, quick and bright and full of mischief.

Dexter might have filled her life with trouble, aye, but with laughter too. And her heart broke just to imagine trying to live without him.

In so many ways, he was her son. Not Maxwell's. Not Mary's.

"Why are you looking at me that way?" Dexter asked, and heaved a great sigh. "Very well so, I will try harder to keep awa' from the man, as you asked. But I think it is a great pity. He can teach me things Master Callum cannot—or will not."

"Oh, aye?" Bess asked faintly. "Like what, pray?"

"Dirty fighting." Dexter grinned alarmingly. "Master Callum wishes us always to put honor first. But there are times a man cannot."

"A man, is it?" But you are only ten, she wanted to say, and knew that did not matter. Young men grew up swiftly on the treacherous borders. And aye, though Callum did try and hammer a sense of honor into this lot, they sprang from men who, for generations, had stolen and cheated their way through life ruthlessly.

How fascinating a man like Aleck Maxwell must be!

"Aye." Dexter crammed the last bit of oatcake into his mouth. "I am on the verge o' manhood. Soon I will tak' over looking after you, instead o' you looking after me. What if a band o' reivers came here and tried to tak' you captive?"

"I would whip out my dirk and do my best to fight them off."

"So you would. But what if they overwhelmed you? If a big, ugly brute had his dirk to your throat? Master Aleck says a stroke to the back o' the brute's legs will cut a vital sinew there, and he will stumble about like a poleaxed steer."

"Does he, so?"

Dexter waved a hand airily. "And many other things. The man is a—a fount o' knowledge."

"A fount of ill advice, maybe." Bess leaned on the table. "Listen to me," she said earnestly. "I have said I do not want you seeking the man out, understand? But if you should, as it seems likely, encounter him, you must be polite. And if you should pick up a few pointers along the way—then aye, a lad needs all sorts of knowledge."

Dexter grinned in delight. "I just knew you'd see it that way."

"Did you, then?"

"Aye. You are what Master Callum calls a sensible woman."

So she was, though when it came to Aleck Maxwell, her good sense seemed to fly from her like a maddened bird.

She waved a finger at Dexter. "I would have you remember just one thing. From a moral standpoint, you cannot accept everything Aleck Maxwell tells you. A man like him—well, he crosses lines you should never violate."

"I understand."

"I hope you do."

"He is a rascal and a bounder."

"Just so."

Dexter appeared to ponder the matter. "Just, who do you think would win in a combat between him and Master Callum?"

Bess did not bother to chastise Dexter for the question; she knew the lads spent countless hours deliberating such things.

She answered swiftly. "Master Callum, of course. I have never seen anyone fight so well as he."

"That is what I said, before I saw Master Maxwell at practice. Indeed, Bess, you ha' never beheld the like."

"Indeed?"

"Aye. And," Dexter leaned his dark head toward hers, "I'm thinking Master Aleck might win just because he is no' so honorable. Sometimes, you ken, a dirty move can be an advantage and turn the fight."

"Perhaps so, Dexter, my lad, but that is not the sort of man I wish you to be."

Chapter Sixteen

Three days passed, and Anald did not return. Aleck told himself the man had far to ride, in order to secure more swords to their cause, and might run into any sort of difficulty out there, given the unrest Mordock Callander had described.

He tried not to chafe over it, but truth be told he felt as unsettled as a roach on a hot griddle.

Too many people crowded the keep too closely here, and a lot of strong personalities, at that. Even though some of the lads had gone, the rest seemed to be everywhere, asking questions and getting underfoot. He enjoyed his encounters with Dexter but quite truly found some of the others, like that wee pillock Ronson, flat out annoying.

Add to that the fact that his men were bored, no matter how many times he sent them out on patrol or set them to drilling, and it made an atmosphere primed for exploding. Things would grow lively, indeed, if and when Danhal Thomson—or aye, anyone else—came raiding. Meanwhile, friction grew.

Even with Anald gone, MacFee looked no happier. No doubt these many years he'd felt the keep his own. He visibly resented having to bow to Aleck in any kind of decision.

Aleck would not be surprised if, at some point, they came to blows.

And then there was Mistress Bess. Holy sweet Jesu, her presence tried him. He both dreaded and desired encountering her, and seemed to do so constantly. To be sure, she and MacFee both worked the lads on a daily basis. And she seemed to haunt the lad, Dexter, with whom Aleck truly did enjoy speaking. Yet fate placed her in his way at every moment, when he brought game to the kitchens, when he tried to give one of the lads advice, when he pursued any number of other errands that occupied him daily.

True enough, he had no business giving any of the lads advice. Yet when he heard one of them boasting or, worse yet, saw him doing something lug-headed, he could not help it. Whatever Mistress Bess might think of him, he was a warrior. His own father had spared him nothing during training. He felt it a duty to do likewise.

Quite apart from that, the tension between him and Mistress Bess screamed aloud. When she came into a room, or out onto the greensward where they had their camp, he could feel it, even if she focused elsewhere. His whole body came to attention, his skin pricking and his heart speeding up. And even though he told himself he would not look at her, would keep his gaze turned on his task and pretend her presence did not matter, he always did look—to find her stormy blue eyes fixed on him also, in an expression that said she either wanted to take his head off with her sword or kiss him until madness ensued. He was not sure which.

He needed to touch her again, get her out of that rough leather clothing and run his hands all over her. He wanted to taste her again, with a yearning so deep it shocked him. That frustration far outshone any other.

If he did not have the woman—soon—he would explode like a rotten log on a blazing fire.

But he would not, could not have her. She believed Mary's lies, believed he'd forced the woman. Aleck had no idea how he could ever convince her otherwise.

And why should he bother? Bess Mowatt counted as just another woman among the thousands. Only she counted as far more, to him.

In an attempt to spare himself, he started going out on patrols with his men. Thus it was, on the fourth morning, he spied Anald returning, riding hard, with three men in tow.

They met on a ridge of land that overlooked the valley. Aleck turned a burning look on Anald and cried, "Three? Ye come wi' but three men?"

Anald waved a hand at his companions. "Others follow behind us—if they mak' it in time. Thomsons are on the way, and I thought, like a fool, ye'd want me at your side."

****

They held a council of war in the hall, the five of them—Aleck, Anald, Callum, Bess, and old William. The three new arrivals, all men Aleck knew, went off to the kitchens for a feed. Anald declared he needed only a flagon of ale, to which he applied himself most diligently.

Without further preamble, he wiped the foam from his whiskers and said, "They ha' already attacked and burned two castles, the Thomsons. Heavy damages, and many slain. The survivors," Anald said with relish, "ha' agreed to stand here wi' us. No' for honor, though. They want their cattle back."

Aleck tried to make sense of it, and failed. "Why

would Danhal Thomson waste his time attacking two other keeps if he has his eye on this one?"

Anald leaned forward. "I ha' a theory about that. I think he is practicing, so to speak, finding out who among his crew will tak' orders from him and how those doughty cousins o' his might, or might not, fall into line. Ye ken, just weeks ago they were busy slitting one another's throats."

"Aye," said Aleck, in dawning horror.

Callum spoke heavily. "What he's finding out is, when they all raise their swords together, they make an effective army."

"Effective as a battering ram," Anald agreed. "None o' those he attacked could stand against them. And ye ken, Aleck, each man along the borders keeps a strong house."

"Aye," Aleck said again, even less happily. Ah, what had he done, taking this place on? All the lads to protect, along with Mistress Anne and Mistress Bess. He eyed her while pretending not to. She'd hurried down from her chamber when the call came and had not taken time to plait her hair. It hung loose down her back in a flow like warm honey. He'd never seen her look so arousing.

But, he reminded himself, Bess was not his to protect and could defend her own life and honor.

"When?" he asked Anald, getting to the heart of it. "How far are they behind ye?"

Anald shook his head. "No' far, lad. We rode all night to keep ahead o' them."

Ah, hell.

"What will they do when they get here?" Bess asked. "Did they set fire to the other keeps they attacked? You say they killed many?"

"All who stood before them. Timothy Carruthers lost his son, Roger. He is," Anald said with some relish, "a very angry man."

"Yet he may no' get here in time," Callum observed.

"True. Of course, a force attacking the Thomsons from the rear would do us no harm."

"How many men will Danhal bring?"

"Wi' all his cousins and the hangers-on, there will be at least three score o' them."

Three score. And they barely twenty or so. And all those lads…

He looked Anald in the eye. "When will they be here?"

"By nightfall, I should think."

"Then we'd better prepare." Aleck turned his mind to being a warrior, shutting the door firmly to aught else. He began to call out orders—men to go watch for anyone approaching the keep, friend or foe. Other men to the gate. All weapons brought to the hall.

Callum MacFee stepped forward and faced him. "This place," he said loudly and clearly, "lies under my orders."

Aleck gaped at him. "What d'ye mean, man? Did ye no' ride out yoursel' to question Lithgow's man over just that? Did ye no' see the paper, signed?"

"Aye," MacFee stood like a rock. "You might own the place. And I will accept your help in defending it against those ravening beasts who come, if only for the sake o' the lads. But I am steward here. No paper in the world changes that. Robert Lithgow charged me and set me to defend this keep. I will do just that, to my dying breath."

Aleck experienced a flash of annoyance so strong it overset his frustration. "Then do so," he shouted. "Stand and die, for all I care. But this place is mine, and I will gi' the orders."

A new look came into Callum MacFee's eye, one Aleck had never seen there before. With deliberation, he eased his sword from its scabbard. "Fight me for the privilege."

"Callum!" Bess Mowatt exclaimed, racing to his side, looking as horrified as Aleck felt.

Anald said in a rumble, "Wha' madness is this, man? We ha' intruders nearly at the gates."

Callum flicked Anald a look of raw dislike, and said nothing.

"MacFee." Aleck strove to remain calm. "'Twill do no good for me to murder ye, or ye me. Think instead o' defending those lads—"

"I am."

"Well, curse me." Aleck scowled. "I do no' see it. Stand down, I warn ye. Once I pull my blade, blood will be shed."

"My point, precisely." Callum bared his teeth. "So far as I am concerned, there are two ways this keep may be defended—yours or mine." With weight, he added, "Without honor, or with it. I ask mysel' which do I want those lads to witness?"

Aleck flushed with anger. They had no time for this. Besides, he did not wish to kill the man.

"Callum," Bess said again, only to be echoed by Mistress Anne who entered the hall.

Callum ignored the first woman and gave the second one a scorching look before he raised his sword.

"Keep back!" he cried. "We will have this out."

And before Aleck could so much as blink, Callum MacFee attacked.

Chapter Seventeen

"Stop!" Bess demanded in a shriek that sounded shrill to her own ears. "Madness, this is madness!"

Both men ignored her as if they failed to hear. Perhaps they did, given their intense concentration.

She'd seen Callum fight many times and knew his uncanny skill with a blade. In the old days, when such tales were sung in a hall such as this one to the accompaniment of a harp, it would have been called magical. Too quick for a mortal's wielding, and too deadly.

She had never seen Aleck Maxwell fight, other than in passing when he sparred with his men. But he had a reputation all through the border marches.

And now he did not spar. Indeed, his face—usually so mobile and full of mischief—had closed into a mask in which his yellow eyes gleamed like those of the feral beast after which he was called.

Bess might not have recognized Callum, either. This man she'd known so long as fair and even-tempered wore a snarl and the determination of a hunter.

It seemed as if both men's frustration rose to fill them, and they determined they would expend it on each other.

Anne flew to Bess's side, her face transfixed by horror, and seized her arm. "Stop them. Stop them!" she begged.

"They cannot hear me." And it was far too late. The blades had crossed and continued to do so in a flurry that crashed on the ears, almost too quick for the eye to follow.

The sound brought others running—men who stood guard at the gate, those in the kitchen, and worst of all, the lads from everywhere. Bess, her gaze fixed to the two dancing men, could spare a glance for none of them.

For they did dance, a set full of deadly grace. Nearly matched in height, they matched their steps also, and the strikes from their swords. So far, no blood had been drawn. That would not last. Callum MacFee was the best swordsman Bess had ever known, so good he rarely raised his blade in earnest, preferring to pass on his skills to the next generation. In her heart, she believed he should be able to better Aleck Maxwell.

But—but did she want to see Maxwell slain?

Someone stepped to her other side. Dexter it was, his eyes wide with both shock and excitement.

"What are they doing?" he asked.

"Just sparring," Bess lied.

"It does no' look—"

Dexter's words were interrupted by another series of clangs. They rang through the hall loudly like chimes, perhaps those more commonly heard in Hell. At their conclusion, Maxwell gave a grunt. A thin, red line appeared on his bulging upper arm.

"First blood!" someone called.

Bess sucked in a breath. "Honor has been maintained!" she shouted.

Neither man heeded her. She broke free from

Anne's grip and rushed forward.

"Enough!" she roared. "Let it be done."

Callum, who had never before touched her in anger, planted the flat of his hand on her chest and shoved. She stumbled back even as William called, "Let it play out, lass. There can be only one cock o' the walk."

She had no chance to protest further. The combat promptly ramped up a notch, the matched steps growing quicker and the blows more definite. The blood on Maxwell's arm welled to a red seam and began dripping on the gray stones underfoot.

"They are going to kill each other." Anne's fingers once more dug into Bess's arm.

Quite possibly. Or they would, indeed, battle their way to the gates of Hell. For if Callum was the best swordsman Bess had ever seen, Maxwell came damned close, and neither man looked ready to back down.

More and more men came in from outside. If Danhal Thomson arrived now, he could stroll right into the keep.

Foolish men, Bess thought. Was ever there anything as foolish as a prideful male?

A sudden flurry of movement banished the question from her mind. The two glittering swords engaged in a wicked show of force, and held. The two men, both with their teeth bared, glared into each other's eyes.

Muscles heaved. Dominance hung on the edges of the blades, and the room went silent.

Just as suddenly, they disengaged, neither man able to overpower the other. With an almost graceful movement, Maxwell spun, raised his blade and swept it at Callum's head.

Bess saw, from the corner of her eye, a figure dart forward. A blur of blue, it looked, moving far too swiftly and far too precipitately for sanity. She had no time to call out before Anne placed herself between Callum and that blade.

"No!" Anne cried out. "You shall not."

Somehow, Maxwell curtailed the blow. It cost him, and he staggered, off balance. The point of his blade caught Anne's wrist, raised to bar the strike.

At the same instant, Callum threw down his sword and caught Anne in his arms from behind. He lifted her almost before Maxwell stopped moving.

Everyone in the room exclaimed. Dexter gave a choked cry of, "Mistress Anne!" Maxwell paled with horror, and the expression on Callum's face as he cradled Anne made Bess's heart skip a beat.

Once more she stepped forward to Callum's side. "Bring her," she told him, "away out o' this."

Callum stared at her blankly before he nodded. They turned and, with a single burning glare for Aleck Maxwell, Bess led the way out of the crowded hall.

****

"What were you thinking?" Bess asked Callum as she tucked a clean white bandage around Anne's wrist. The wound had proven miraculously superficial. Such a blade as Maxwell wielded could well have severed Anne's hand. But as she knew, a sword blade was notably filthy. They would need to watch carefully for poisoning.

"Me?" Callum returned. "Me? Why do you no' ask her that?"

He'd hunkered down beside the bench in the solar

where Anne lay and had not budged from the place the whole time Bess cleaned and dressed the wound. Now he gazed into Anne's face with a tenderness that belied his angry words and disguised nothing.

"Foolish lass! You might ha' been killed."

Anne gazed back at him. "As might you. And what should I have done then? Callum MacFee, I would rather die a thousand times over than see that happen."

Suddenly, Bess felt very much in the way. She rose with the basin balanced in her hands but could not resist speaking. "You are each as mad as the other. Callum, what good would it do for you to kill Maxwell or him you?"

"'Twas not about sense," Anne answered for Callum. "It was about power."

"Dearest lass." Callum reached out and cupped Anne's cheek in his hand so tenderly tears came to Bess's eyes.

She did not need to witness this. She might want to, but these two deserved at least a few moments alone.

Still carrying the basin, she exited the solar, only to meet Dexter on the stairs.

"Is Mistress Anne all right?" the lad asked anxiously.

"She will be." Bess drew a breath. "Where is everyone?" Only silence came up the stairs from the hall.

"Master Maxwell sent his men out, back to their posts."

"And the lads?"

"He set us to drilling outside, but I—"

"You'd best go, then."

Bess did not know who'd come out on top in that

little tussle just past, but Maxwell had returned to giving orders, and he had the paper to back them, did he not?

Dexter's gaze moved past Bess to the door of the solar. "Might I see Mistress Anne?"

"Later." On top of the other things he'd witnessed this day, Dexter did not need to see what Bess hoped took place in the room behind her. "You run off, now."

Only one person occupied the hall when Bess reached it. He sat on a bench by the fire, trying rather awkwardly to tie up the wound on his bicep, using one good hand.

He lifted his dark head when Bess appeared, and the quick, feral gaze fastened on her.

"Is she all right?" he echoed the now-departed Dexter.

"She will be," Bess said again. "But I must compliment you on nearly slaying a fragile woman."

"How was I to know she'd do somewhat so utterly foolish?"

"You and Callum were the fools. What good will it do any of us for you to spill each other's blood?"

His gaze eased. "Nae good at all," he conceded. "I am no' proud o' myself. Trust me, I am usually far more careful."

"Then sit quietly, while I fetch clean water."

Somewhat to her surprise, he obeyed. She emptied the dirty water outside, where a crowd of lads did their best to imitate the combat they'd just witnessed, and fetched more from the kitchen.

Ah, now, she thought as she returned to Maxwell. She must contrive to touch him, to bind his wound, without displaying any hint of attraction. That might prove a challenge indeed, were she not still so flamingly angry with him.

Still, as she sat down on the bench at his side, she caught his scent—warm and dusky. It seemed to set her very senses alight.

"Sit still," she told him unfairly. He had not moved, and his eyes watched her movements carefully.

The wound had bled all down his arm. He'd made a poor attempt at cleaning it. Bess did better as she sponged the blood away.

He had freckles on his arms. She wondered if they extended everywhere.

"Did you mean to kill him?" she asked in an effort to focus her anger.

"Nay, just show him who is in charge."

"Well, I hope you are pleased with yourself."

He grimaced. "I ha' already said I am not. And I hope ye ken I could never raise a blade—or a hand—to a fragile woman like Mistress Anne. She is the very picture o' gentle womanhood."

"But me? You would raise a blade to me?" Bess's fingers stopped moving against his skin. Their gazes met.

"Ye are no'—" he halted abruptly.

She grimaced in turn. "I am no' what? Gentle? Or womanly?" She did not know what made her ask the questions, but neither could she hold them back.

"I was going to say, ye are no' fragile, nor unversed wi' combat. Bess, ye maun know I think you the most womanly female I ha' ever met."

"I am as different from ladylike Anne as night from day."

"Aye."

"I wear no skirts, I do not dress my hair upon my head or rouge my cheeks—"

"Ye be, by far, the most beguiling woman I ha' ever seen, ever touched—"

Following the words with the deed, he cupped the back of her head and brought her mouth to his. The kiss started out hungry, almost savage, a raw claiming rather than an indulgence. It softened swiftly to something hot and languorous, Maxwell's tongue once more claiming Bess's mouth and setting up that seductive rhythm.

Suddenly the taste of him overwhelmed her, his scent surrounded her. The world narrowed to this one moment, this one man.

The cloth fell from her hand. Her fingers smoothed over his bicep, up his shoulder, and tangled in his hair.

So, she thought a bit wildly, this is how it happens, how a woman who has kept control of her emotions so carefully goes a-wrong. She meets a man like this, who can seduce her with a single touch, a single kiss, and she becomes willing to offer him anything.

When Aleck broke the kiss, they both breathed raggedly. He pressed his forehead to hers and gazed into her eyes.

"Never doubt, Mistress Bess Mowatt, I find ye all woman under those leathers, and I'd sell my very soul to get ye out o' them."

Bess swallowed hard. As a compliment, it was neither lovely nor melodious. But she would accept it from this man.

This man.

"Beside ye," he went on, "a woman such as Mistress Anne pales to insipid insignificance."

"Better," she said aloud.

He grinned. It was a rogue's grin that invaded his golden eyes and sent a jolt straight through Bess.

"I am no' the man for pretty words. But ye, my lass, could wring me dry."

Bess had never lain with any man. Though her knowledge of what occurred in the bedchamber might be severely limited, she had no doubt what he meant, and heat rose to her face.

He raised his hand to cup her cheek. "So what are we to do, eh, Mistress Bess?"

"Naught." Gently but determinedly, she disengaged from his touch and glanced around the room. Thankfully—miraculously—they remained alone. No one had witnessed how shamefully she behaved with this man.

Her cousin's rapist.

"We shall do naught at all."

Chapter Eighteen

"I can no' be around the woman," Aleck complained to Anald as they paced the wall of the keep together, supposedly on lookout. "Quite plainly, I canna' be in the same room wi'out losing my head. I tell ye frankly, Anald, I ha' never experienced the like."

Anald glanced at him, his gaze for once entirely serious. "That is no' like ye, lad."

"I ken."

"Women ha' chased after ye all your life."

"They ha' chased me, aye." Rarely enough had Aleck been interested in getting caught. He'd allowed himself to get snagged by that vixen, Mary Johnstone, and look at what had come of it.

Yet for all the beguiling attraction between them and the skill of Mary's clever tongue, he'd kept his heart out of her grasp.

This matter with Bess Mowatt, he suspected, might be completely different.

"Now," he told Anald bitterly, "I am after chasing her. And she will no' fall into my arms. She believes I raped her cousin, and naught I say can persuade her otherwise."

"Aye, and you a right persuasive man."

"Usually."

"Still, lad, most women do succumb to persistence, at least in my experience. They are that flattered a man thinks so highly o' them, they eventually melt."

Aleck shot him a burning look.

"Ha' ye done more than kiss her yet, lad?"

"Nay." Though those kisses were seared into Aleck's mind along with all their accompanying sensations. He paused along the wall and ran a hand through his hair.

"She is determined to run from ye, then."

"Even when I kiss her, she holds something o' herself awa' from me. 'Tis as if she's fire, wi' ice underneath."

"Ah." Anald clapped him on the shoulder. "Ye be suffering, and no mistake."

Aye, and he should stop with moaning about it, put his feelings away, and behave like a man. Lay aside the conviction that if he did not have Bess Mowatt to himself, and soon, he would burn up into ash.

Anald asked, "What d'ye think o' Mistress Anne's actions during yon combat?"

Aleck looked at his friend sympathetically. "I think she's in love with MacFee, rushing to protect him that way. And I think you will ha' to set your feelings for her aside. She—"

An interruption occurred then in the form of a rider, coming hard across the greensward—one of Aleck's men.

"They come! They come! Thomsons!"

Aleck swore bitterly under his breath. Now he would indeed need to set every other consideration aside.

If he could.

****

Aleck and Anald made it down off the walls

140

swiftly and met the rider before his feet hit the ground. Geordie MacAlvin, his name was, one of the men newly arrived.

"Wha' is it, man?" Aleck demanded. "Wha' did ye see?"

Geordie's face, slick with sweat, shone in alarm.

"A large force o' men. Most o' them mounted, but some afoot. Coming as fast as the runners can manage."

"How far off?" Anald grunted.

"They've made it through the ford at Dalweedie. They'll be here by nightfall." Geordie gulped breath. "The rest of our scouts come just behind me."

Aleck turned to Anald. "Ride out to meet them. Get everyone else inside, wi' aught o' value—arms, game."

He turned and found Callum MacFee at his side. Since their combat, he had to admit he'd avoided the man, had barely looked into his face. Aleck still wanted to know which of them had the stronger sword. Not likely to find out now.

Would MacFee take his orders? Or would there be strife within as well as without?

He told MacFee, "Mak' sure Mistress Anne is safe upstairs, and the lads also." He hesitated. "I do no' suppose there be any sense asking Mistress Bess to stay there with them?"

"Did I hear my name?"

She stood at MacFee's shoulder, fully armed. She appeared a bit pale but steady, and her eyes glittered.

Aleck dismissed MacFee from his mind and, turning to Bess, seized her by the shoulders. He looked into her face. "Is there any use asking ye to keep out o' harm's way?"

"Harm's way?" she repeated, going stiff beneath

his hands. "'Tis a raid, no' a winter's gale."

"I know that."

"What use am I, if I do no' fight?"

What use was she? Warm within his arms, heaven beneath his lips, a balm against his heart.

But he could say none of that. Instead he shook her slightly and growled, "'Tis no' the fighting worries me. Ye be competent wi' a blade in your hands, aye. But if aught goes wrong, if these walls should fall, ye stand to be captured. And then ye, and Mistress Anne, face a fate worse than any wound."

She lifted her chin and looked him in the eye. "Then I think it my duty to make sure these walls do not fall."

Despair touched Aleck's heart. A confident man, he rarely experienced that emotion save when he thought on his lost son. Now it assailed him with unexpected potency.

"Will ye no' at least hang back to guard the lads, and Mistress Anne? Your blade will be valuable there." And he would, at least, be able to concentrate on the fight.

"Assign someone else," she tossed at him. "There is somewhat you do not understand, Aleck Maxwell. This keep has belonged to me and Callum a long while. Just because you come waving a paper in our faces, that does not change what is in our hearts."

He could understand that. Trouble was, he could not accept her risking her safety because of it.

"Stubborn Englishwoman," he growled.

"That I am. Best not forget it."

****

Bess climbed up to the solar, wondering at what

she'd seen in Aleck Maxwell's eyes. Anger, aye, right enough. Outrage because she refused to follow his orders. But there had been something more that she could not so readily identify.

She reminded herself, not for the first time, he was a reiver—not unlike these raiders who now came to attack them. He would have her believe he worried for her virtue, even though he had, himself, forced Mary and begat upon her his child.

The fact that she, Bess, loved that child as she loved no one else in this world changed nothing. Well, aye, maybe it sent her up to the solar now, not to stay but to check that everyone else would remain there.

They'd taken places in the room that had become Anne's own domain, the lads who were left, along with Anne and three female servants. Bess did not envy Anne the coming ordeal. The chamber already felt overcrowded and overfilled with both eagerness and anxiety.

The lads, especially the older ones, thought they should be allowed to fight. They looked like so many young wolves trapped in a cage. The women appeared plainly frightened.

Dexter rushed up to Bess when she came in. "What's happening? Must we stay here?"

"I am afraid so. I want all of you to guard those here and obey Mistress Anne."

Jamie, one of the oldest lads, stepped forward. "Surely we are to be included in defending the keep?" he asked aggressively.

Bess looked him in the eye. "Aye, should the worst happen and our walls be breeched, you will fight at the door of this chamber and on the stairs, if necessary, to protect Mistress Anne, along with Cook, Elspeth, and Kate."

"Do you think that will happen?" asked one of the younger lads uneasily.

"No, I do not. We have some of the best blades in the borders down below. But understand this: we do not await a mere raid, which comes in the night, the theft of cattle or sheep. These men approach in broad daylight. They must know we have seen them. They come to take possession of the keep."

The lads murmured. Jamie bowed his head. "You can rely on me, Mistress Mowatt. I will defend Mistress Anne to the death."

Dexter rolled his eyes. Far more likely, Bess thought, they would all kill one another while waiting for the Thomsons.

She turned sympathetic eyes on Anne. "A word, if you please."

They stepped to one side, and Bess placed her mouth at Anne's ear.

"I am sorry to leave you in the midst of this. Try to keep them occupied, and away from the windows."

"Occupied! How?"

Cursed if Beth knew.

Anne's eyes looked wild. She clutched Bess's arm. "I am worried for Callum."

"Callum can take care of himself."

"But he will toss his life away if he thinks he must. And I—I cannot live without him. Bess, I cannot lose another man I—love."

"Have you told Callum that?"

Anne shook her head. "I dare not. I do not know how he feels for me."

"He adores you." Bess squeezed Anne's hand. "Tell him how you feel. Do it now while you may. Would you like me to send him up?"

"Here?" Anne glanced at the lads, who now argued over when Danhal Thomson and his unsavory crew would arrive. "In front of them?"

"On the stairs, if need be. Let me send him up."

Anne bit her lip and shook her head. "I would not wish to distract him. But look after him for me, Bess. Please look after him for me."

Chapter Nineteen

"Are the lads safe?" Aleck shot a close look at Bess as he worked beside her. They stockpiled weapons all around the walls. Fortunately, the keep had a well-furnished armory, and Aleck saw no lack thereof.

Callum MacFee had done a fine job of maintaining the keep over the years, he had to admit. Seemed somewhat a shame that after giving his heart to it so long the man had to lose the place. But such was the way of life. A man lost much he valued.

In reply to his query, Bess made a face. She had scraped her hair back out of her eyes and braided it tightly, ready to fight. She looked grim, and steady. And so lovely it made his heart ache.

"They are safe for the moment, at least from everything but each other. Trapped in that chamber together, I do not know how long it will take them to come to blows. You may as well know, they do not all get along. Some actively hate each other."

Aleck smiled. "Like Dexter and Ronson MacNab." He sobered. "Dexter says Ronson taunts him for being a bastard. A strange thing, since ye say he's your cousin's son."

Bess's gaze fled his hastily. "His parents' union was not a legitimate one."

"Aye, so. But his father acknowledged him?"

"He did, but he's—gone now. And his mother has

had little to do with the lad since he was small."

"And, his mother's name?"

"Why should you ask that?"

"I merely wondered if I know her."

"Margaret. Margaret Watson."

Not Mary, then. And why did he persist in asking? Why not just accept his son had died at birth? It was as if some inner, vital instinct shouted it down.

"Does she no' worry for him, this Margaret?" he asked.

"She has moved on and lives elsewhere, out o' the country," Bess said hastily. "'Tis I raised him."

"Ah." It explained how close they were, and why he'd never heard of Margaret Watson. "So then," he leaned against the wall, "you never wanted to wed and have bairns o' your own?"

She straightened and gazed away over the rampart as if searching for approaching reivers. They were out there, Aleck had no doubt. But evening now drew down, and it looked like they would wait, after all, to attack in the dark.

"There never seemed time. Nor opportunity." Bess shook her head. "Who would wed a woman like me, who chooses a sword over an embroidery needle?"

I would. Aleck did not say the words aloud. He didn't dare. He took a terrible risk being alone with the woman for, as he'd told Anald, alone with her, he ached to touch. The fire, it seemed, never lay far below the surface.

Momentarily forgetting the danger that surrounded them, he lowered his voice and said, "Surely ye maun ken how bonny ye be."

Her gaze flew to his, arrested, and full of disbelief.

"Ah, Master Maxwell, keep your outrageous compliments to yourself. They will not work on me."

"Work?" he repeated, stymied.

"I do not intend to fall into your arms again nor allow you to—to take such liberties as before. There is grave and serious business at hand."

"So there is." And, so, what was he to do with the need? This relentless ache that made him want to be close to her, watch the light flash in her eyes, and catch her scent. Aye, she must be well past marriageable age, and a while on the shelf—surely past five and twenty. He did not care. And despite the sword and the leather clothing she wore, he could scarce believe no man had thrown himself at her feet.

For she could easily be wooed out of those leather breeches. And then…

She shifted uneasily. "Why do you look at me that way?"

"What way?"

"As if, as if—" Having no words for it, she shook her head again.

As if he wanted to consume her? Get her naked, her skin smooth against his naked skin, and set her alight so the two of them burned up in glorious flame?

"Because I enjoy the looking." He reached to cup her cheek but she danced aside, wary as a wild fox.

"Nay, I meant what I said. That will not happen again."

Aleck went suddenly still, deadly serious. "Ye will look after yoursel', Bess Mowatt, once the attack begins. I may no' be able to protect ye, in the heat of the fight."

"I need no man to protect me. I need no man at

all."

So she thought. But Aleck intended to prove her wrong.

****

When Bess went upstairs to say good night to Dexter, she found the lads' quarters miraculously quiet. She'd felt certain they would all still be up and talking, far too excited to sleep. But at least some of the commotion had died down.

Dexter slept in a small cell of his own. Some of the lads shared quarters and so had Dexter, for a time, but it always seemed to come to quarrels and name calling. He had been sharing with Jock Callander till the boy's father took him home. So only one of the cots in the narrow chamber remained occupied when Bess stepped in.

Dexter, not sleeping after all, promptly sat up. "Has it started? The attack—"

"Not yet." He'd left the stub of a candle burning—against rules, but she would let it go this time. She went forward and sat on the edge of the cot. Looking at the lad—her lad—her heart contracted with love.

His sheets were in a restless tangle, and his black hair stood out ruffled all over his head. His eyes glowed with what might be trepidation.

"Master Maxwell has men watching all along the walls and standing firm at the gate. We will know when they mean to begin the attack."

Dexter relaxed a hair. "That is all right, then. Master Maxwell will look after us."

"Master Maxwell, all his men, Master Callum, and me—you have all of us standing between you and harm."

"Aye."

Bess hesitated. "You like him, do you? Master Maxwell?"

Dexter's face lit. "Aye. He is brave and so funny. He talks to me—really talks—as if I'm a man already grown. I wish...I wish he were my father."

Bess promptly lost all her breath.

"I wish," Dexter went on earnestly, "I had a father. Then the other lads would leave me alone. But most of all I wish my father were Master Maxwell."

"You had a father," Bess said faintly. "Everyone does."

"But I canna' speak o' him, or boast about him as the other lads do. I never knew him. So I am no' as good as the others."

"Dexter, my love, that is not true. You are every bit as good as any among those lads. Better, in fact."

"I am no'."

He sounded so certain that Bess's heart broke in her breast. How could she convince him? How when, day by day, he was prey to his companions' slurs and jeers?

She said, "A man must make his own way in the world, by his words and deeds. In the end, 'tis that makes his measure."

"And his forebears. So Ronson says."

"Oh, and will you listen to him? He is good for naught but pummeling."

Dexter gave his devil's grin which, to her dismay, Bess now saw very much resembled Aleck Maxwell's. Then, abruptly, he sobered.

"Will the attack be very fierce?"

"'Tis hard to tell before it begins. Hopefully we

will be able to repel them, and make them think again."

"Aye."

"They will not expect us to have so many men as we do, and more to come."

Dexter gazed into her eyes. "Must you fight?"

"You know I must."

"Mayhap you could stay safe with Mistress Anne and me."

"That is not my place."

His expression crumpled. "But what if you should fall in the fighting? And Master Callum—I ha' no one else. Wha' would befall me?"

He cast himself into her arms. She gathered him in tight as she had when he was much smaller, when he'd scraped his knee or bumped his nose during some scramble. He clutched her just as fervently, as if grasping his whole world.

"Och, love," she murmured, "that will not happen."

"It might. The other lads can go home, like Jock. I h-have no home."

What could she say to him? Before Robert Lithgow's death, she might have assured him his great uncle would take him in. To be sure, his mother did not want him, and Bess could think of nowhere else he would not be pushed aside and neglected.

An image of Aleck Maxwell swam into her mind. If he knew Dexter to be his son, he would take him in, in an instant. She knew that to her bones.

But did she have the right to reveal a secret not her own?

Did she have the right to keep a father and son apart?

For the first time, she grasped her uncle Robert's

dilemma, and why he had perhaps acted as he had, in granting the keep to Maxwell. He had not revealed Mary's secret or betrayed her trust. He had gambled that, thrown into close proximity, Maxwell and Dexter would find each other.

She should do the same. Trust in fate, if it had a role, and in the strength of the blood.

"There now," she stroked the lad's rough curls. "The chances of both me and Master Callum falling in any fight are quite small."

"You think so?"

"I do. Now, quiet yourself and try to sleep. This may be the last peaceful night we see for some time."

"Aye."

She tucked him in and kissed his brow as she'd done when he was small. She went downstairs with a weight on her heart.

A number of Maxwell's men sat in the hall, Maxwell among them. Maxwell's gaze lifted to her as soon as she entered the room, and a chill crept up her spine. Or was that a thrill of titillation?

He discussed strategy, no doubt, with his men. Bess crossed to a table and poured a cup of ale. Before she could drink, Maxwell left his companions and joined her.

"Mistress Mowatt, is somewhat amiss?"

She might have held her tongue. If she wished to speak with anyone about Dexter, she could find Callum, even though he probably paced the walls, searching for danger. She should definitely not confide in Aleck Maxwell, yet the words came from her, worried and low.

"The lads are on edge tonight."

"Ha." He tossed his head, so like Dexter it made her stare. "Everyone is on edge tonight. Imminent attack will do that to a man."

"You believe it is imminent?"

He gave a grim smile. "My ears are constantly stretched for a cry from the walls. There will be little sleep this night."

"Is Callum up there?"

"He has just gone out, as I ha' just come in. If it reassures ye, 'tis a clear night, and the moon is up."

"Why should that reassure me?"

"Mistress Mowatt, I am a reiver. I ha' made many such raids, and I tell ye, I love best a wee bit o' rain and fog."

"I see."

"That does no' mean we will fail to hear that cry before morning. Danhal Thomson is no' me, nor I him."

Bess frowned. Morning seemed terribly far off. "It is Dexter who concerns me," she said.

Maxwell's attention quickened. "Dexter?"

"He fears that both Callum and I may fall during an attack and he will be thrown, friendless, upon the world."

Maxwell grunted. "Callum will no' fall. He is far too virtuous and too stubborn." He appeared to contemplate it. "Too well skilled, also. And ye will no' fall."

"Because I am also too well skilled?"

"That, and because I will let no harm befall ye." His hand brushed her back, just a fleeting touch, yet comfort flowed from it.

His eyes met hers again. "Believe me."

She wanted to. Part of her did. Yet Mary insisted

he'd forced her. How could she trust such a man?

He took a step nearer, and her breath suspended. "Bess, would ye like me to speak wi' Dexter?"

She should say no. Her duty lay in keeping him as far from Dexter as possible. Instead, she nodded. "But not until morning. I hope he's sleeping now."

Aleck smiled wryly. "Aye, it can wait for morning."

If morning ever came.

Chapter Twenty

Morning arrived, the sun pushing its way off the shoulders of the land into an achingly clear sky, and Callum MacFee came down off the walls. Aleck met him at the entrance to the hall.

Things between them remained far from settled. Their dispute had merely been suspended for the duration of the attack. Having had a taste of the man's skill, Aleck did not know if he could best him—unusual for him. MacFee might be an uncommon man with the sword, as well as uncommonly controlled in his emotions. But his animosity showed every time he looked at Aleck.

No exception now. MacFee gave a glare of loathing even as he made his report. "They are out there, right enough. Waiting. We had glimpses once it began growing light. Besides," he shrugged his shoulders, "I can feel them."

"Waiting for some cover, mayhap? Such as mist or rain?"

"Mayhap. Have you slept?"

Aleck shook his head. "Up and drinking."

MacFee's gaze sharpened. "Is that wise?"

"It quickens the senses."

MacFee snorted.

Aleck told him, "Ye'd better catch some rest now. I will go up and keep watch. But I maun speak wi' someone first."

"Whom?"

"Surely that is my concern."

MacFee wanted to argue it. The angry words fair trembled on his lips. Nay, their quarrel definitely was not over. But, choosing his battles, MacFee nodded. "I will no' ha' my head down long. Call me if it begins."

"I will."

MacFee moved off. A shiver traveling the length of Aleck's spine told him Mistress Mowatt had entered the room. He spun to face her.

She looked ill-rested. Once more she'd braided her hair tightly, prepared for the fight, but her pale face and troubled eyes betrayed her anxiety.

Aleck crossed to her side. "Good morning, mistress. Well, we came through the night."

"This waiting will destroy us all."

"Part o' Thomson's game, no doubt. He must ken we know he's out there. He is testing our nerve."

"He is a right bastard, then. What am I to do wi' those lads all day?"

"Set them to drilling in the forecourt." Offhand, he offered, "I am due for a turn upon the walls. But would ye like me to work wi' them a short while, after?"

She hesitated. The woman did not like accepting his assistance, just as she did not like the way she caught fire every time he touched her. She wanted to despise him, but she didn't, not quite.

He added, by way of persuasion, "I will speak wi' young Dexter first, if ye like."

"Very well. He is still up in his chamber, the second on the right."

Aleck took the stairs two at a time and rapped on

the thick oaken door. A fine dwelling, this, and one in which he might not mind making a home, once the dust settled.

But he'd have to defend it first.

Dexter came to the door still dressed in his night shirt, with his dark curls all tumbled. He looked young and vulnerable, and Aleck experienced a queer sensation in the region of his heart.

"Master Maxwell?"

"A word, Master Mowatt, before ye go down to your breakfast."

Alarm flared in the boy's blue eyes. "The attack—has it started?"

"No' yet. Believe me when I say ye will hear when it starts. Might I come in?"

Dexter swung the door wide. The room, small and barren, boasted but two narrow cots, one of which had clearly not been occupied, and a single chest. No windows, no comforts of any kind.

Aleck seated himself on the unused cot, wondering how to begin. He had little experience with children, but it felt different with this lad, comfortable. Honesty, he thought, would prove best.

"I hear ye be uneasy about your future."

Dexter backed up and sat on his own cot. It lay wildly tumbled, as if he'd had very little sleep last night. "Who told you that?"

"I had a word with Mistress Mowatt."

"She should no' ha' told you." Dexter's face flushed a ruddy hue. "'Tis not—not manly to worry."

"Is it no'? I maun be no' much o' a man, then, mysel'."

"You?" Dexter's eyes widened. "You are a braw

man and warrior, indeed."

"And yet, I am concerned for wha' may come. Only a fool would no' be."

"Truly?"

"Most truly. A man wi' any kind o' wit examines the possibilities, does he no'? And then these possibilities begin to niggle at his mind."

"Aye. Just so."

"But I am fairly confident we can handle Danhal Thomson and his ugly crew. We ha' the advantage o' these walls, ye ken. And a good number o' experienced warriors."

Some of the tension went out of Dexter's shoulders.

"So ye see," Aleck continued in as bland a tone as he could manage, "I do no' think ye need worry about losing the folk ye—well, those ye love."

"Aye, but Master Callum—he will be at the forefront. He would ne'er hang back or spare himsel' out o' concern for the rest of us."

"So he would not."

"And Mistress Bess—" Dexter's face suddenly crumbled. "She is all I have. I ha' lived wi' her all my life."

Aleck's voice softened. "She's been a mother to ye."

Dexter nodded. Tears filled his eyes.

"What if I promise ye I will tak' special care to look out for her in any battle? Would that ease your mind?"

Dexter nodded. "Will you?"

"I will." He intended to do so anyway. His every instinct demanded it. But if saying so could chase the fear from the lad's eyes, he'd speak the words.

"Thank you." Dexter launched himself from the cot, and suddenly Aleck had his arms full of boy. Dexter clutched him tightly, and his head, very like a boulder hurled by a catapult, smashed into Aleck's shoulder. "I trust you, I truly do."

The queer sensation squeezed Aleck's heart still tighter. "Ah, now," he crooned. "I will do my best. And I will tell ye this, lad… Look at me, now."

Dexter raised his head. His gaze met Aleck's with total attention.

"Should the unthinkable happen to both your guardians—and I am no' saying it will—then ye shall come to me. As my ward, ye understand? So ye ha' no need to worry for your future, whatever comes."

"I would like that very much. But I would like to stay here wi' Mistress Bess and Master Callum most o' all."

"I would like that best, also." Aleck would not remind the lad the keep now belonged to him, and whether or not Bess and MacFee stayed lay at his discretion.

Instead he tousled the lad's hair. "Get yoursel' dressed, now, and come down to breakfast. There's to be drilling on the forecourt."

"Will you work wi' me?"

"Just as soon as my watch up on the walls is over, aye, lad, I will."

****

The rain moved in just before nightfall. Bess climbed up to the ramparts where Aleck Maxwell once more stood on watch. So far as she could tell, he'd taken little rest this day, having kept watch this morning and worked with the lads most of the afternoon.

He quickened when he heard her foot on the stone, and his gaze enveloped her, glowing golden in the fading light.

"Any movement yet?" she asked as she joined him.

"Nay, but it will come tonight."

"How do you know?"

"Danhal Thomson's no' all that patient. Besides, I can feel it." His shoulders twitched. "This is just the sort of night I would choose."

"Have you taken any dinner?" She had no right to feel concerned for him—to feel anything for him—but if battle came, he needed to be in good form.

"I had a wee bit o' bread and broth before I came back up."

She let her gaze pan the countryside, so familiar and yet now so riddled with menace. "Are you sure they're out there? I see nothing."

"Ye are supposed to see nothing. But oh, aye, they're there. See that stand o' fir trees just left o' dead center? Twice ha' I seen a glint o' light from there. Someone's been careless."

"How bad will it be, when it comes?"

He shrugged, then turned his head and looked at her. "Bad. As I told ye before, I would like it if ye stayed wi' Mistress Anne and the lads, no' because I think ye canna' fight, but because I do. They need someone to guard them. Ye might hold the top o' the stairs quite well."

Seeing the desperation in his eyes, Bess relented. "All right, I will guard Anne and the lads. But 'twill not come to that, surely? Thomsons will not break through the gates?" Bess's throat went tight.

"No, probably not tonight. But I ha' men enough ye can be spared for the post." He paused before saying, "Young Master Dexter is worried about losing ye. Your presence will go far to reassure him."

"Aye."

"I think we will be able to repel them from the walls, for a time. But Thomson's doubtless brought a large force."

"What about the gates?" They were double, one inside the other, with a narrow walkway above.

"Aye, that's our most vulnerable spot. If he breaks through there, 'twill become interesting."

"Can we not parley?"

"Talk to him?" Aleck laughed. "Ye do no' ken Danhal Thomson. He's a reiver to his bones."

"Like you."

"No' like me. Whatever ye might think o' me, Mistress Bess, I do no' harm those weaker than myself."

Except defenseless young women.

"Nor do I kill for pleasure. Danhal Thomson enjoys both."

"Oh, Jesu," Bess whispered.

"As soon as the attack starts, I will go down and defend the gate, wi' a stout party o' men."

"Have you thrashed that privilege out with Callum?"

"Callum does no' come into it." Aleck drew himself up. "'Tis my gate, and I will defend it. No' but I welcome Master MacFee's sword by my side."

Sudden fear clawed at Bess's belly, and she knew how Dexter felt. She could lose Callum—close as a brother to her. She could lose this man beside her.

Unbearable.

All at once she wanted to press her way into his arms, she wanted to kiss him one last time, feel the heat of him wrap around her. But the walls were well populated, and eyes watched from everywhere. So she merely stood where she was, her heart pounding much too hard, and said, "God guard you, Aleck Maxwell."

"And ye, Bess Mowatt. And ye."

Chapter Twenty-One

"Sweet heavens!" Anne raised her hands and covered both her ears. "I cannot stand the racket. Who would think 'twould be so loud?"

All the lads turned their eyes on her, and Bess—stationed not at her assigned place atop the stairs outside the solar but at the large window—winced. Never had she thought to see the composed, serene Anne come to pieces, but it had occurred. Bess supposed she should have expected it. Anne's beloved husband had died in a raid like this one, and their circumstances must bring back dire memories.

And aye, the clash of weapons and the shouts and cries sounded unnaturally loud. Men fought all along the walls, but the worst of the attack centered at the front gate, and the sound funneled up the stone stairs. An intense battle, indeed.

Bess glanced at Dexter, who sat hunched and miserable. Aye, well, all the lads looked unhappy, some because they itched to join the fight and some because they feared they just might have to.

Anne's jangled nerves certainly did not help.

"Master Dexter," Bess requested, "please sit beside Mistress Anne and recite to her your lessons."

"My...what?" Dexter's jaw dropped, and everyone else stared, including Cook and the two female servants, still billeted there.

"Reciting your French verbs should do the trick. You never do know," Bess peered out through the window, "when you may need a command o' the French tongue."

"I canna'," poor Dexter said huskily, even as he moved to the seat at Anne's side. "My mind has gone blank."

"All the more reason to fill it with something."

Ronson MacNab spoke up. "My da says we will all be speaking French someday, if Queen Mary has her druthers. He says she's near as bad as the damned English queen."

"That's treason, that is," said another boy.

"'Tis no'. Scotland should remain Scotland, and a curse to both the English and the French."

Just like that, they began arguing again, squabbling fit to drown out the din from below.

Bess turned her attention back through the window, even though she could in truth see little between the mullions. Did Callum fight down there? Did Aleck Maxwell?

Impossible to tell on a night so dark. Danhal Thomson had, indeed, chosen his moment well. Rain and mist clouded the forecourt. Torches flanked the gate, but they struggled to burn in the wet, and she could not tell if the battle went well or badly.

Behind her, the discussion intensified. Each of the lads, it seemed kept an opinion and did not mind voicing it. Soon, Anne occupied herself trying to restore order.

Bess started when someone bumped her side. Dexter, ever disobedient, had abandoned his place beside Anne and tried to peer through the panes.

"I can see naught."

"You should get back out of danger."

"So should you," he retorted. "Can you see Master Callum?"

"No."

"Or Master Maxwell?"

At the sound of his name, Bess's heart accelerated. She assured herself, not for the first time, she need not worry for him. He was not hers to fret over.

"The gates are holding," she told Dexter—the one thing of which she could be certain. "If either of them has taken an injury, he fights on."

"Maybe," Dexter suggested, "you could go down to the hall and see."

Maybe she could. The hall, so they'd agreed, would be where the wounded were taken. She might take a wee peek, just to reassure Dexter.

Of course, Maxwell had bidden her stay here.

She did not take orders from Aleck Maxwell.

"Guard the door," she bade Dexter. "You have your sword?"

He seemed to grow three inches. "I do."

"Then stand firm. I will be right back."

Aleck Maxwell, so she told herself as she pelted down the stairs, full bore, should know better than to expect her to stay shut away in ignorance of what passed. For the sake of those she guarded, she needed to keep abreast of what transpired.

The doorway that opened to the forecourt lay just opposite the foot of the stairs, with the gates beyond. Two of Maxwell's men guarded the doorway. They turned strained faces to Bess as she landed.

One of them said, "Lady, ye should no' be down

here." He sounded uncertain. Some of Maxwell's newer arrivals had never seen a woman in leathers, armed with weapons, and did not know what to make of her.

"Get ye back upstairs," said the second man, "wi' the others."

Ignoring them, she continued forward. "How goes the fight?"

"Fierce."

"Any wounded?"

The first man jerked his head toward the hall, which opened to the right. Bess tiptoed to the door and peered in.

Three men occupied the place, none of them Aleck Maxwell—or, she hastily added, Callum MacFee. Two were men of Maxwell's whom she did not know, both appearing only superficially wounded, one being treated by William. The third lay bandaged and insensible.

William shot Bess a look. "I thought you were supposed to be guarding those upstairs."

"I am."

"Ye maun ha' a damned long reach."

"We needed to know how the fight goes."

One of Maxwell's men answered, "Ye be in no danger yet, mistress. They'll no' get through the gates this night."

Bess longed to ask about Maxwell and dared not. *Be satisfied with what you have learned and go back upstairs. Our wounded are few enough.*

And Aleck Maxwell meant little to her, save that he was Dexter's father. And, as such, surely of warrantable importance.

She let that thought die away even as the clamor

from the gates grew louder. One of the injured men rose to his feet.

"I ha' better get back to it."

Old William gave him a hard nod. To Bess he said, "And you ha' better get back to your post, lass."

She went, pelting back up the stairs to the solar, only to encounter an astonishing sight. Anne, perhaps tiring of the argument within, had somehow restored order. Bess found her sitting in her chair, listening while one of the lads recited a string of French verbs, and the other lads waited their turns.

Dexter moved aside and admitted Bess to the room.

"All's as well as may be expected below," she assured him. "Not many injuries yet."

He brightened. "'Tis good, that."

"Very good, indeed. Go take your turn reciting for Mistress Anne."

She did not tell him this night was but the beginning of their troubles. Or that she suspected they would all know their verbs very well before it was done.

Chapter Twenty-Two

The light of a sickly dawn bled through the mist, and Aleck Maxwell at last lowered his sword. He hurt from head to foot and would give a year off his life for a draught of ale.

Wounds stung on his cheek, thigh, and forearm. His knuckles had been slashed and bashed more times than he could number. But he'd held the gate.

He glanced at the man who stood beside him and hastily amended: *they'd* held the gate, he and Callum MacFee.

"They are falling back. At last," he muttered, and MacFee shot him a sharp look.

"It maun be odd for you, this," he said.

Aleck lifted a brow in query.

A wry smile twisted MacFee's lips. "You are used to being on the other side, battering your way in, aye?"

"Aye," Aleck admitted ruefully.

"How does it feel, to stand in defense?"

"Difficult." But thank God and all the holy saints Danhal Thomson had decided to withdraw with the arrival of morning. Of course, he and MacFee had taken a toll on Thomson's fighting force, with a good deal of help from the walls. But he needed time to lick his wounds, catch his breath. Get that draught of ale.

Lay eyes on Bess Mowatt.

He ached to see her, even more than he ached for rest. All through the fight amid the sweat and the struggle, she'd remained in his mind.

Almost as if he fought for her. And the boy.

Well, and he did, more or less. Yet it made a strange proposition for him to be battling for the sake of anyone but himself. As strange, aye, as fighting to defend rather than attack.

"Better go get those knuckles tended," MacFee said, even though he sported wounds every bit as lurid as Aleck's. "I'll get some fresh men at this post."

"Fresh men?" Aleck muttered. They had none such.

MacFee gave a rare grin. "Fresher than we."

"Ah, aye."

Tottering a bit, Aleck took himself off to the hall. Thronged with men and echoing with voices, at first it looked every bit as confusing as the scene outside.

Two of his men greeted him, and Anald hurried up. He'd taken a slash to the forehead during a critical moment in the battle, and gore splashed his face, dried in patches.

Aleck blinked at him. "Holy Jesu, clean yoursel' up, man. Ye'll frighten the lads."

Anald grinned, his teeth looking very white amidst the gore. "They ha' no' come down yet."

And would not, if Bess Mowatt had a say. Aleck swept the room, hoping for a glimpse of her. The longing inside him, still rampant, urged it.

"She has no' come down either," Anald told him wickedly, interpreting his state of mind with ease. "That ham-fisted old fart, William, is doing the nursing. I would rather wait and see if Mistress Anne will tend me."

Aleck swore with feeling. "Will ye no' give that

up? She belongs to MacFee. And 'tis no time, this, for pushing the man."

"Does she belong to MacFee, though?"

"Ye ken she does."

"He has no' spoken for her."

"I believe they have an understanding. One of the heart."

Anald pretended to look shocked. "Since when d'ye speak o' the heart? Och, and ye maun ha' taken a blow to the head in yon fight."

Aleck gave him a glare. "I need a mug o' ale."

"Breakfast might be more appropriate."

"Aye, but I ha' been wanting the ale all night."

He went and found a cup. The female servants, released from the solar, began bringing out bread and cheese. He and Anald sat and waited for their turn beneath William's rough-and-ready hands.

Anald nodded at Aleck's mug. "Best drink that while ye can." The expression in his blue eyes looked unnaturally clear. "Wha' d'ye think o' Thomson's intentions? I think he means to settle in for the long siege."

Aleck shook his head, then wished he hadn't. it still rang from last night's clamor. "What makes ye say that?"

Anald grunted. "Instinct, along wi' the fact that if he did no' mean to settle in, he would never ha' broke off the attack at sunrise but would ha' kept hammering at us, hoping for a crack in our defense."

Aleck contemplated it unhappily. "But we ha' our advantage, more men on the way."

"If they come, given our situation." Anald reflected briefly. "I am no' certain I would." He nodded at the ale. "So, enjoy that while ye may. We might soon run out o' everything."

Aleck swore bitterly. Suddenly the much-desired ale tasted sour in his mouth. Och, to what had he committed himself? What had he taken on? As MacFee said, he should be the one outside, battering the walls. Not the poor sod struggling to put up a defense. He did no' like—

"Is it over? Are they gone?"

The voice, strident, came from his elbow. Aleck swiveled his head and saw Mistress Bess enter the hall.

He came up to his feet as if hauled by ropes, his weary body responding despite itself. She looked angry, distressed, and so tantalizing his despair fled on a rush of heat.

Anald gave what sounded like a chuckle and stumped off to take his turn with William.

Bess's gaze moved over Aleck slowly. It started at his head and went downward, lingering at the gash on his cheek and the rents in his clothing.

"Are you badly injured?" she asked.

Did she care? Had she spent any worry for him last night, or did all her concern center on the defense of the keep?

He shook his head and countered with a question of his own. "How are the lads?"

"Anxious and impatient. Frightened, though they do not want to admit it."

"Aye."

She edged closer. He caught her scent, and his senses, already battered, swam. "Is it over?" she asked. "Have Thomsons been driven off?"

He wanted to laugh but would not. The distress in

her eyes prevented it, and he shook his head again, regretful. "'Twill no' be so easy as that."

"Easy? What we heard last night did not sound easy. And you do not look—"

"Danhal Thomson took some injuries, as did we. He will be back again at nightfall, if not sooner."

Dismay flooded the stormy eyes. "How long? How many nights like that one?"

"I canna' say."

"Anne will never endure it. She lost her husband, you see, in just such a raid."

"I am sorry for it, and for her. But this has only begun."

Bess swore softly before asking in dread, "What am I to do with the lads? Tell me that."

"Put them to their lessons. Drill them as ye can." Aleck ached to touch her, if only in reassurance. His fingers twitched before he disciplined them. "Fear it as ye may, mistress, this is in truth a very good lesson for them. In our world, this is what they will face, either from inside or without."

"Well, then," she snapped just before she turned on her heel and left him, "I do not think much of our world."

****

Bess stood at the highest window of the east watch tower, huddled up against the cool air that flowed through the aperture, which boasted no glass. The keep had been built with a tower at the corner of each parapet, a place for men to keep an eye on the far countryside. She knew they did just that now, somewhere above her head. So it had been throughout this seemingly endless day.

The lads had proven a handful and no mistake, soon growing edgy and restless in the solar, at each other's throats once again. She'd spoken to them sternly and had even called Callum in to speak to them, all to no avail. She'd broken up no fewer than three fist fights, and Ronson MacNab had drawn a dirk on Jamie Hume.

'Twas but day one.

She'd needed to get away, if only for a few precious moments. The top rooms of the towers—small and barren—served for little more than storage. She did not care. Here, sounds from below became muted and distant.

The danger, though, remained.

She peered out at the land below, well known to her but now containing an element both foreign and perilous. They would come soon. The battle would resume.

She twitched and tried to duck the thoughts thronging her mind. So much could happen before the new day arrived. Men would be wounded. The gates might fall.

As might Aleck Maxwell.

That thought spurred a wild protest in her breast. She remembered the look in his tawny eyes when she'd approached him in the hall this morning—those feral eyes that, she fancied, softened when they rested on her.

Softened, and burned.

Fool, she chastised herself. How could he do both? It did not even make sense. But then nothing about the way she felt for that man made sense.

Desire—aye, well, desire was just that, a craving of the body. It could be disciplined. Only she hadn't been able to discipline this desire. It ran rampant through her blood and dominated the thoughts in her mind.

And she had to admit desire did not make up the whole of what she felt for Aleck Maxwell. He proved nothing like Mary's lurid descriptions of him, a seducer and scoundrel. Oh, he might seduce her, Bess, right enough. But he did not seem the calculating abuser Mary had described.

Bess admired far too many things about him. His quick mind, and the wry humor that often flooded his eyes. His kindness and patience with the lads, and the way he treated Dexter, with respect. His courage—

Oh, what if he did fall this night? It could happen. Given, he did not appear hampered by the wounds he'd taken last night. She'd inspected him as carefully as she could and decided they looked superficial.

But any warrior could fall in such a fight.

Her heart began to pound, and suddenly she could not catch her breath. She had to see him before the fighting began. Better, she should fight at his side. That way she'd know what befell him, moment by moment.

She needed to go down now and tell him so. How dared he forbid her from fighting? Had she not trained at arms just as he had?

She spun from the window, and the tower door opened.

"There you are," Anne said. "By heaven, Bess, everyone is looking for you. Poor Dexter is half frantic."

"I needed a few moments alone, away from—from everything."

"I can well understand that. But next time, a word to someone, me at least."

"I regret worrying everyone."

"Come down now." Anne shivered. "'Tis cold here, and we have been ordered back into the solar."

Ordered? Bess bristled.

"I will come down." She followed Anne out. *But not to the solar.*

She greeted Dexter first, to set his mind at rest, before leaving the hall and going out into the forecourt. She nodded at Callum in passing, and he frowned at her. She found both Aleck Maxwell and Anald Robertson at the gates, with a number of other men.

The gates had been constructed at the end of a narrow chute, to be defended by a small contingent of men, and were overlooked from the walls on either side. Arrows could be shot down, and rocks tossed onto attackers. Now Aleck and Robertson worked at wedging stout wooden beams against the oaken panels, as reinforcement.

Aleck looked astounded to see her at his elbow. "Mistress? Ah, so ye ha' been found."

"Aye." She looked him in the eye. "And reporting for duty."

"Eh?" Both men stared at her.

"I am wasted guarding the solar, at least before anyone breaks through that." She gestured at the gate. "I am a fresh sword, and a skilled one."

Robertson laughed. "Argue that, Aleck," he said.

"I will." He squared up in front of her. "Ye be needed at the solar."

"I am not."

"Dexter needs ye. Would ye worry him by placing yourself at peril?"

Robertson chuckled and walked away, signaling

the other men in the chute, and affording the quarrelers at least a modicum of privacy.

"I do not wish to worry Dexter. But—" *But I cannot bear having you so far from me and risking yourself.*

"Bess, that lad's already fretting over what will happen to him if he loses ye and Callum. Ye need to be within his sight as long as possible."

Bess. He called her Bess. Highly improper, but it sounded so sweet on his lips…

"If it comes to hand-to-hand fight—"

"Then ye will battle. We all will." He pulled her to him roughly, his body coming into hard contact with hers, and bent his head. The kiss felt hard also, searing hot and far too brief. "Let me go into this fight knowing ye be safe."

Bess backed away from him, and he released her shoulders. She might believe he cared for Dexter's welfare, aye. But did he expect her also to accept the wild premise he cared for her? This devil of a man, this reiver.

She met his gaze and wondered at what she saw there. Concern, aye, overlaying the desire. And something more that caused her heart to beat double time.

Very softly he said, "Please, Bess, keep yoursel' safe. If no' for Dexter's sake, then for mine."

She fled.

Chapter Twenty-Three

"That gate's too heavily damaged," Callum MacFee pronounced in a tone that brooked no argument. "'Twill never hold through the night."

Aleck glanced at him. It had been a long day, and not an easy one. He felt sore and weary, and had no patience to spare for MacFee's unbending attitude.

He'd lived the whole of his life—nearly thirty years—taking things as they came to him, refusing to worry too much in advance of events, but by all that was holy, he felt worried now. And just when he got things squared in his head, he did not need MacFee coming along, declaring his opinions.

"'Twill hold," he replied shortly. "We ha' reinforced it, see, here and here."

MacFee refused to look impressed, which ramped up Aleck's impatience.

"I know this place, as you do not," MacFee declared. "Every stone o' it, every lock and walkway. 'Tis I should be making these decisions."

That again? Aleck's nostrils flared on a wave of genuine anger. Outside, night gathered on the shoulders of the hills and crept out from the woodlands. The two of them—he and MacFee—had met on the walkway that overlooked the gate in question—the outer, which had taken such a battering during their second night's fighting.

"Do ye truly think I would risk the safety o' all who shelter here?" he asked MacFee.

MacFee gave him a hard, brown stare. "The reputation you hold is no' that o' a man over-concerned wi' those in his charge."

With unstinting honesty, Aleck admitted, "I ha' never before had anyone in my charge, to speak of." Just his men, and they—a ragtag bunch of cronies and kin mostly of Anald's ilk—came and went as they pleased. "'Tis a new experience for me. That does no' mean I will do poorly at it."

MacFee gave a grunt worthy of Mistress Bess at her most disparaging. Ah, and why did she once more insist on invading Aleck's mind? She'd been there all the day, off and on. Now even the prospect of her glaring at him heated his blood, despite his weariness.

He wished he could see her—touch her, kiss her—even once before the fighting started up again. Because a man did not know what would happen during combat. He might not get another chance.

He sighed and looked MacFee in the eye. "I ken fine ye be angry and canna' understand why Lithgow placed this keep in my hands instead o' yours. I canna' understand it either. And we canna' ask him. Ye will ha' to accept it and trust me to do my best, defending everyone here."

"Trust you?"

"Aye," Aleck returned steadily. "For 'twill do no one any good for us to be at odds." Not waiting for MacFee to answer, he directed a sweeping look out over the countryside. Shadows began drawing out across the sward, and the land cradled the dark to its bosom.

Soon. They would come soon—he could feel it.

"I suggest," he said, "ye go and speak a fond farewell to your lady."

"My lady?" MacFee stiffened.

Aleck smiled ruefully. "Ye think I canna' see how ye feel for Mistress Anne? Man, 'tis as clear as morning dew."

MacFee, looking confounded, said nothing.

Aleck went on, "I'm thinking this will be a hard fight."

"Aye. I'm thinking the same."

"So ye'd best speak your feelings now, whilst ye may."

MacFee pressed his lips together and thought about it. "Mistress Anne—she has a grief on her heart that prevents her welcoming my suit."

"Has she? The death o' her husband, aye?"

"Aye."

"But that is the past. This is the present, and we ha' no guarantee of a future."

MacFee grunted. "Wha's made you into a damned philosopher?"

"The prospect o' what might happen this night."

"Aye, so." MacFee shot another look out into the dark. "Then mayhap I'd better do as you suggest."

He made off, and Aleck, with a glance that assured him the gate remained well-manned, went also.

To follow his own advice.

He found Mistress Bess in the solar, which overflowed with boys. She looked harassed and as if her patience had been tried to the utmost, which Aleck did not doubt. The lads had been difficult to keep distracted and occupied this day, being filled with both excitement and trepidation.

Bess's hair had escaped its plaits and spilled down her back like a river of warm honey. She had a smudge on one cheek, and a tear in the hem of her tunic.

She looked so lovely it hurt. Odd how she could make him ache, this woman, just at sight of her.

Dexter saw him enter the room and ran over, his eyes lighting up.

"Master Aleck, did you come to say good night?"

It would not be a good night. But Aleck returned the lad's smile. "That I did. I want ye to be sure and stay here, once ye hear the fighting begin. Aye? And listen to Mistress Bess. Do no' give her any grief, understand?"

Dexter nodded gravely. Aleck resisted the impulse to give him a hug, here before those others, and tousled his hair instead.

"Now, go snag her for me, will ye? I need a word wi' her also."

Bess had not seen him. Settling a dispute between two other lads, she stood with her back toward the door.

"Quick now," he told Dexter. He did not have long.

Dexter darted forward and grabbed Bess by the elbow. When she looked around and saw Aleck, her expression changed—lit and brightened, almost like Dexter's.

His heart rose impossibly in response. He longed for that look in her eyes, would give anything for it.

Swiftly, she crossed to him, wariness replacing the gladness as she came. "What is it? What is amiss?"

"Naught. I wished only to speak with ye before the fighting begins." He closed both hands on her wrists and asked desperately, "Where might we be alone?"

She examined what lay in his eyes and seemed to make a quick decision. "Come."

They went along a corridor and up the narrow flight of stairs to an empty tower room. The small space lay dark. Aleck did not care. As soon as they stepped inside, he drew her into his arms.

She came willingly and, as their mouths met, reaching avidly for each other, she twined her arms around his neck. Heat poured through him, accompanied by tenderness, baffling as it was strong. He rarely felt such softness, and never coupled with this kind of hunger.

He plundered her mouth, setting up a rhythm with his tongue that matched what the rest of him craved, a full invasion. She surrendered herself to him until she could surely get no closer, and for several glorious moments the world went away.

When the kiss broke at last, he trembled like a horse that has run too far. She drew away from him—but a hair—and said, "That is not speaking."

"Eh?"

"You said you wanted to speak with me."

"So I do." He kissed her again, diving still deeper, needing to emblazon her flavor upon his senses for later, when they must be apart. He ran his palms down her back, a heated caress, and cupped her buttocks to draw her still nearer, so she might feel all of him. Ah, and her trews molded to her derriere in the most delightful way.

But it made her gasp. "We should not—"

He rested his forehead against hers. "We should. We truly should. I wanted to say to ye—Bess, I wanted to say—" Ah, God, he couldn't even think straight. "I would like a truce between us."

"Truce?"

"Aye. Now, before I go into this fight. I ken fine wha' ye think o' me. 'Tis no' a good opinion. Ye believe I'm the sort o' man who would force a woman, that I forced Mary—"

"Aye." She tried to pull away; he held her tightly.

"'Tis no' true. What can I say to convince ye 'tis no' true?"

"Naught. She told me—"

"Bess, she lied."

"Why?"

"I do no' ken why. Maybe she was ashamed o' our meetings or wanted to guard her reputation. Maybe she did no' want to admit she'd given hersel' to her father's enemy, a Scot."

"She said you waylaid her. Stole her maidenhead. She told me how she struggled and wept—"

Carefully, Aleck informed her, "She had no maidenhead for me to steal."

"I do not believe you." Again, Bess tried to break free from his grasp. Again he held her.

"Mary confided everything to me. We were close as sisters—closer. I would sooner believe you lie to me than she."

Aleck winced. How could he change her mind, this woman who attracted him so completely and affected him so deeply?

Could he destroy her belief in her friend, whom she trusted? Was there aught he could say?

He gazed into her blue eyes. A storm raged there, one brewed of equal parts outrage and passion.

"Ha' ye never caught Mary in a lie?" he

challenged. Surely she must have. In his experience, the minx lied the way she sought to wrap folk around her fingers—continually.

But Bess shook her head. "We sat together, she and I, and she told me the tale of what you did to her, accompanied by tears. 'Twas no' easy for her, that telling. Why would she lie to me? Especially about such a terrible thing."

Aleck shook his head. "We met the first time by chance, aye. After that, by design—her design. I took what she offered. What man would not?" Aleck had a sudden vision of Mary shedding her clothing for him, in the green bower at the bottom of the hill. Her white limbs and heavy breasts, the wicked gleam of invitation in her eyes.

He'd been nineteen, and she no older. But she'd taught him things he'd never imagined. Where she'd learned her skills, he could not say.

After the first expenditures of passion had begun the complaints—he did not think enough of her. He would not come running every time she bade him. He refused to say he loved her.

Because he did not love her. What he felt toward Mary had been lust, pure and simple, and aye, perhaps the reiver's instinct to take.

He'd been wrong in that. As he'd learned over the past ten years, women were not for taking but for cherishing. Though he'd challenge the devil himself to cherish Mary Johnstone.

"Lies," Bess stated. "Naught but lies fall from your lips. Mary was an innocent lass when you ruined her. A respectable maiden."

Aleck wanted to choke. He could not change the

notion that had been in Bess's mind these past ten years. Aye, he saw that. Yet he needed her to believe him.

"Bess," he said, desperate, "I do no' want to go off to this fight wi' anger between us. Wi' doubt or...or your opinion held hard against me."

Once more she attempted to step away from him. For the third time, he held her where she was.

"Whatever ye may think o' me, let us forge a truce here, now. Say ye will gi' me a fair chance to prove the man I am."

"Persuade me, you mean." Her eyes glowed with rage and another emotion Aleck could not name. "Ply me with your kisses and try to get from me what you had from her."

Ah, and Aleck could not deny he wanted this woman beneath him, wanted to plunge into her, mold their bodies into one, and assuage this ache that beset him each time he so much as looked at her. But he wanted her hot and willing.

"I ha' never forced a woman. I will no' start now."

"Nay, you will charm me into it instead, or so you think." She laid both palms against his chest and pushed. This time, he released her.

"Go," she told him. "Go and defend this place you've usurped. A reiver's all you'll ever be."

Chapter Twenty-Four

Callum came down off the walls sometime in the midst of the night, to speak with Anne. Bess heard him at the door of the solar, where both women waited, having sent the lads to their rooms a while since.

Not that the lads could be expected to sleep, given all the racket. Bess had done little during the intervening hours but pace, replaying the scene in the tower room over and over in her mind. How she'd felt with Aleck Maxwell's arms around her. How he'd tasted, and the expression in his golden eyes.

What had she seen there? Desperation. He wanted to convince her he had not lied. Possibly because he wanted more kisses.

Not necessarily because the tale he gave her was the truth.

Mary would have told her if she'd been meeting with him. These were exactly the kinds of things they confided in one another. They used to love talking about the young men who inhabited their world in those days—relating how an attractive young groom had caught an eye, or an exchange of smiles with a guardsman.

They'd been so young, and both of them pretty enough to turn heads. That was before Bess, wanting to make a place for herself and wee Dexter, had plunged head first into training at arms and left things such as skirts and rouged lips behind.

A miracle Aleck Maxwell so much as looked at her now. But she could not mistake the heat in his stare, and she'd tasted genuine desire in his kiss. It had burned her to her toes.

She knew what he wanted. She wanted it also, and it shocked her. She'd never shared more than a stolen kiss with any man, had never wanted to.

Why this man, above all others?

When Callum came to the door of the solar, her heart leaped, thinking—hoping—it might be Aleck. But they had not parted on the best of terms, and she soon recognized Callum's voice.

Had something dire happened below? Had Thomson's men broken through the gate? Had Maxwell fallen? Och, God, no—

She swayed where she stood, her heart beating a strangled tattoo beneath her leather jack. Anne stepped out into the corridor, and Bess's ear caught enough of their conversation to calm her immediate fear.

"—had to see you," Callum said, "if only for a moment."

"You're bleeding. Here, come in and let me bind up the worst of your—"

"No time for that, and 'tis not what I need."

The ensuing sounds betrayed that Callum kissed her, and Bess backed up even as she acknowledged she could offer them no real privacy. She turned her eyes away, but could still hear their whispers.

"Och, Callum! Callum—"

"Hush, my lady. Just let me hold you. I canna' stay long."

"How goes the fight?" Anne asked, with

trepidation.

Callum did not answer, his silence more eloquent than any words.

Swiftly, Anne pressed, "The gates—have they fallen?"

"Nay, nay."

Not yet. This time, Bess heard what he did not say.

Oh, sweet Jesu! What would befall them all if they were overrun? Anne and Callum, Dexter and Aleck Maxwell. How did Maxwell fare now?

"Hush," Callum repeated. "Beautiful lass, I just needed to come and tell you—tell you how I love you. I regret I wasted so much time holding back wi' that truth. I canna' imagine why I waited. And now—"

"Och, Callum! We will have many days together yet. Years—"

"I pray so. I pray so, lass. List, I maun return to the gates. Stay safe, and may God guard you—"

He embraced her, hard and fast, before tearing himself away and running back down the stairs. Bess heard his feet on the treads. Anne turned, and her gaze locked with Bess's.

Tears flooded Anne's eyes. "It goes badly," she gasped. "He came to say farewell."

"It must go badly," Bess agreed, and her body snapped to well-practiced attention. "You stay here. Rouse the lads and the servants from their beds. Gather them close here. Arm the lads, and push whatever furniture you can across the doorway."

Anne stared. "But…you?"

"I go below to join the fight."

"Nay, Bess, you cannot."

"Mine is an extra sword." It might not turn the tide,

187

but how would she ever forgive herself if the keep fell and she had failed to do all she could in its defense?

"Callum will not like it," Anne began.

Neither would he like losing the fight at the gate, but Bess did not say so. Half filled with resolve and half with dread, she gave Anne a quick hug.

"Aye." Time for no more. Bess pelted through the door in Callum's wake.

****

Blood streamed down Aleck's face from a cut just below his hairline and seeped, annoyingly, into his eyes. He'd taken the wound some time ago when several of Thomson's men, led by Danhal himself, had scaled the gate, now in ruins and nearly broken through. Aleck, fighting with Anald and MacFee at his side, had succeeded in repelling them, but barely.

He did not remember taking the slash to the head and, in the heat of the moment, felt little pain. But by God, the blood in his eyes irritated him. He spat and swore aloud over it.

Thomson had staged a canny fight, and no mistake—one far from over yet. Aleck, raising his sword once again, wondered how many hours remained before dawn and whether Danhal Thomson would call off the attack then. Not if he thought he had them on the tip of his sword and ready to fall.

But Aleck could not think about that now—he could not let that happen. Thomson had ranged his men all along the walls with siege ladders, which had the effect of spreading the defenders thin. True, only two or three men could fit into the narrow chute between the gates, but the demand upon their numbers meant few men remained available to swap out and give the defenders relief.

For most the night, it had been him, Anald and MacFee, though MacFee had ducked away a few moments ago. Back now, Aleck saw with a rush of relief. The man might well be a sanctimonious prig and at odds with him over ownership of the keep, but by God he could fight.

The three of them fought now at the top of the inner gate—the outer had all but fallen, brought to grief by a stout battering ram some time ago. Thomson's men kept swarming their position, trying to come up and over. The three defenders, balanced on a walkway, beat them off repeatedly.

Aleck's sword arm felt like lead, and his heart pounded a desperate rhythm in his chest. He'd passed through exhaustion some time ago and felt mostly numb. And he'd lost count of the wounds he'd taken.

But the swords just kept coming. As swiftly as they beat back the attackers, more appeared. All it would take—

The thought fractured when Anald, fighting beside Aleck, turned to him in alarm—Anald, a bull of a man, fairly resistant to wounds.

He stared in horror as a blossom of red blood appeared on Anald's chest. Aleck swore bitterly.

"Back, get back!" Aleck imposed his own body between that of his friend and the attackers. A swift strike to Anald's opponent had the man falling back into his comrades.

But more came. Ah, God, they still came.

"Go!" He shouted at Anald again, in terror. He shot a desperate look at MacFee. Had he seen? The grimace on MacFee's sweaty face told Aleck so.

Just the two of them, then, shoulder to shoulder, as Anald stumbled down the stone steps that flanked the gate and the narrow walkway.

Beneath them, the stout oak of the inner gate shuddered as, working in the narrow space, Thomson's men maneuvered the battering ram past the remains of the outer gate and into place.

Danhal Thomson, at the fore, looked up and caught Aleck's eye. "You," he called. "I am coming for you!"

A terrible, dark sensation took hold at Aleck's heart. He refused to admit to desperation. His father had taught him, years ago, a man who despaired invited his own defeat. But och, with but two of them…

Abruptly, a shoulder bumped into his. Like a miracle, someone had climbed up and taken Anald's place.

He expected it to be one of his men, or even old William—the aged man had grit. He did not expect to encounter the stormy blue gaze of Bess Mowatt, full of defiance.

Protest arose, promptly oversetting his despair and replacing it with alarm. "Wha'!" he gaped inelegantly. "I told ye—"

"I know what you said." She set her jaw. "But I have a sword. And you need every sword, aye?"

"But ye be a—"

"Woman? Try and forget that for the time being."

He could not. Even if he met his death this night—and it seemed quite possible—it would be upon the memory of how she felt in his arms.

"This is my fight as much as yours," she declared. "And those here mine to defend."

No time to argue it further. But Aleck raised his

sword with new vigor. Her presence and her courage lent him that.

He battled, then, to protect not only the keep but she who fought at his side.

Chapter Twenty-Five

"Aleck, are you all right? Are you with us still?"

Someone shouted in Aleck's ear. He wished most earnestly they would desist, because apart from the shouting, all else had gone quiet. The attack seemed to have fallen away for now. Beyond the inner gate they'd held—*held*—the outer gate lay deserted, if in ruins, and gray daylight flooded in.

He stared into the face of the person shouting at him. Short—he was short with a blur of honey-colored hair and a face full of concern. Nay, she—it was a she, not a he, and she had blood on her face.

He remembered it then—Bess Mowatt appearing like the answer to a prayer at the turning point of the battle, and fighting at his shoulder like a small whirlwind. They'd beaten back the attackers, and his men, on the walls, had fired on them. He did not remember that part very well, just Bess at his side, feeling like part of him.

"Hurt." He put out a gentle hand and touched her face. "Ye be hurt."

"As are you." She grimaced. "Your face is all bloody."

Perhaps she did not shout at him after all; mayhap his ears merely rang from the unaccustomed silence. He turned to Callum MacFee, also beside him. "Have they gone?"

Callum, looking as filthy and exhausted as Aleck felt, clapped him on the back. "For the time being. Come, we maun get our wounds tended and make repairs to that gate whilst we may. They've withdrawn to the trees. I do no' think they are finished wi' us."

"Nay," Bess agreed. "Callum, you go reassure Anne and the lads. We will be right behind you."

Callum nodded and went. Aleck eyed the woman at his side. "I should be angry wi' ye."

"Should you?" She cocked a brow in return. She had blood in her hair, and the wound on her cheek gave her an oddly jaunty air. But beneath it she looked near as weary as he felt. "What of the fact I saved your life not once but three times?"

Had she? Sometime after she'd taken the place at his shoulder, his mind had gone blank. He'd kept fighting by instinct, on the pure need to protect her. Not surprising she'd protected him, instead. Nothing about this woman should surprise him.

He reached out and very gently caressed her cheek. "Ye might ha' got yoursel' killed, Bess."

"As might you." She swallowed. "And then what would I do?"

"Or I?" He leaned forward, needing her kiss as much as he needed breath, but she drew away. "Not here, where everyone can see."

"Where then?" For out of his weariness came one desire—to touch her, to taste her, to make her his completely.

"Come." She caught his hand. Men already gathered beneath them, prepared to begin repairs on the gate. "To the kitchens. You cannot let the lads see you looking like that."

"Like what?"

"Wearing a mask of pure gore. Come," she bade again.

He went meekly, knowing he would follow her anywhere. Into the kitchen, into another battle, or into Hell itself. It didn't matter. Should a man not always follow his heart?

The kitchen, by some miracle, lay empty for the time being, and Bess found water warming at the back of the fire. She pushed Aleck onto a stool with disquieting ease and said, "The women must still be upstairs. No matter: I can clean you up before they get here."

She dipped water from the kettle into a basin and found a clutch of cloths. When she stood over him and began to sponge his face, he sat complacent for a number of reasons. He felt too tired to move. He hurt too much. And he wanted her to touch him.

Almost tenderly, she sponged away the blood—much of it dried—and carefully probed the wound.

"This is deep and has bled much."

"It's stopped now." He did not care. The sensation of her soothing him made him close his eyes. The scent of her, so near, made him think of other things: her breast at his lips, her strong body arching against his. Having her fight at his side the way she had made her feel part of him. How much more so, if he were to plunge into her...

"There, that's better. What other injuries did you take?"

Aleck opened his eyes. Despite his weariness, a mischievous smile danced over his lips. "D'ye mean to tend them all?"

"If I can."

"Here, then." He touched his rent jack. "And here." He brushed his thigh.

"I see no wound there."

"Ah then, I must be mistaken." He wanted her fingers there. Or her lips. Och, how he—

"But your poor knuckles." She lifted his hand to her lips and all his senses went on alert. Before he could think twice about it, he captured her hand in turn and pressed a heated kiss into the palm.

"Blessed lass. I should, aye, be angry wi' ye, but ye appeared like a miracle, and fought like a dream."

She quirked a smile and snatched her hand away. "Perhaps now you will afford me some respect."

"Respect? Is that what ye want o' me?"

"It is."

"I will gi' it to ye, then, and plenty more." Capturing her by the elbows, he brought her down to straddle his knees, facing him. He needed her kiss the way he needed air. Tenderly he cradled her head in both hands and claimed her mouth for his own.

He expected her to fight it, to begin with her protests and excuses. Someone might come in. They would shock her students. Instead, she opened to him, invited his tongue in, then stroked it boldly with her tongue. He fell into her, the way a dying man might fall into eternity.

He rose for her despite his aching body. His need, pooled just beneath her splayed thighs, strained against the fabric of his trews desperately.

She broke the kiss at last and gazed into his eyes, a look as intimate as the kiss itself.

"I should finish tending you."

"So ye should." Slip to her knees between his legs, free him from his confinement, and provide him ease. What wouldn't he give?

"The one on your chest first, I think."

She made as if to rise, but he caught her and held her in place. "Bide a moment, Bess. I—"

By God, he wanted to tell her he loved her. Because he did, he did. His heart had decided so, up on that wall during the time his rational mind had gone away. He'd come out of it loving this woman so much he ached for it.

Yet how could he tell her so? How, when she believed the very worst of him, when she still accepted Mary Johnstone's lies instead of his truth? She would not welcome such a declaration.

Her blue gaze, full of storm, inspected his face closely before fastening on his eyes. She tipped her head. "You...what?"

"I want ye." Another truth, and one that should, by now, be obvious.

She flushed, and a new expression invaded her eyes. Speculation? But she said, "Do you truly think me such a fool?"

Maybe.

"I am a maiden, untried," she confessed. "Why should I give myself to you, of all men?"

"For this." He kissed her again and felt her melt against him. Even if she wanted to, she could not hide her desire, or shield herself from such heat.

But she broke away from him and leaped to her feet. "You call this respect? This is the honor you afford me after I fought at your side? Would you seek to turn me into a trollop?"

"Nay, Bess. Nay, I did no' mean—" He stood also, with such haste he knocked the stool over.

Her eyes glowed with rage. "But you expect me just to shed my clothes for you? Allow you to ruin me? You are all Mary said, and more."

She crashed from the room, leaving him standing pierced to the heart, with a wound that rivaled all his others.

Chapter Twenty-Six

"Will you please hold still? If you do not, I swear I will call upon William to tend you. Would you prefer that?"

The threat from Anne snapped Bess back to attention. She stood nearly naked in her bedchamber, the one place they would not be interrupted, while Anne treated her wounds.

"No, I would not," she muttered. The last thing she wanted was for old William to see her thus. So she did her best to still her body—her traitorous body—but it required almost more discipline than she possessed.

Because she still wanted him—that reiver wolf with the warm mouth and the amber-colored eyes. Despite the suggestion he'd made.

Well, to be fair, it had been more a statement than a suggestion. *I want ye.* She heard it again, and gooseflesh came up all over her body. It was not as if he'd invited her to meet him somewhere so they might be alone and he could pluck her, even as he had Mary. If such a place existed in this benighted stronghold.

The tower room. That thought popped unbidden into her head.

No, no. No!

If she were honest, she supposed Aleck Maxwell could be forgiven for his mistaken opinion of her, given the way she'd allowed him to kiss her and had kissed him in return. And given how she'd perched on his knees that way, so she could feel…

Oh, aye, she knew the facts of life. She understood what occurred between a man and a woman. She might even go so far as to say she would not mind seeing Aleck Maxwell stripped right out of his clothing, and that the idea of having him upstanding for her proved a heady one.

"What is the matter with you?" Anne asked. "Are you in pain?"

"Aye." Pain of the heart and the mind.

"I am that sorry to hurt you. Perhaps I truly should call William. I do not like the look of this wound across your ribs."

Bess, distracted for the first time, looked down at herself. All in all, she'd come through the terrible fight at the gate fairly well—just that scratch to her cheek, a long, skittering cut to her left arm, and knuckles near as battered as Aleck's. Only the wound across her ribs—a sword swipe—truly troubled her. It had bled through her half-chemise, in which she still stood, and her shirt also.

How could she have let herself be distracted by Aleck's kisses while still she bled beneath her clothing?

Because his kisses were so sweet. So hot and deep. When he kissed her thus, it felt like he claimed part of her soul.

"Please do not call William," she begged Anne. "I will try to hold still."

Anne's eyes filled with compassion. She pressed a folded bandage to the wound. "I am sorry I snapped. It was a difficult night, listening to the fighting while worrying for Callum, and you. What was it like, up on that wall?"

"Terrible." Bess relived it all again. The sheer terror brought by the prospect of being overrun. The strength of having Aleck at her side. He'd been her courage as well as her reason for fighting. "Loud. Frightening."

"Bess, lass, you have a courage I will never possess." Anne gently smoothed the bandage. "But promise me you will not go up there again tonight."

Bess turned her face away. "I must find clean clothing, some without holes in it."

"Bess, you must not—"

Bess spun to face her. "I will, if he—if they need me."

Anne's expression changed. "He? Please tell me this is not about Aleck Maxwell."

" 'This'?"

"This show of valiance."

"It is about defending the keep and all in it."

"Bess, my dear, I can tell you find him attractive. I can see that by the way you look at him. But have you forgotten what that man is? A reiver, who steals and murders for gain."

"I've not forgotten."

"I suppose it must be a heady experience, fighting beside someone that way. I understand it can bond folk to one another. I suppose 'tis no different for you."

Bess pulled fresh clothing over her head before joining Anne on the bench at the foot of the bed.

"May I speak frankly, Anne?"

"Of course." But Anne's eyes betrayed her trepidation.

"I am indeed attracted to Aleck Maxwell—to the

look of him." As well as the way he moved, and spoke, and laid his hands on her. "Not—not to the man, himself." *Liar*. His courage attracted her, and the clever way his mind worked. His kindness with Dexter. She asked Anne plainly, "What does a woman do with such desire?"

Anne turned rosy red.

"I only ask because you are more experienced than I am," Bess stumbled on. "You were wed, and have— well, been with a man. And I know you long for Callum."

"Lord, Bess!" Anne pressed both hands to her burning cheeks. "What passes between a man and his wife in their marriage bed is a sacred thing, given in trust."

"Aye. You would never go outside the bonds of marriage, then?"

"I would not. Well…" An honest woman, Anne considered it. "If we thought the keep should fall, and Callum and I would have no hope of an opportunity in the future—I might then." Anne bit her lip. "Because if Thomsons break in, there is no telling what they may do to us, as women. And I would have Callum first."

"Ah." Definitely a consideration. Whom did Bess want to be her first? Some merciless reiver or—the reiver wolf? Aleck might have lied to her about forcing Mary. But to be fair, she had lied to him also, about the death of his infant son.

Mayhap that made them even.

She gave Anne a crooked smile. "I do not doubt you would have some difficulty persuading Callum. His morals are higher even than your own."

Anne nodded gravely. "He respects me."

Maxwell did not respect her, Bess, despite all her demands. If he did, he would never seek to follow through with the promise she'd seen in his eyes.

"What is it like," she whispered, "lying with a man—for the first time?"

"Geoffrey was very gentle with me."

Bess doubted Aleck Maxwell would be gentle. He would be hot and hungry, all-consuming. Any discomfort might well be lost in the heat of her own passion.

But why contemplate such a thing? It would not—could not—happen.

She got to her feet. "I must go down and reassure the lads. Dexter will be anxious to see me."

"So he will. But, Bess…" Anne caught her hand. "Thank you for your service on the walls last night. I am grateful, more than I can say."

"Then, pray, do not threaten me with William again."

Chapter Twenty-Seven

Bess found Aleck Maxwell and Dexter seated side by side upon a bench in the hall, their dark, tousled heads nearly identical. Seeing them that way, it seemed their relationship cried aloud, and her heart leaped into her mouth.

But no one else paid them the least heed. The hall thronged with men and boys. In one corner, William still tended the last of the men. The female servants, having reappropriated the kitchen, went about serving breakfast. There were not enough places for people to sit.

Dexter's face lit when Bess wove her way across the room to him. So, she could not help but notice, did Aleck Maxwell's eyes. They both stood when she reached them, and Dexter threw himself into her arms.

"Are you all right? Are you sore injured? Master Maxwell was just telling me how brave you were—the hero o' the hour."

"Well, I would not say that."

Aleck's gaze met hers. "I am no' certain we would ha' held the gate without ye. Here, sit beside the lad. Take my place."

So he meant to disregard what had passed between them in the kitchen, did he? To ignore the angry words she'd hurled at him, and to pretend he respected her.

Hence the courteous look in his eyes as he gestured

to the bench. But the courtesy covered something else, far hotter. By God, her anger hadn't discouraged him, not a whit.

But she sat and put her arm around Dexter, who cuddled in tight. To the lad she said, "I have been well tended by Mistress Anne. Only one of my wounds troubles me."

Dexter's eyes shone. "Master Maxwell was just telling me how courageously you fought, with no thought for yourself."

"We all fought hard," she acknowledged. "Master Callum was unflinching, a true hero."

"I am that glad you are all right. I maun have the best teachers in the world!"

"Ah, then." Aleck reached out and tousled the boy's hair. "What a warrior ye will be."

"I hope so, I truly do."

"No need to worry about that yet," Bess said hastily. Fathers—and, she suspected, mothers—sent their sons to men like Callum for training because the prospect of seeing them bashed, battered, and injured proved so painful. She could not send Dexter away. But the thought of him facing what they had last night fair turned her cold.

"Aye," Maxwell agreed. "No need to rush things. Here, let me go get us some breakfast."

He stepped away, and Bess could not help following him with her eyes. Oh, how he moved—shoulders squared, and with just the slightest swagger, the picture of confidence. And that despite all his wounds.

"Bess?" Dexter spoke from the circle of her arm. "I truly do like Master Maxwell."

And should a lad not like his father? Watching them together, it seemed to Bess that blood spoke to blood.

"Did you see his hands?"

"Aye." She had raised those battered knuckles to her lips.

"He must ha' fought gey hard."

"So he did."

"Bess, some o' the lads are saying the gates nearly fell last night." Dexter's troubled gaze met Bess's. "Is it true?"

There had been moments when Bess was sure they must. But she could not tell the lad that.

"The marauders fought hard." And she assured him, "We fought harder."

"But what will we do when they come back tonight?"

A good question. Bess's weary body ached at the prospect. "We will repair the gates before they return and will be ready."

Dexter thought about that. "What will happen if they do break through?"

Bess's stomach muscles tightened at the very thought. "Ah, well, they shall steal what they can, eh?" Probably set fire to the rest. Perhaps take hostages from among the lads. Rape the women and put the surviving men to the sword.

"Will the keep then belong to Danhal Thomson?"

"Aye, most likely."

"It is just...I canna' remember ever living anywhere else."

"I know, lamb." If this ordeal frightened her, how much more terrifying must it be to Dexter, who stood to lose everything? "But you must trust in us."

"What is this about trust?" Maxwell, returning with their breakfast, cocked an eye at Bess and lifted a brow.

She said, "Dexter is fretting a bit about whether we can hold off the next attack."

"Never doubt it, lad." Maxwell gave Dexter a wink, and passed the food into his hands. "Sit and make sure Mistress Mowatt eats every bite o' hers, aye? She needs her strength."

"What of you?" Bess could not help but ask. She wanted him beside her, on the bench. "Here, we can make room."

"Me? I'm awa' to get repairs started on those gates. Dexter, lad, get her to eat—and rest a while."

And did he not need rest also? You would not know it, to look at him. He turned on his heel and went off, still managing to move with that cocky grace. If he thought Bess would meekly rest while he labored elsewhere, he had better think again.

****

The outer gate, where they'd fought so hard last night, lay in ruins, severely damaged. Aleck found Callum there ahead of him, looking cold and steady in the morning light. MacFee wore a white bandage on his head that gave him a ludicrously jaunty air. After fighting beside this man for so many hours, Aleck did not know what to think of him. MacFee carried a reputation, though very different from Aleck's—the light against his darkness, it might be said. Yet they'd battled against their attackers as if they could anticipate one another's thoughts and actions.

Aleck climbed to the place where Callum stood, the same narrow ledge they'd held last night, and saw blood on the stones. His? Callum's, or Bess's? it did not matter. Callum MacFee might be the last man Aleck would choose for friend, but they were now linked most surely.

"How bad is it?" he asked, though he knew just by looking.

"Ah, bah—I am standing here wondering how we ever beat them off." MacFee shot him a look. "Can you tell me?"

"I thought 'twas your valor."

"And I thought 'twas yours."

"Must ha' been Mistress Bess's, then."

MacFee gave a rare grin, so wide it might split his face. "Has there ever been such a woman? I will admit, I wanted to throttle her when I saw her come up here, but by God I was proud o' her."

"Ye taught her to fight?"

"I did."

"Then ye should be proud."

"She should ha' stayed back guarding the solar, where she'd be safer."

"I do no' think Mistress Bess is the kind o' woman to stay back." Aleck thought of her in the kitchen, kissing and embracing him with not just her lips but her spirit and her will. She'd not held back then. And she'd held nothing back in the anger that followed.

"Well, if we do no' get this mess right by nightfall, all her valiance will count for naught."

"'Twill take longer than that to rebuild the outer gate."

"You're right there, man. I am thinking it better to use the pieces of the outer gate to reinforce the inner. Then we can man the wall more heavily there," Callum pointed, "and there, so we can fire down on them when they come pressing in. What's our casualty cost? Will your friend Robertson be able to fight?"

"I am no' sure. We ha' two men dead and so many wounded I ha' not the fingers to number them."

"Who are the dead?"

"Two o' mine." Aleck named them. "Jim had a new, young wife. I owe her a debt now."

"If he had a new, young wife he should never ha' come reiving," Callum pronounced.

"Too late to chastise him for that now. All I can do is see she wants for naught, and her child, should she be carrying."

"I maun admit, Maxwell, you surprise me. For all I had heard o' you, I did no' expect such a sense o' duty."

Aleck looked Callum in the eye. "A man's children are sacred. I would never do aught but right by one."

Callum gave him an odd look before directing his gaze out over the countryside. "At last, something upon which we agree. Come, Maxwell, we'd better get this gate repaired, for I ha' a whole slew of other men's sons to defend."

Chapter Twenty-Eight

"Bess, you should no' fight. You will be hampered by that deep wound to your ribs, and you have taken little rest this whole day long."

Aleck paused at the top of the stone stairs when he heard MacFee's voice issue from the doorway of the solar. He'd come up to locate Bess, intending to tell her that exact thing. Seemed MacFee had beaten him to it.

But Aleck had learned enough about Mistress Mowatt to tell MacFee's dictatorial, if concerned, tone would not win her compliance. He felt no surprise at her stark reply.

"Nor have you. You've spent the whole day repairing the gate and, I suspect, barely took time for a decent meal."

"It needed to be done."

"Precisely."

Callum, with no notion Aleck stood virtually behind him, said, "Whatever Maxwell's claims, I still feel responsible for this place. If it falls, 'twill be my fault."

Quick and steady, Bess replied, "Then perhaps you know how I feel. So long as Dexter is here, I will defend him in any way I can."

Aleck could not keep back a thrill at that declaration.

MacFee said, "Then defend him. The danger o'

those demons breaking through the gate tonight is greater than ever. Stay here and guard the top o' the stairs. I will assign you two men. Three o' you should be able to hold the place, at least for a time."

An instant of silence ensued before Bess spoke. "Do you not expect the repairs to the gate to hold, Callum?"

"I do no' ken what to expect. But I feel your sword will be put to best use here."

"I agree." Aleck stepped forward, and MacFee spun to face him.

Bess gave Aleck a glare. "So you would."

Ignoring her combative tone, Aleck said, "I ha' just come from seeing Anald, who insists he can fight. I suggest I assign him a place here wi' ye. There is no man I trust more, when his back is to the wall."

"Aye," MacFee agreed, "and perhaps William. The lads know and trust him. 'Twill prove heartening for them, should the worst come."

He gestured toward the solar. Peering within, Aleck could see the lads gathered there, in a knot by the far wall, with Mistress Anne and the female servants already in attendance.

He picked out Dexter's dark head among the others, and a queer ache seized his heart. He wanted a word with the lad before he went to this fight.

Bess lowered her voice and narrowed her eyes on Callum's face. "So you expect the worst?" she pressed.

MacFee gave a hollow laugh. "You were on that wall wi' us. Need you ask? But I will ha' your word, Bess, you will hold the place I assign you, this night."

"And I," Aleck chimed in.

Bess tossed her head. "When the two o' you start

agreeing, I have no chance. Very well, I will defend the solar—with my life, if need be."

Callum nodded. "Now I wish to go say a farewell to Anne. Just in case…" He swallowed the rest of the words.

Bess stepped aside to let him pass, and Aleck faced her.

He gave her a crooked smile. "Perhaps we should speak a farewell also."

For an instant, terror flashed in her eyes, as quickly veiled.

Aleck stepped closer and took her hands. "It has been an honor knowing ye, Mistress Bess Mowatt." A searing pleasure kissing her, though he did not say so. He would never forget those kisses nor the way she felt in his arms, through this life and beyond.

Her gaze clung to his. In a soft voice she said, "You do not expect that gate to hold."

"I told ye, I do no' ken what to expect."

"But you fear the worst."

"We barely held it last night, and we now ha' fewer swords, and a lesser bulwark. But you can believe I will shed the last drop o' my life's blood to protect ye." He nodded toward Dexter. "And him."

Her eyes widened. "But…why? Why us? You barely know us, and—"

"I know ye." And loved her. Should he tell her so? Should he speak the words now, while he had the chance?

Would she think him mad, if he did? She believed him a rascal, a reiver—a rapist. Would she welcome such words from him?

He clenched her fingers tight. "God be wi' ye, Bess

Mowatt. And know that even though I do no' fight beside ye this night, my heart remains wi' ye." As near as he dared say.

And she surprised him, this woman of iron courage and flaming passion. For her expression abruptly softened, and she came forward into his arms.

As an embrace, it proved fierce indeed. Bess's arms clutched him hard around the middle, her head pressed into the place just above his heart.

Aleck closed his eyes on a wave of mingled love and possessiveness so powerful it uplifted him. If he had to spend himself this night—spend his life's blood—at least he'd met her first, had this, touched and kissed her. If he died, it would be for something worthwhile.

"I would rather fight at your side," she whispered. "At least that way I would know what is happening to you."

Did that mean she cared? Dared he hope so? "But ye ha' given Callum your promise to stay here." And he had given Anald instructions to keep her here, if he could.

"Aye."

"Guard Dexter for me." He kissed her quick and hard, not the kind of kiss he ached to bestow but more the promise of one. For one glorious instant she clung to him, her hands clutching at his tunic, before she released him and turned back to the solar.

Within the chamber, Callum and Anne also embraced, which had drawn the attention of the lads. Callum spoke to Anne, his words low and intense, and she nodded once before releasing him.

Aleck crossed the room and herded Dexter from

among the other lads. The boy looked at him in alarm.

"What is happening, Master Aleck? Why does Mistress Anne weep that way?"

Aleck hunkered down so he could meet Dexter eye to eye. "List to me. The fight is about to start again. Whatever happens during these next hours, I want ye to be strong, aye?"

"Aye." Dexter looked frightened. "Will we be overrun?"

"Not if I can prevent it. Whatever does happen, ye will be brave."

"I will."

"Look after Mistress Bess, if ye can." A tall order for any man, much less a boy of ten.

But Dexter drew himself up. "You may rely on me."

Aleck grinned. What a lad—a son of which any man might be proud.

Dexter grinned also, then threw himself into Aleck's arms much as Bess had. Very low, in Aleck's ear, he said, "I wish I were your son."

A wish Aleck could only echo.

****

Guard Dexter for me. During the ensuring hours, Bess heard those words over and over again in her mind. Why should Aleck Maxwell charge her with such a task? True, he and Dexter seemed to have bonded. But Aleck had no idea Dexter was his son.

The truth of it, though, cried so loudly to Bess she could scarcely believe no one else had noticed. They did not look alike, nay, save for their dark heads. But the resemblance lurked just below the surface. It emerged in their identical grins, in the way they held their heads. It lay, often, in the expressions that filled their eyes.

Guard Dexter for me. The words implied Aleck had claimed Dexter for his own. Perhaps his heart had.

The reiver's cub.

That, and nothing else—certainly no sense of obedience—kept Bess at her post through the clamor of the night that followed, though she longed to be elsewhere. She ached to know if Aleck fought on—if Callum did—and to put her own sword to their defense. Yet she understood what it was to love Dexter, to put his welfare ahead of all else. So she held her post despite her desperation.

Impossible for anyone to sleep while listening to the battle below. Impossible, even, to ease. The window of the solar had been shattered; they could see nothing through the dark.

She feared the worst.

Anald Robertson, who should not be on his feet, clearly shared Bess's deep concern. He paced the hallway outside the solar like a caged beast, visibly aching to be elsewhere. William, the other of her fellow defenders, took a calmer approach, leaning against the wall and lowering his eyelids to slits.

"How can you endure it?" Bess asked him at one point. "Go below and bring us back word of how things stand."

He'd given her a look then that contained nothing lazy. "I took my orders to stand here, lass, and so I will do."

"But—"

"Aye, waiting is hard. But d'ye know how much waiting I've done in my long life? And I'm still here, so

I must ha' done it right."

Anald Robertson, hearing him, bared his teeth in a smile. "So long as you can fight, old man, when the moment comes. I ken fine Mistress Bess can. So Aleck told me."

"Ye've no need to doubt me," William retorted. "My sword will be ready." He nodded at Bess. "Just ask her."

"We will stand," Bess said. If the worst came, they would have no choice. "And nay, Master Robertson, you need not worry about our William. But what of you? Master Maxwell said you took a sore wound, indeed."

"I've a wound here, to my chest," he admitted. "That will no' stop me fighting."

Bess asked again, "Will you no' go down and find out what happens at the gate?"

He gave her a long look, shot another at Anne, among the lads inside the solar, and nodded. "I will."

William began to protest before turning his head away. "None o' my affair."

Robertson clattered off down the stone stairs. Bess stood clutching the balustrade at the top, staring after him and listening to the clash of weapons, hollering voices and, aye, screams, floating upward.

How much longer till dawn?

Before she could calculate an answer to that question, Anald returned. He'd been flushed red when he went down; he returned pale and with sweat on his brow.

Bess gasped, "How goes it?"

He exchanged one long look with William before he said, "Stand ready."

"But—"

"Stand ready, I say. Here with me, shoulder to shoulder. I'll tak' the middle, you, old man, on my left."

Bess seized his arm. "Has the gate fallen?"

He looked grim. "No' yet. But the defense hangs by a thread."

"Who survives? Callum?"

"Aye."

"And—and Maxwell? Does Maxwell fight on?"

Anald turned his eyes on her. What Bess saw there made her knees go weak. More than anything, she wanted to run down those stairs, to find him, to lay eyes if not hands on him.

Guard Dexter for me.

She must stand.

Chapter Twenty-Nine

"Stand. Stand!" Aleck had shouted the word so many times nothing remained of his voice, save a hoarse croak. Numerous defenders had filled the place beside him—where, last night, Bess had fought—and had gone down, one by one. Now only he and Callum remained, in a space that required three.

Danhal Thomson's men kept coming. Like an evil dream, they swam toward the gates without apparent end. Aleck's mind, which seemed to have lost most of its capacity for thought, dimly reasoned Thomson must have called in more men. Either that or his dead must have gained the ability to rise and fight on.

As for the keep's defenders—those stationed on the walls, either side of the gate, had stopped firing. Dead? Too sore wounded to carry on the fight? He did not know. It felt as if he and Callum fought alone.

How much longer?

He could not feel his sword arm. It rose and fell to his command by sheer willpower, and the breath rasped dangerously in his lungs. Aside from the exhaustion, he remained miraculously untouched. A scrape here or there, and his knuckles bled freely, cut to the bones. Only yestere'en's wounds hampered him.

That would not last. He expected to die here at his post. When?

He spared a thought—not the first by any means—

for the woman and lad behind him, up in the solar, and his heart fair strangled with despair. He wanted to hold Bess in his arms one more time. He wanted a chance to sponsor Dexter, to see him grow into manhood.

Not that Dexter didn't already have a fine patron.

Aleck shot an assessing look at the man fighting beside him. Unlike him, Callum fought injured, and badly. Gore from a wound at one shoulder trickled steadily down his chest, and he cradled the other arm—fortunately his left—against his body. Dislocated? Broken, perhaps, from one of the falls he'd taken. Impossible to say, but if Callum went down, he, Aleck, could never hold the gate alone.

Upon that thought—that fatal thought—the gate once more shook, as Thomson's men brought the battering ram into position. The very walkway shuddered, and the sound of splintering oak filled the air.

Aleck gave a cry with his broken voice and, from the corner of his eye, saw Thomson's men swarming the broken gate. Ugly visages came at him out of the darkness; a sword struck Callum, who at last crumpled like an axed tree.

And went down.

For a single moment, Aleck stood alone, facing a throng. Again he thought of the woman and the lad up in the solar.

Fight strong. Guard him for me.

****

They all heard the cries and the splintering of wood when the gate fell. Old William swore bitterly, and Anald at last paused in his pacing. Bess drew a deep breath, and—suddenly, dismayingly—her life passed before her mind's eye.

She had never thought to die thus. Once she'd been an ordinary girl, running wild over the hills with her cousins and friends. Then a young woman, expecting naught more than marriage, children. Then Mary's supporter and confidante, entrusted with Dexter's care.

Dexter had become all.

Now, she would spend herself for him, here on the stones at the top of the stairs.

She turned her head and, over her shoulder, engaged Anne's horrified eyes. "Arm the lads."

****

Thomson's men came up over the remains of the gate like an evil tide, shedding red. Aleck quite deliberately shoved Callum off the walkway—it was either that or see the man's throat cut where he lay. Then he lifted his sword—the sole barrier to the overrun of the keep he'd fought so hard to defend.

He should have known the first invader up and over would Danhal Thomson himself. The man came with his sword lifted high and his teeth bared, the whites of his eyes showing, in a frenzy. Calling on the vestiges of his strength, Aleck met his blade with a grunt that came all the way from his soul.

Keep them safe, keep them safe.

Was it a prayer? A silent battle cry? No time to tell. He'd faced Danhal Thomson in the past, once or twice—on both sides of the attack—had stolen his cattle and, on one memorable occasion, his sword. But now Aleck had nothing left.

Nothing but the will to protect.

That had him baring his own teeth, meeting Thomson's crashing blows again and again. He could hear someone screaming, and behind Thomson's ugly head he saw the sky begin to grow light.

Dawn. He must hold out for the dawn.

Suddenly, a ruckus out beyond the gate caught his attention. Thomson heard it too, and half looked round. Aleck took advantage of the distraction to deliver a blow of his own, up under Thomson's sword, that had the man reeling back.

Then Aleck felt himself falling, falling into a pit of darkness so deep he might never surface again.

****

"Wha' happened?" Even to his own ears, Aleck sounded drunk. His tongue felt too big for his mouth, and he hurt all over, as if he'd been thrashed by a team of cattle drovers—his head worst of all. Waves of silence washed over his ears like rollers upon a shore. After days of battle, that just did not seem right.

He opened his eyes and saw a worried face suspended above him. A young face, it bore generous smears of dirt and had a head of wild black hair, and frantic eyes.

Aleck's mind, which seemed to have taken a severe pounding, supplied a name. Dexter.

"Bess!" the lad bleated. "He's alive."

Bess. The name Aleck most wanted to hear. But all this must be a dream. For surely he lay in a bed, in a quiet room, with everyone for whom he most cared nearby.

Or were they all dead?

He engaged Bess's eyes and repeated in a croak, "Wha' happened?"

She smiled. Och, and it would be worth clawing his way back from death for that smile. She knelt down at the side of his bed and put her arm around Dexter.

"Rescue happened. And at the last hour, no less."

He questioned her with his eyes. His throat felt too dry and too sore for speech.

"Your cousins arrived. At least, that's who they say they are. Some of your cousins," she amended. "Their leader says his name is Dunston Kennedy."

"Ah." Aye, Dunston had promised to come, so Anald said, once he settled a few affairs of his own. "He took his time."

"But he did, so you must acknowledge, arrive at an opportune moment. He said he and his men had word of Thomson's attack. They rode hard through the night and hit the attackers from behind, just after the gate fell."

God almighty, that had been a near thing.

Aleck reached across the blanket that covered him, for Bess's hand. She slid her fingers into his.

"All was confusion, there at the end," she said. "I thought us done. The lads," she smiled a bit mistily at Dexter, "were prepared to fight."

"I wanted to come down and stand beside you," Dexter told Aleck. "Bess would no' let me."

"Someday, lad," Aleck said, speaking it like a prophecy. "Someday we will fight together."

"Not too soon," Bess stipulated.

Aleck croaked, "Callum? He was sore wounded. I shoved him off the wall at the end, so Danhal Thomson would no' cut his throat."

"He's alive," Dexter sang. "Mistress Anne attends him."

No doubt MacFee would enjoy that. "What a man in a fight! Nae quit in him."

"Nor in you, by all accounts." Bess's gaze moved over his face in a way that warmed him right through. For that instant, despite all the confusion and pain, Aleck wanted for nothing—everything life might offer lay within his grasp.

"Thomson?" he asked.

"They took their wounded and fled. No one seems certain whether Danhal survives. If not, his body was taken with the other dead. And you…" Bess paused and her fingers tightened on his. "You are miraculously unharmed, save for a mighty whack to your head that put you under."

"Unharmed?" he echoed in disbelief.

"Aye." Dexter grinned. "Folk are saying 'twas magic protected you."

Magic, Aleck conceded, or the sheer desire to return to the ones he loved. But perhaps they were one and the same.

Chapter Thirty

"Are ye planning to lie there all day like a wee lass, or get up on your hind feet and greet me like a man?"

The jeer came from the doorway of the room where Aleck lay—Mistress Bess's own chamber, so Dexter had confided to him—and peeled Aleck's eyelids open out of a light doze. Posed there, leaning against the jam, he beheld his cousin, Dunston Kennedy, big as life and a welcome sight.

The border marches, he reflected, fair teemed with cousins. That tended to happen when clans made marriage alliances over the centuries, then quarreled and broke them. A volatile breed of men—and women—bred wide-reaching blood relations, some spanning the border.

Dunston Kennedy had always been one of Aleck's favorites. A strapping fellow with flaming red hair and an acerbic sense of humor, Aleck enjoyed sparring with him.

Never so much as now.

"Ah," he croaked in his ruined voice, "and seeing your ugly face may ha' me hiding under the bed."

Dunston grimaced. "And here was I thinking after saving your grand new keep for ye, I might receive a warm welcome."

"Welcome." Aleck managed a grin. "I ha' no doubt ye not only saved the keep but my life also."

Dunston moved to the seat beside the bed where Aleck lay, rattling as he came. He'd put aside none of his weapons and, as Aleck knew, liked to go well armed. He now wore his sword and, Aleck spied, at least three knives.

His tawny gaze moved over Aleck with swift and well-disguised concern. "Are ye sore injured, that ye lie there sleeping while other men guard your walls?"

"Other men?"

"I, mysel', ha' just come down from watch." Dunston gave a nod at the door. "I near had to fight my way in to see ye, past that fierce half-lass, half-warrior out there."

Bess.

Dunston quirked a brow. "Something I should know?"

Aye, she's mine, Aleck thought.

"An unusual woman, though a bonny one," Dunston went on. "I do no' think I ha' ever seen—"

"She's mine." Aleck said it aloud this time.

Dunston tipped his head. "Aye?"

"She just does no' know it yet."

"Aye, well. I suggest ye get up off your lily-white arse and do something about that. My men ha' been eyeing her like she's the main course at a banquet."

"'Twas she ordered me to stay here, under threat o' dire consequences." He'd tried to get up last night, anxious to walk the walls for himself. The look in Bess's eyes had kept him from pushing the matter. What had he seen there? Concern? Protectiveness? Did it mean she cared?

"Did she come wi' this property you've inherited?" Dunston asked. "And why should Robert Lithgow leave this place to ye, anyway?" He drew himself up. "Why no' me?"

"I'm no' certain." Aleck shoved higher against the pillows behind his back. Bess's pillows. The bed where she slept. The very idea had him growing hot.

He asked Dunston, "What be the state of the defenses?"

"Good. Thomson's withdrawn for now. I sent my men out to scout, and not an ugly man o' his company's to be seen. No one seems to know whether Danhal is alive or dead. My men, along wi' what's left o' yours, are keeping close watch."

"And Callum MacFee?"

Dunston's expression grew thoughtful. "An interesting man is MacFee."

"I would not be alive were it no' for him."

"Nor he but for ye, from the sound o' it."

"So he lives?"

"Oh, aye, and lies in the care of the lovely Mistress Anne. She guards him closely, and will admit no one to the room. 'Tis said when the old man, William, offered to doctor MacFee, she fair beat him off wi' a stick."

"Ah." Fortunate MacFee. Aleck would no' mind Bess beating folk off, for his sake. "I am that glad he's all right."

"'Tis soft you're turning. Where's the reiver wolf I ken so well?"

A movement at the door caught Aleck's eye. Peering around Dunston's ugly head, he spied Bess looking in, and his mouth went dry.

"I'm that grateful for your help," he told Dunston, "and your timely arrival. Go get yoursel' some breakfast. I want a word wi' Mistress Bess."

Dunston looked round and quirked an eyebrow. "I see the way of it. Do a man a good turn, and he shrugs ye off for the sake o' a bonny face." He got to his feet and sketched Bess a surprisingly courtly bow. "I wish ye joy o' him, mistress. He's a cantankerous cur, and no mistake."

Bess's eyes flew to Aleck. Once Dunston went past her out the door, she took his place beside the bed.

Ah, and what to say to her? Should he tell her how he'd clung to the thought of her—and Dexter—the whole time he'd battled? How she'd never left his mind, and his desire had been all to fight and protect her, to hold her in his arms one more time? Should he tell her he loved her, as he'd failed to do before the battle? For he did, he did. But he meant little to her, save perhaps an erstwhile rescuer and a man who'd forced her cousin and then lied about it.

"How does your head feel?" She spoke before he could. "You cracked it wide open when you tumbled from the wall. It bled copiously, and I feared—well, 'tis a terrible amount of blood to lose."

Was that why he felt so weak? He did not often take long to recover from battle. Not this long, certainly.

He told her, "I will get up soon. I need to see to the defenses."

She sniffed. "Your cousin seems to have that well in hand. A very definite sort of man."

"Ah." Had Dunston and Bess already had a run-in? "He's a scoundrel, but I am glad he arrived when he did."

"As am I." Her storm-blue eyes inspected his face. "Was it a near thing? The keep falling, I mean."

226

"A very near thing." He'd been alone on that wall in the end. "'Twould ha' gone hand-to-hand in here. Ye. The lads."

"I was prepared to fight."

"I do no' doubt it. But I did no' want to see ye, or Dexter, at risk. How fares Callum? Dunston says he is in Mistress Anne's care."

"Aye. He took a fearsome blow just above his heart, plus lost two fingers of his left hand."

"But he will recover?"

"Anne and William both say so. Anyway, I believe he is too stubborn to die."

Aleck grinned, despite himself. "The lads must ha' got a terrible fright."

"And, I suspect, a valuable lesson. The idea of battle seems bold and exciting until it is at the door."

"I will get up and go reassure them. I do no' want them to get the idea a warrior lies about after a fight, like—like some beached sea creature."

"Wait, please. I have somewhat to say to you, first." She extended her hand across the bedcovers and gripped his. "Thank you. Last night proved a lesson to me also. I never realized how much I love Dexter till I stood there forming part of a final barrier between him and harm. I would have fought my best for him, but I do not know if my best would have kept him safe."

Aleck drew a breath. "If ye feel any gratitude for me—"

"I do."

"Then I pray ye, hold the words of thanks, and grant me one thing in return."

Caution flooded her eyes. "What is that?"

"A chance, a fair chance, Bess. Dismiss what ye

think ye know of me—what ye heard from others in the past, and judge me as ye find me. The man I am."

"And if I fear I cannot trust my own judgment? If 'tis clouded by things like—like my gratitude and…"

She let her voice trail away, apparently unwilling to utter the word attraction. Aleck knew they both felt it, quick and vital, alive even now in the room.

He'd never in his life experienced its like. It made up part of why he loved her, but not all.

"I will no' deceive ye, Bess."

"No?"

"Nor will I harm ye. Why should I fight in your defense, only to turn round and hurt ye in any way?"

"I do not know. Perhaps—perhaps you do all this in order to seduce me." Her gaze probed his with honesty impossible to dodge.

With like honesty, he returned, "I desire ye, Bess. That much must be plain."

"And that is what you do—take women and ruin them."

"Not ye." He lifted his hand, still in hers, and pressed it to her cheek. "I would sooner die, Bess, than harm ye."

She froze. In her eyes, he saw that she fought a battle every bit as fierce as what he'd faced last night. At length she wetted her lips and said, "I am no child, such as was Mary when you ruined her, but a woman grown. I make my own choices."

"I would have it no other way." He wanted her to want him, as a woman wants a man. He wanted her to burn for him as he did for her—with every heartbeat.

A moment longer she fought with her emotions. Then she leaned forward and covered his mouth with hers.

As a kiss, it started tentative, almost gentle. But heat flared quickly, a spark to dry tinder, and even as his lips parted beneath hers, she dove into him. Thorough, that kiss was, and he could taste her desire, barely held by threads of restraint.

She ended it much too soon, and gazed into his eyes. "I no longer know what sort of man you be, Aleck Maxwell. I am not even sure I care. But remember one thing: I give what I give as a free woman and only when I so choose. No man will ever force me."

He did not want to force her, God knew. He wanted her wrapped around him, pouring her heat into him as she'd just done, desiring him more than breath.

"Now," she told him, "get up and go reassure those lads. And…" She hesitated only one instant. "If I should invite you to stay with me here this night, remember it is at my invitation."

Aleck forgot to breathe. "Here? Tonight?"

"Aye. But do not let it go to your head."

Chapter Thirty-One

And what devil had prompted Bess to invite Aleck Maxwell to share her bed tonight? Bess questioned the impulse even as she followed him down the stairs to the hall, where most of the company gathered.

Not one but several answers sprang to mind. She felt grateful to him, without question. But a woman did not hand her virtue to a man out of mere gratitude.

And if she followed through with her offer this night, she would indeed be handing him her virtue. It was true, what she had told him. She'd never yet—despite her advanced age—lain with any man.

Despite all she knew and feared she knew about him, she wanted Aleck Maxwell to be her first. More terrifyingly, she suspected she wanted him to be her only. If she never had any other man before she died, she wanted this one.

That could not all be laid at the feet of desire, though she was learning just how powerful desire could be—a primal force, deep and prepossessing like the need to survive.

The great hall, crowded with wounded, those new arrivals not on guard, and the overly excited lads, swallowed Aleck when he came in, the way an estuary swallows a rivulet. Everyone greeted him at once, pounded him on the back, and congratulated him on his great feat of defense.

Callum—who should not be out of his bed—rose from the table where he sat in company with Anne and William, to greet Aleck. To Bess's surprise, the two men embraced one another heartily before engaging in serious conversation.

When you fought with someone, Bess knew, when you nearly died beside him, a bond formed—even between these two, who'd started out so much at odds.

Dexter ran forward and fastened himself to Aleck's side, interrupting whatever words he and Callum exchanged. The light in Dexter's face mirrored so exactly what Bess saw in Aleck's at the sight of the boy, she caught her breath. Surely someone must see the resemblance between them.

Her feet took her to their sides; she tousled Dexter's hair and drew him against her.

"Do not bowl Master Maxwell over, lad."

"I do no' mind." Aleck smiled.

And at the same instant, Dexter cried, "I am but that glad to see him up and moving."

"As I am glad to be." Aleck returned his grin. "An exciting night was that last, eh? Come have breakfast wi' me."

"Will you tell me all about it?" Dexter asked. "How did you and Master Callum hold the gates alone?"

"Come," said Callum surprisingly. "Let us go find some breakfast and a place to sit together."

Without a backward look, Aleck went. Bess crossed to sit with Anne, who looked pale and sleepless and sat with her chin in her hand. She gave Bess a dour look. "Men."

"They are a sore trial, and no mistake," Bess

agreed as she sat down. "How sore are Callum's wounds?"

"Bad enough that he should not be on his feet and playing at silly beggars." Anne paled further. "I thought I'd lost him, Bess. When they carried him in covered in blood, and with two fingers missing, I thought—ah, Jesu! I'd only just managed to tell him how I felt for him, and I feared him gone."

Bess availed herself of Callum's abandoned cup of ale. "You did tell him, then?"

Anne nodded. "Aye, much good it did me. It did not keep him from risking himself, nor persuade him to spare himself now, either."

"Men are bullheaded," Bess agreed judiciously, "but that is perhaps also what makes them so strong. And makes us so—so helpless before them."

"You? Helpless?" Anne focused on her intently. "Bess, what have you done?"

Bess lowered her voice so William, on the other side of Anne, would not hear. "Only told Aleck Maxwell I want him in my bed. Tonight."

Anne's lips parted in an "O." Rarely did Bess see her startled from her customary poise, but so she appeared now. "You? Him? But you said—" She broke off. No fool, Anne; shrewd kindness appeared in her eyes.

Bess tossed her head and spoke under cover of the noisy room. "I know very well he is unsuitable. The last man I should choose." For reasons to which Anne was not privy. "But I am ten years past my prime and have never been with a man. Who else would want me? Who else has shown any interest? Anne, there came a moment last night when I thought we would all die—

you, me, Callum, Dexter. If Maxwell will have me, I will have him."

Anne swore softly, a word never learned in any lady's company. She took a judicious look at Maxwell before studying Bess again. "You have told him this?"

"I have invited him to—to stay with me tonight."

"And he agreed?"

Had he? Not in so many words. She'd issued the invitation like a challenge, with conditions. He had not actually accepted.

Her cheeks flamed with incipient humiliation. What if she'd read him wrong? What if he'd been, still, half out of his senses when she kissed him?

But nay—there could be no mistaking the heat that flared between them when they touched one another, when they kissed. Bess wanted to toss herself into that heat, to burn up in it regardless of the consequences.

Anne appeared to reach a conclusion. "Finish your breakfast, lass," she said briskly, "and come with me."

"Where?"

"To my chamber. You can scarcely welcome your chosen swain to your bed clad like a warrior, can you?"

"No?"

"Indeed. We will see you fitted out properly, and will begin with a bath."

****

"This is foolishness." Hours later, Bess stared at the image in the glass that stood in one corner of Anne's chamber. The woman there wore a borrowed white night rail trimmed in lace, and her hair flowed over her shoulders in a river of gold. She looked demure, virginal, and nothing like Bess Mowatt. "I scarce recognize myself."

She rarely wore her hair down. It got in the way when she trained the lads, so she'd become used to braiding it in a tight plait or bun. Sometimes it fell down on its own, becoming an annoyance more than anything.

She'd not realized quite how long it had grown.

What would Maxwell think of it? Of her, decked out like some bartered bride. Nervous energy skittered through her at the prospect. Fallen beneath Anne's care, she'd barely seen him this day long. It had taken an absurd amount of time to get the water heated for a bath. Anne had spent still more time fussing over what Bess should wear.

As if that mattered. The way she understood it, at least from overhearing the talk of fellow warriors, the goal was to shed all clothing as swiftly as possible so that pertinent areas might come into contact.

Maxwell quite likely wouldn't show up anyway. As she reminded herself over and over again, while the day sped by and turned to evening, he hadn't actually agreed. And she'd had no opportunity to speak to him since. He'd spent the day walking the walls, inspecting the fortifications, and talking with the wounded—all with Dexter at his side. Bess didn't feel particularly happy about that situation, either, but did not know how to prevent it.

Things so rapidly slipped away from her...for better or worse.

She narrowed her eyes at the woman in the mirror and tried to imagine Aleck Maxwell's reaction to her. Would he think her hair bonny? And her body, unaccountably softened from how it usually appeared— would he want to touch? Cup one of those breasts in his large, battered hand? Caress the exposed skin?

Anne spun her around. "You are perfect. Now you'd best go to your chamber and await him. You want him to see you thus, when he arrives."

Bess went suddenly breathless. "What if he does not arrive?"

"He will."

"'Twill be so humiliating, to sit and wait."

"He will, lass."

Bess gnawed her lip. She was not used to waiting but to acting on her own. "I do not feel like myself."

"You are a different self, that is all. Now go." Anne's gaze fell. "Callum will be here soon."

"Here?"

Anne lifted her gaze. "You are not the only one who hopes to spend the night in a man's company."

"Oh! But—" Would Callum do such a thing? He lived by strict morals and would never disparage Anne's reputation. But he'd nearly died. They all had. It sharpened and clarified things in the mind.

"Why did you not say?" Hurriedly, Bess gathered up her clothing and other belongings.

Anne shrugged delicately. "I do not know what may pass between us. He is sore hurt. If he does no more than sleep in my arms, I will be content."

Bess nodded, absurdly embarrassed. Anne had been wed to her beloved Geoffrey; she knew what to expect. Bess had but a vague notion.

"I want to know I am his, and he mine," Anne added simply.

Ah, and Bess had no hope of that. She could not even say whether she wanted Aleck Maxwell for her own.

She just wanted him—clad like a strange parody of herself or no.

"Good luck." She kissed Anne on the cheek.

"And you, lass."

Bess crept off to her own chamber, convinced she would spend the night alone.

Chapter Thirty-Two

Aleck never should have sat up so late, drinking ale. For one thing, his battered head and bruised senses did not need further addling. For another, Bess Mowatt had invited him to spend the night with her, in her chamber.

Had she not?

For the life of him, he couldn't be sure. Her kiss had promised it. Her words, if he had them straight, seemed much more equivocal. Then, there was the fact that she detested him.

It didn't help that it had been hours since he'd so much as caught a glimpse of the woman. No hot glances from those stormy blue eyes, to encourage him. No sweet, whispered suggestions—if he could imagine Bess Mowatt confiding suggestions to his ears. He found he could not.

What if he presented himself at her door, seeking a bed, and she screeched at him, making accusations about Mary Johnstone all over again?

But now, Callum rose to go to his bed. The lads were long in theirs, and Aleck had no excuse to sit up. Other men covered the watch. He could go to the walls, just to check.

Or he could take himself up to Bess's door, and see what happened.

Sudden longing overwhelmed him—the same that

had occupied him the whole night he'd battled at the gate. To see her, touch her, catch her scent.

So what if she turned him from her door?

What if she did not?

That thought had him hard and ready, despite his bone-deep weariness. He suspected Bess Mowatt might rouse him so even from the grave.

He had a glimpse of Callum slipping through a door down the corridor from Bess's. His eyebrow quirked. Mistress Anne's door? Well, well.

And what of him? Should he knock? Faced with the arched oak panel that sealed Bess's chamber, he did not know. He put out his hand, all the knuckles bandaged in white, and pushed. If she wanted him here, she'd leave it on the latch, would she not?

The door swung open without a sound, and the scene inside burst upon him. Bess sat beside the fire. But…was that Bess? She wore a garment familiar enough to him—a woman's night rail—though he'd never seen her clad in anything but trews and leather. The room glowed with warmth, the bed where he'd wakened this morning turned down, and she…

She glowed also, the firelight sliding down the length of her loosened hair and warming her skin. She leaped to her feet and turned with that hair fanning around her like molten metal. Her eyes blazed with emotions he could not begin to name.

That look stopped him where he stood with his hand still against the door, stopped him as even Danhal Thomson's sword had failed to do. They gazed at one another, and his lips parted before he spoke. "Mistress, am I welcome here?"

She stirred so the white gown fluttered around her,

and even clear across the room he saw her pulse flutter in her throat. "Aye," she said. "You are most welcome."

****

At last! It had seemed an age to Bess, waiting by the fire. She'd been able to hear voices from below— *men*, she thought again—but had more or less decided Aleck Maxwell would not come to her door this night. In fact, she'd just been about to take the door off the latch and crawl into bed alone when it swung open, silent as a dream.

He looked like a dream also, standing there with the firelight washing over him. In the days of Bess's youth, back when she'd cared about such things, she'd had a vague idea of male perfection that she carried in her mind.

Aleck Maxwell might not fit that far-off image, but och, he looked perfect to her eyes.

Black hair all in disarray, amber eyes narrowed, mouth held tight. Wide shoulders tilted slightly toward her, shirt open at his strong throat. A variety of white bandages—one on his head and several on his fingers splayed against the door.

Bess's heart began to pound high and hard. She wanted those fingers at her breast. Och, Jesu, she wanted them between her thighs. She wanted them everywhere.

"Bess, ye look—" Words appeared to fail him.

She rushed in with, "I ken fine I look ridiculous, do I not? This was Anne's idea of—"

"Ye're gey beautiful." His voice sounded rough and sent a wave of heat over her that pooled in her belly. He stepped in and closed the door behind him.

"Secure the latch," she whispered.

"Eh?"

"Make sure no one can come in." Sometimes, Dexter did. She would not want the lad to see—ah, what? Her legs began to tremble beneath her.

Aleck did as she asked with careful hands. When he turned back, he looked thoughtful. But he crossed the room to her, as if he could not keep away, a bee drawn to honey.

What was a woman to do in these circumstances? What should she say?

He reached out and took her by the elbows. His hands felt warm, and he engaged her eyes determinedly.

"Bess, are ye sure about this? I would no' ha' there be any doubt between us. I will no' ha' ye say later wha' ye say of me and Mary."

Och, and did he have to mention Mary now, when Bess fair vibrated with desire for him? Bess did not want to think about Mary. She did not want to think at all.

With an unintended edge, she asked, "Would I be here, all trussed up like a goose and waiting for you, if I were not certain?"

His mouth twitched. "Women are strange creatures. They may say one thing and mean another."

"I expect I shall have to show you, then." She leaned forward and kissed him. She meant it as an act of defiance—defying her own fear—but as soon as their mouths met the hunger came leaping.

A sigh came from her throat and a growl from his as he pulled her into his arms. The kiss that began as an act of daring turned into something far more, hot and consuming, an instant demand.

If Bess trembled, so did he. She could feel the quiver of his muscles as he drew her body against his, like those of a stallion that wants to run.

He splayed his hands across her back, hot through the thin fabric of her gown—one went up to bury itself in her hair at the back of her head, so he could kiss her more deeply. The other found a place lower down.

Bess had never been touched so by any other man. Aye, she'd been knocked onto that derriere often enough by warriors with whom she sparred. She'd been nudged and bruised and battered. With those things, she could cope.

This—

"Bess." He came up from the depths of the kiss to speak her name. "Och, God, Bess, sweet Jesu—"

Aye, and his mind seemed every bit as blasted as hers; he was raving. She gazed into his eyes, and what she saw there stabbed her to the heart. Desire, oh, aye, enough desire to set the bed aflame. But something more—a depth of feeling such as she'd never imagined beholding in any man's eyes.

So bright she could scarcely meet it.

She lifted her hands and cupped his face. She closed her eyes before she kissed him again.

Take me, she thought. But of course he could not hear her. Or could he? Perhaps so, for with a groan of desire, he lifted and carried her to the bed.

Suddenly, she wished she'd snuffed out some of the candles. For if she understood the way of these things, he would now remove her lovely gown. And then he would see her body—scarred and muscled where it should be soft and smooth.

And she would see his.

This time, the desire overwhelmed her. She squeezed her eyes shut again.

"Bess? Bess, look at me."

"Nay."

"Bess, I want to be certain 'tis me ye are wantin'."

She opened her eyes. He'd deposited her on the pillows and knelt on the mattress beside her. Close, so close she could reach out and touch his hair, slide her fingers inside his shirt and feel his warm skin.

"Who else?" she asked simply. There existed no other man in all the world whom she would invite into her bed. Only him. Only this.

Suddenly, modesty did not matter, nor did embarrassment, nor shame. There was only the heat in his eyes and the throbbing inside her, this desperation for him.

"Touch me," she bade. She rarely asked men for anything. She considered herself too strong, too independent. But that rule, too, seemed to have dissolved in this heat.

He brushed the fabric of the gown with his fingers softly, almost gingerly. His fingertips moved across her breast, and her every sense roused.

"So bonny. Ye are so bonny."

Ah, God, surely he could find something better to do with his mouth than pay her compliments? Aye, she wanted him to find her beautiful, every bit as beautiful as she found him. But the hunger inside her left no room for patience.

Gazing at him earnestly with wide eyes, she asked, "Are we not supposed to remove our clothing, then?"

He laughed, sounding surprised. "Aye, Bess. Och, aye. Only let me show ye."

Chapter Thirty-Three

Bess expected to feel awkward when Aleck drew
the night rail off over her head and bared her body to
his gaze. A moment of truth she considered it—a price
to be paid for the rest of what she wanted from him.

She did not anticipate the tenderness in his touch
when he untied the ribbons at her neck and lifted the
garment. Nor the wave of staggering, blinding intimacy
when his eyes found her naked flesh for the first time.

He caught his breath, and his white-bandaged
hands hovered for one moment, as if afraid to touch,
before he brushed the softness of one breast. Bright
light rose in a bubble to Bess's head, and her world
abruptly narrowed to those fingers—touching her—in a
caress that seemed to link the two of them.

"Look at ye," he murmured. "All strength and
softness."

And scars. But she did not think about that then,
too busy holding his amber gaze with hers,
experiencing the feelings pouring through her, tasting
what would come. No dream, this, but a reality such as
she'd barely dared imagine.

"Show me," she echoed his words, and pressed her
mouth to his.

The hunger, aye, leaped up rampant, but the tender
intimacy remained. Perhaps she need not fear what he
thought or that he would not find her feminine enough.

Because for these moments, she belonged to him in a way she'd never belonged to anyone else, and he to her. Nothing more existed.

He kissed her deeply while palming her breast, and it set her further aflame. Her body, seeming to know far more than she did, set up a primal demand.

Aleck broke that kiss far too soon for her liking and reared up over her. "Wait."

She did not want to wait. She wanted him closer rather than farther away, and then closer still. But he began stripping off his own clothing, which rendered Bess silent with awe.

Aye, she'd seen her share of half-naked and even mostly naked men. She'd certainly seen Callum stripped down to the minimum at practice, as well as most of his warriors. Even old William, all sinew and tanned hide.

Aleck Maxwell was no William. And what she saw compared to no other man, not even Callum.

Broad shoulders and a deep chest, liberally stubbled with a pattern of black hair, narrowing to a lean waist. Muscles on his belly that rippled when he moved, and arms that displayed brawn with little bulk. A complement of scars that removed all shame for her own.

Vaguely, she registered the sound of his clothing hitting the floor beside the bed—jack, belt, and the slap of the leather trews from which he wiggled before her eyes. Muscular thighs came into view, along with his manhood.

Oh, sweet God, oh, Jesu, och, so that was the whole of it.

The whole of it.

Of course, she'd suspected how a man's most favored appendage must look. She'd even had partial glimpses when, neglecting her presence, a companion relieved himself against a wall, or a tree.

Naught like this.

It made of Aleck Maxwell a feral thing—well, he'd always been that. A reiver wolf. But now she'd admitted him to her own private keep; he had gained leave to breech the last of her defenses.

Armed with that dizzying intimacy.

She didn't fear much. At this moment, desire assured she didn't fear him. But och, the sight of him, entire, took her aback.

Naked, he lowered himself onto the bed atop her, and she could feel all of him—his skin, rough and hot against hers. The weight and power of him.

His eyes sought hers persistently in the golden light.

"Bess, are ye sure?"

For answer, she twined her arms around his neck. Aye, her body knew what to do, if she did not. There might well be rules to this game of give and take, but she had no patience for them. She pressed her body to his and, with no clothing in the way, they fit together perfectly, curve and hollow. The weight of him—that curious, thrusting weight—settled between her thighs as if they'd done this a thousand times.

But he did not breach her, not yet. He began moving, yes, but only to kiss her first on the lips with quick, hungry kisses and then on the throat, moving downward. She quivered beneath him, in response, her eyes squeezing shut once more.

When his mouth, hot and wet, closed on her breast,

she near died from the pleasure of it. The circle of intimacy seemed to tighten around them until only the tug and caress of his lips and tongue existed. When he found his way to her other breast, she moaned. When he moved down her belly, bestowing kisses all the way, she wanted to weep.

She longed for him back in her arms, ached for the delirious weight of him upon her, but when he gently parted her legs, when he kissed the inside of first one thigh and then the other, she forgot to breathe or to think.

He spoke then, his voice a rough rasp. "I am sorry, lass, I canna' wait. I will try and be gentle."

Bess cared little for gentleness, then. When his body once more covered hers, she felt half wild for him. Accustomed to battling her way through the world, she had little fear of blood or pain, so she fastened her mouth to his and invited him in.

The rest of it happened in a flurry of heat, still accompanied by that blinding intimacy. The victim of passion, Bess knew only that she wanted him inside her. And when, mouth fused to mouth, he at last slid home, it felt right and bright, and victorious.

He withdrew all too soon and lay half collapsed on top of her, his breathing ragged. Sensation still poured through her, so powerful she barely registered the wet warmth on her belly.

But he said, babbling in a way she'd never imagined he could, "I did no' want—Bess, did I hurt ye? I did no' mean to—"

Was he a man who worried about hurting the women he plucked? It had not seemed so, yet the intimacy, still wrapped around them, assured it.

She told him, "No pain. There was no pain." Thinking about that, or trying to, with the warm mush that used to be her brain, she mused, "Perhaps I lost my maidenhead during one of the falls I took, during combat."

"Perhaps."

"I have never—"

"I ken." He eased himself down onto the bed beside her. Warm firelight flickered over him from behind, tipping the black of his hair with red. Bess could not see his face. Did she want to?

He began again, more determinedly, "I did no' want to leave ye my seed. That is why—"

He reached down over the side of the bed, pressing her into the mattress, and came up with his shirt, which he used to mop her belly. She realized what she felt there was part of him—that part which could make a child.

Like Dexter.

Shock went through her, like the kiss of lightning. Her euphoria threatened to shatter.

She'd just given herself to the man who'd forced her cousin and left her with a child.

And she didn't care. She didn't care.

She'd never in her life wanted anything the way she wanted this man. She suspected she'd trade her conscience or even her immortal soul for the scent of him, the feel of him touching her. For this sense of binding that erupted between them.

Already she wanted him inside her again, hot and vital. What did that make of her?

A woman, after all.

But he stirred. Having finished cleaning his seed

from her, he stirred and made as if to rise.

She heard herself croak, "Do not go."

"What?"

"Stay. Stay the night."

"Eh?" He seemed unable to comprehend what he heard.

"Here. With me."

"Bess. Bess." He cupped her chin in one bandaged hand. She wanted him to kiss her then, so much it shook her.

"Please, Aleck."

He made a sound in his throat. Refusal? Assent? No matter, for he kissed her, a sweet, leisurely kiss, and the world once more slipped from her grasp.

Nothing mattered while he remained here with her. Not Mary, not Dexter, not what tomorrow might bring. For ten years, she'd denied herself and neglected her own happiness for the sake of others. On this one night, she would have what she wanted.

Whatever the cost.

Chapter Thirty-Four

Aleck Maxwell surfaced from a light doze at the demand of his body, and with a single thought clamoring in his mind.

He lay in Bess Mowatt's bed, both of them naked and with her tucked into the crook of his arm. A marvelous warmth suffused him, not all of it physical. He'd had other women, a few, in spite of his caution following the disaster with Mary Johnstone. But he could not remember staying to sleep with one, after.

Not even Mary. Nay, for theirs had been clandestine meetings, quick, daring things, and soon over. Just long enough for him to give her a child.

A mistake he'd not made since, and would not make now. Even though the connection with Bess, when he plunged into her, felt so deep and so complete he'd found it near impossible to keep from giving her everything.

Which is why, insisted the thought that beat at his brain, you should tell her you love her. You should give her that. Make her see this was different from any act you've ever performed with any other woman.

Ah, and would Bess Mowatt, who now slept so sweetly in his arms, welcome such words from him? Aye, passion had overtaken her, a short time ago. Passion, as Aleck knew, proved a powerful mistress. It had turned Bess hot and willing beneath him, made her quiver and cling to him. But that didn't mean she regarded him as aught but the man who'd ruined her cousin.

If she still believed that. Did she?

He could not wake her and ask. He dared not hear the answer. He would not destroy the peace that encircled them.

How long had she slept so trusting against his shoulder, her warm breath stirring the hairs on his chest? All the candles had guttered out, and the fire burned with a low, orange glow. He could hardly see her, but och, how beautiful she was to him.

Strong, his Bess—strong yet soft. No need for artifice to color her cheeks or lips, now swollen from his kisses. No fine clothing necessary to enhance her limbs or those high, firm breasts, likewise swollen. From her long, brown eyelashes to the scars on her hands, she was real.

Perhaps that explained why she called to him, to something so deep inside him he'd never suspected it existed. And why his love for her was likewise so real, and deep.

Tell her, you fool. Aye, he'd been a fool in the past, right enough. He'd made mistakes; he'd been selfish. Waking Bess and telling her he loved her might be the most selfish of all.

His body wanted her again. Indeed, that had roused him. He wanted to kiss her, taste her, kindle the fire that so easily erupted between them.

Show her they belonged together.

She'd begged him to stay with her, here in her bed the night, to sleep with her. What did that mean?

These last days had been filled with fear and

uncertainty, culminating in the battle and the near loss of the keep. What if nothing more than relief—and the need for release—had driven Bess into his arms?

He understood that kind of need. All men did. But, by heaven, he wanted more from her than physical satisfaction. Aye, he had a reputation. A reiver, a taker—a user. Who would have imagined one woman could make him want to give instead?

He drew her closer in his arms and, coming half awake, she raised one hand to his cheek in a caress. Her touch went through him and filled him with tenderness.

A strange emotion, that, both gentle and powerful, near as primal as the need to have her again.

She murmured wordlessly and pressed her body to his. Warm, and willing, even still half asleep.

"Bess."

"Kiss me."

He did. Her mouth met his, hot and open, and he dove in. Instantly, she came alive. Ah, God, how they fit together! Bodies, minds, spirits. He'd never imagined such a sense of belonging.

He wanted to make that feeling last, this time. He wanted to indulge her, show her how varied their pleasures could be, and likewise indulge himself. But the flaming heat of her body called to his, and anyway, he suspected a lifetime with this woman would never prove long enough.

"Bess—"

"Hush."

She arched her body against his and, his desire interpreting hers perfectly, he claimed her breast. Disregarding her own command, she began mumbling a string of words—or perhaps they were imprecations—

beseeching him for more. Had he the control to give her that?

When he abandoned one breast, giving the swollen nipple a last caress with his tongue, she seized his head between both hands in protest. "Nay."

He laughed, gave the other nipple a kiss in passing, and moved to position himself between her thighs.

She reared up to look at him then. In the dim light, her hair made a honeyed river all around her, and her eyes glowed with demand.

"Part yoursel' for me, Bess. Let me in."

As he had earlier, he nudged her thighs apart. The scent of her very nearly made him lose all restraint. But she parted for him sweetly, with obedience he suspected she rarely offered. He parted her curls gently and thrust one finger inside.

She arched from the bed, her strong body responding for him. Two fingers, and she gave a strangled cry.

"Ah, God—"

So tight. She was so very tight. His member throbbed at him in demand. But he thought not of himself now. He wanted to give pleasure to the woman he loved.

When he bent his head and replaced his fingers with his tongue, he nearly forgot even that. The taste of her flowed at him—wild honey—and he reveled in it, reveled in the way she quickened, and in learning the most intimate secrets of her body. He wooed it, wooed her, until she suddenly convulsed in a breaking storm.

He wondered then, as he crawled back up her body with her flavor still on his tongue, if those sleeping in the other rooms around them heard her cry out, if men would come running with swords drawn. If so, they would find him once more mounting her, pumping into her moist heat until he convulsed also, and they became one.

No one came running. Their breathing quieted, and the silence contracted, closing them in. He might ask for no more from life than this.

Yet a little thought niggled at his mind. He'd failed to maintain his control. For the first time in ten years, he'd broken his own rule and given her his seed.

A fatal act, as he well knew. He'd not done that since his days with Mary, and look how that had ended.

Ah, but surely once would not matter. Once would not give Bess his child. He and Mary had gone at it like rabbits. And produced a child whose existence—or non-existence—had haunted him ever since.

Out of the soft silence, Bess spoke. "I never knew. That is, I never heard tell a man could kiss a woman—thus. There. I rarely speak of such things wi' other women. Well, one does not. And men do not talk about it either, do they? At least, not in my hearing."

Aleck should hope not. Men did talk, as well he knew. But they had words to describe what he and Bess had just shared, words with which he imagined she had no familiarity.

"'Tis a thing in which a man and woman might engage, if they care about one another, Bess. No' somewhat to talk about."

"An intimacy?"

One of the deepest. "Aye."

"And you showed it to me."

Aye, and what did her clever mind make of that?

He nearly said it then, told her how he loved her

and would do anything to please her, all within his power.

She spoke first. "I did like it. Nay, but *like* is too weak a word for such pleasure. Tell me, Aleck, does it work the other way round?"

"Eh?"

She ran her fingers down his chest, over his belly into the nest of black curls between his thighs, and cupped him. "Might I pleasure you with my mouth?"

He promptly went still, and breathless. "Aye. Och, aye." His voice did not sound at all like his own. And, God, he should be spent, unable to rise for her.

Yet, miraculously, he did.

"Ah," she said, not without a touch of mischief. "Let us see."

Chapter Thirty-Five

"There have been no sightings of Danhal Thomson or any of his men," Dexter informed Aleck, standing straight and tall. "I ha' been on the walls since sunrise, keeping watch."

"Have ye?" Aleck wanted to ruffle the lad's hair but did not wish to denigrate his great dignity. Dexter appeared to have grown overnight, and his blue eyes held a glint of steel.

"Aye. Wi' so many of our warriors sore hurt, Master Callum gave us leave to patrol and keep an eagle eye."

Master Callum. And who was he to be giving orders? The man who'd stood beside Aleck in defense of this keep, and nearly given his life, that was who.

Did it truly matter which of them gave the orders? Aleck trusted Callum, and providing the lads a role seemed a fine idea.

"Where is Master Callum?" he asked, glancing around the hall where the men, mostly injured, took their breakfasts.

Bess remained upstairs, along with the better part of Aleck's good sense. After what had passed between them, he found it difficult to focus on anything else.

Dexter answered, "Master Callum was down earlier, but went back to his bed." He widened his eyes and lowered his voice. "In Mistress Anne's chamber.

The lads are saying all sorts o' things about it."

"Are they?" Aye, gossip was gossip everywhere. Aleck wondered if the lads knew where he'd spent his night and speculated on what had happened there. He did not wish to damage Bess's reputation with her charges, which was why he'd bidden her stay in her chamber and come down later.

But Dexter only asked, "Are Master Callum and Mistress Anne now wed?"

"Not precisely." Though Aleck wished them joy of one another. MacFee deserved it, as did the lady. He said, "I suspect, Master Callum being sore hurt, Mistress Anne but wanted to keep an eye on him during the night."

"Oh." Dexter looked relieved.

"Now, come up to walk the walls wi' me, and show me how ye ha' been keeping watch."

"That I will."

****

Bess frowned at herself in the beveled glass that stood in one corner of her chamber. Usually she left it turned to the wall, having little desire to view her appearance. Well-worn leathers and tightly braided hair left little to admire.

But now, having shrugged back into Anne's crumpled night rail, plucked from the end of the bed at dawn when she bade Aleck farewell with a lingering kiss, she needed to take a look.

Did she appear any different? The lacy gown definitely made her seem so, as did her hair, hanging loose all the way past her bottom. She appeared more— feminine. Or perhaps that was just the way she felt.

For she had discovered a woman existed inside her,

one she'd never guessed she harbored. Aleck, with his kisses and his unexpected tenderness, had tapped into her, drawn her forth, and set her aflame.

If Bess donned her leathers and braided up her hair tightly enough, would that woman once more disappear?

Bess needed her to. For with the light of day came enough clarity to show her last night had been madness. A wonderful, ripe, delightful delirium she could not permit to occur ever again.

Aleck Maxwell might be many things. The most beautiful man she'd ever seen or hoped to. Brave and strong, and unexpectedly gentle—with Dexter and with her—but he was also Dexter's father and the man who'd begotten him by force.

Bess had wanted her one night, her chance to find out what it meant to be a woman, and she'd gotten that in abundance. Three times. She'd chosen Aleck Maxwell for the task, knowing she could not have him, could not keep him. That, in her own mind, had been the bargain.

She'd trusted him with her body last night. She could not trust him with her heart.

At least now she knew she was a woman—all woman—in the company of a man such as him. Perhaps she could have chosen better, given herself to someone other than the man who'd forced Mary. But for once in her life, she'd wanted what she wanted.

And she'd never before wanted anything like Aleck Maxwell.

How to keep from wanting him again?

Aye, and there was the question.

The door whispered open, and Bess spun, half

hoping he'd returned, that she might have just one more chance to taste him on her tongue.

But it was Anne who slipped in, a tentative look on her face. "Lass, is all well?"

"Aye." Bess shot a final, doubtful look into the glass before turning her back on the image. Another time, another woman. "And you?"

A smile broke across Anne's face, so radiant it outshone the morning sun. She nodded.

Bess need ask no more. She recognized that look of a woman in love.

Only…she didn't love Aleck Maxwell. She could not possibly.

Anne glanced at the rumpled bed. "He was—not too rough with you, I hope."

"Neither rough nor demanding." Indeed, all the demand had come from Bess. Aleck had but given her that for which she begged, even the last time, when his hot seed filled her mouth. Oh, God, such intimacy. Such bliss!

"And how is Callum this morning?"

"Sleeping. I persuaded him back to bed, though not before he insisted on going down to check with the men. But you—are you sore?"

She was, but far less so than following a brisk practice, if in different places.

Impulsively, she seized Anne's hands. "Tell me, what do you do with the desire? I thought—I thought having him would quench it, like a cold drink after a long ride. It has not."

Anne regarded her kindly and shook her head.

Bess went on, "I need to put him away from me now, Anne. To put the desire away."

"Ah, well." Anne towed her to the settle in front of the fire and sat down. "That is not so easily done."

"So I do learn." Bess contemplated it and bit her lip. "Tell me, what am I to do? What, when I see him again?"

"If I had an answer for you, Bess, I would share it. For months on end did my longing for Callum dog me. So steady, so strong, so handsome." Anne's cheeks flushed. "So maddeningly bent on protecting both my person and my honor."

Bess searched her friend's face. "Before the attack, you told him that you love him."

"Aye. I scraped up the courage for that. And he confided he did return my feelings. But when I saw him brought down from that wall and thought him dead—I tell you, Bess, that swept away every other consideration. I have already lost one man I dearly loved. I know how short life can be. That is why—" her cheeks flushed—"when I had him alone last night, I did not hesitate, even though he should well have been taking his rest."

Bess squeezed Anne's fingers, still in hers. "But Callum is a good man. An honorable man, worthy of your trust. Whatever happens, he will do right by you. Aleck Maxwell—he is a reiver and has used women ill in the past." She could not confide Mary's secret, even to Anne. "It torments me, thinking I have chosen poorly." She shook her head. "Yet that does not keep me from wanting him."

"Ah, lass—the heart chooses where it will, as does the flesh, it seems."

"How am I to face him?" Bess asked again. How gaze into those amber eyes without wondering if he remembered all she'd done—the abandon with which she'd offered herself to him, nothing barred. The heat of his mouth between her legs, the eagerness with which she'd tasted him. Those breathless moments when their two bodies became one.

Anne told her, gravely now, "There is no going back from it."

Not what Bess wanted to hear.

Anne jiggled her hands. "I fear you must face what you have done like a woman. Courage, lass!"

A woman changed forever. One who had made a terrible—and wondrous—mistake.

****

As soon as Anne made her way back to her chamber, and Callum, Bess dressed in her leathers, braided her hair, and prepared to face Aleck Maxwell. But when she reached the hall, she found him not.

The big chamber looked like an exercise yard for walking wounded. Almost all the men wore bandages. Some of them, unfamiliar to her, must have been among those who'd chased Thomson's company into flight. The lads circulated freely among them, talking and fetching their requests. Perhaps not a good situation, but with so many other battles for Bess to fight, she swiftly abandoned that one.

The lads, like the rest of the keep's residents, had been through a fright. Let them learn from the other side what it meant to be warriors.

She happened upon Anald Robertson, who gave her a wide grin from his place at one of the tables.

"Ah, my wee sister in arms. How does this victorious day find ye?"

"Victorious?" Bess echoed uncertainly.

"Aye. Did we no' chase off a horde of rampaging reivers the other night?"

Bess shook her head and glanced around. "Where is Dexter?" The one lad she did not see.

"Wi' Aleck—who, I suspect, should no' be out o' his bed."

No, he should not. He should be lying on his back like a man slain while she, Bess, worked her way slowly and deliciously down his body.

"That knock he took to the head—" Robertson wagged his own head sorrowfully.

"Aye." Perhaps Aleck would remember none of what they'd shared last night. Perhaps he'd think he imagined it all in a fevered dream.

Now, if only she could go and knock herself on the head…

"Where are they?"

"Keeping watch up on the walls. Bets are being laid all 'round as to whether Danhal Thomson will marshal his forces and return."

Bess, well-versed in the habits of fighting men, fixed him with an interested eye. "What are the odds?"

"Depends on whether Danhal Thomson be alive or dead. Opinions are undecided. Some say they saw him take a fearsome blow from our Aleck's sword just before the reinforcements arrived. His men bore him awa', after."

Our Aleck.

"Others say his pride will bring him back, even if he's dead." Anald grinned.

Stubborn men.

"So," Robertson concluded, "a careful watch is being kept by all who can keep their feet—I mysel' just came down."

"Nothing?"

Robertson shook his head. "Nothing. Yet."

"Ah. And where did you place your bet, Master Robertson?"

"I think he'll be back. And we'd damn sure better be ready when he comes."

Chapter Thirty-Six

A fresh wind blew up on the battlements, sweeping in from the far distances. It seemed to clear Bess's head as she climbed and the stone walkways came into view.

A number of men patrolled there. The two nearest turned and gave Bess such speculative stares she wondered if everyone knew where Aleck Maxwell had spent last night.

Did they place bets on that too? Whether she'd been a virgin, and whether he would lie with her again tonight?

She could tell them he would not. Whatever else happened, she couldn't so risk her heart.

But mayhap they merely kept watch, after all, for they nodded at her and looked away. Bess knew neither of them; they must have arrived with Aleck's cousin.

"All clear?" she called.

"Aye, mistress, so far."

She let her eyes range along the walkways. There—two dark heads, one belonging to a considerably taller body than the other. Aleck and Dexter stood gazing southward, the most likely direction for Thomson's men to appear, if they would.

Home, for her—England. But she no longer had any home save this one. And that belonged, now, to the very man she wanted to avoid.

So why did she push past the two guards and strike

off toward him? Because she wanted to check in with Dexter.

A fine lie.

Aleck Maxwell drew her even more surely than he had before. Indeed, she tried to halt on the walkway, to turn back. Her traitorous feet refused to obey.

As the guards had, Dexter looked up and saw her. His face bright, he ran to her, straight into her arms. "Mistress Bess!"

The feel of him in her arms assuaged some of her ache. She ruffled his hair and planted a kiss on his head before raising her eyes to the man who followed him more slowly.

And what did she see in Aleck Maxwell's tawny eyes? A measure of caution that matched her own. Longing that matched hers also? For the life of her, she could not tell.

He gave a slight bow and bade her, "Good morn, mistress." Just as if they hadn't spent the night feasting off one another, close as flesh could be.

To cover her discomfiture, she gestured at the countryside beyond the keep. "All clear?"

"So far. This provides a glorious outlook. Master Callum has done well to cut back the forest so far."

"Master Callum is a careful man."

"I am that glad of it. And, Mistress Mowatt, how does this day find ye?" His gaze probed her, as if for hurts—her breasts, her legs—all the places he'd touched.

Heat rose over her in a wave. Och, how was she to manage this relationship? How coexist with him?

She fixed him with a steady stare. "None the worse for my recent experiences."

He smiled, which further heated her blood. Och, what a smile the man had—wondrously beautiful, with just that hint of wickedness.

What did he expect? That they would spend the next night together? She must make it clear they would not. But she could hardly say so in front of Dexter.

His son.

And oh, they looked so similar, standing there side by side in the morning light, she could not deny it. Dexter had swiftly learned from his chosen hero—how to stand, how to level his gaze. How to wield his courage with both hands.

And that was only right, was it not? A lad should learn from his father, if he could. Was that not, perhaps, what Robert Lithgow had intended?

"I am that glad to hear it," Maxwell said. "We need hale bodies to stand watch. Eh, lad?"

"We do. Mistress Bess, I will stand wi' you, even as I ha' stood wi' Master Maxwell. He says the best way to learn is to do."

"Master Maxwell speaks truth."

"We need eagle eyes, and the lad has a pair." Aleck clasped Dexter on the shoulder, and Dexter grew taller still. "Now, ye go down and tak' your breakfast wi' Mistress Bess, lad. I suspect she will no' eat unless ye do. And," Aleck's gaze scorched Bess again, "she maun be famished, after all her exertions."

Bess's lips parted and stayed that way. How dared he?

"Standing guard out front o' the solar, I do mean," he said smoothly.

"Ah," Bess managed. "But are you not famished, yourself?"

"I am, that." Once more his gaze touched her mouth, and her breasts. "But I had a pot o' ale to partly quench my need."

Ale would not do it; that she knew. Suddenly, Bess needed naught so much as to distance herself from him and the emotions he prompted.

"Aye. Dexter, come."

"But—"

"You can have a bite to eat with me, and then bring somewhat back up for Master Maxwell."

"Aye, so." At that, Dexter proved willing. He promised Maxwell, "I will be back soon."

****

Aleck stared into the far distance and sought firmly to discipline his flesh. Pain, as he knew, might be overcome. Desire, at least the sort he felt for Bess Mowatt, proved a far more difficult prospect.

He had only to be near her, only to look at her, in order to grow hard. He wanted to give her, all over again, what he'd given her last night. To spend himself in her so deeply they became one flesh.

He didn't think he'd experienced that, ever, with any other woman. Aye, well, he'd never been in love with anyone else.

Now she thought to deny him, deny what she felt for him. He could see that in her stiff bearing, read it in her eyes. Having had what she wanted, she was done with him.

And how does that feel, my fine reiver wolf? So he asked himself, not without irony. He'd seduced women in the past, made them want him, only to walk away after. Aye, and Bess had seduced him last night—laid claim to all his senses. His heart.

He wanted to spend the rest of his life with her. But…how?

He certainly couldn't let her distract him from the task at hand, which happened to be defense. This place was his to guard, and everyone in it. He might confer and even cooperate with MacFee, but responsibility rested with him.

Ah, speak of the devil, and he came walking. For here, along the stone rampart, came Callum now.

"MacFee, wha' are ye doing up from your bed?"

"Just checking."

"Were ye no' up here earlier?" While he, Aleck, had still been abed with Bess.

"Aye, and I've taken a rest since. All clear?" Callum turned his eyes out to search the sward, slope, and forest.

"Aye, as ye see."

"We maun get the gates repaired today, at least one of them." MacFee grimaced. "Both may be far too ambitious."

We. Aleck found the word reassuring. He may not have started out liking this man but liked him now, full well.

"Aye, right ye are, and I was just thinking the same."

"We will need lumber, and that means a foray to the forest, for we've already used everything to hand."

Aleck regarded the outlook again. "Risky."

"Aye."

"Whom can we send who's not injured?"

"Only your cousin's men." Callum withdrew his gaze from the scenery to fix Alex with a hard stare. "Can we trust them?"

"We can. Dunston may be a quirky bastard, but he will do me no wrong."

Callum nodded. "I will go, then, and assign a work crew."

"Ye will go back to your bed."

"Och, man." Frustration broke from the usually well-controlled MacFee. "How can I lie there when so much needs to be done?"

"'Tis the very reason. I do no' like the look o' those wounds. We need ye hale and hearty, not swaying on your feet."

"I am no'—"

"Besides, would ye wish to worry the lovely Mistress Anne? She maun be frantic, wi' ye awa' out o' her sight."

"About that, I do no' doubt you've heard the men's tongues wagging, discussing what has happened between us. I mean to wed wi' Anne just as soon as she'll have me."

"Och, man, your morals are none o' my concern."

"They are, when I've a house full o' young lads looking to me. I've been charged wi' instructing them, and no' just in warfare. But I would no' expect you to understand."

Aleck bristled. "Why not? Because I've the moral sense o' a rutting cur?"

"You're a reiver, and one whose reputation speaks for itself."

Aleck drew a breath in an effort to discipline his anger. "I'd better tell ye now, before ye hear it elsewhere: I spent last night in Mistress Bess's bed."

Callum stared, and his hands balled into fists. "What?"

"Before ye knock me down, 'twas by her invitation."

"Was it, by God?"

"Aye. And," Aleck stated firmly, "I mean to ask her to be my wife."

Callum gaped and gave him a long glare before breaking into unexpected laughter. "I wish you luck wi' that! She'll never accept you."

"Why no'?"

"She's ne'er accepted any suitor, and you, of all men?"

"Am I no' as good as anyone else?"

"Nay." Callum spat the word deliberately. "No' in her sight, you are not."

Chapter Thirty-Seven

The men restructuring the gate worked all night. The crew included anyone able-bodied enough to labor, which included Aleck Maxwell. And that, in turn, kept him from Bess's bed or from any attempt at gaining it.

A great relief, for she'd not intended to allow him there. And also, a great disappointment.

But she would not dwell on that. Instead, she set about gathering the lads who, now feeling part of the defense, refused to go to bed, and on trying to console Anne.

For Callum, despite his injuries, had returned to work. And Anne worried accordingly.

"What's to do with such a man?" she fretted while pacing the solar. "He will not listen to reason."

"They will none of them listen to reason. They are men."

Despite Bess's best efforts, half the lads remained up on the walls. Given, their young eyes saw well in the dark. Already there had been two false alarms caused by deer sightings.

Others of the lads, including Dexter, who insisted on staying close to Aleck, minded the torches that lighted the work at the gates.

Bess could hear their voices all the way up in the solar, calling to one another for tools, the men's voices deep and the lads' higher but no less intent.

"Two fingers Callum has lost," Anne lamented as she trod the floor in front of Bess's chair. "How can he bear the pain? And, you ken, if he is out there working, he will not keep those bandages clean. What of his other hurts?"

Anne began to weep, an action so unlike her Bess rose and towed her to a seat.

"Here, now. Callum is strong and, for all he's a stubborn male, the most sensible man I know. 'Tis you, Anne, are exhausted. Why do you not go to your bed?"

Anne raised a tear-streaked face from her hands. "Without him?"

Aye, and there lay the crux of it. The reluctance to face an empty bed, so Bess must admit were she honest, had kept her up this night.

"List to me, Anne dear. He will come to you when he is able. But he will come. This is Callum of whom we speak." Not a wild reiver used to taking what he wanted without a thought.

"I do not doubt he loves me, Bess. But my heart…my heart fears. After losing one husband I loved so well—I thought I would never recover. Should Callum take poisoning in those wounds, should he fall from the wall, or should another attack come while we are vulnerable—I could not survive it."

Bess's stomach muscles tightened. She tried to imagine something happening to Aleck—the ultimate something—and never again being with him. The loss of his smile, quick and bright. Of any chance to exchange words with him, or kisses. The loss of the unaccountable comfort she found in his company.

She could not allow him to matter so much to her—she simply could not.

But her hands trembled. She drew a quivering breath. "Would it reassure you if I go out and make sure he is well?" He, to Anne, might mean Callum. For Bess, it meant someone else for whom she felt concern.

Anne brightened. "Aye." Indignation kindled in her eyes. "Remind him I exist, if you will."

"I doubt much he's forgotten. In Callum's mind, no doubt he lingers out there in order to protect you."

"I know. He is a fine man. 'Tis why I love him."

And what, Bess wondered as she left the solar and ran down the stairs, if a man was not so fine as Callum MacFee? For few men were. What if a woman chose to give her body, and her heart, to a man she'd learned to hate long before she ever knew him?

She feared her heart had slipped from her grasp at some point during last night's pleasured frenzy. Possibly when Aleck Maxwell had kissed her so deeply it felt like their souls fused together. Maybe even before that, when he'd lifted the night rail over her head with such tenderness. Surely, surely when he entered her and they rocked together on strong waves of sensation.

She understood how Anne felt. At the same time, she envied Anne, who knew she would have Callum again.

The front gates teemed with bodies and ordered confusion. Bess found Callum right in the midst of it all, giving instructions just as if he hadn't recently had a passing acquaintance with death.

The outer gate had already been rebuilt, or at least framed in. The men now labored over the inner, and it took Bess an inordinate amount of time to catch Callum's eye.

"A word," she called when she did, and jerked her

head.

To her surprise, he came immediately, a look of concern settling over his sweaty features.

"Wha' is it?" he demanded. "Anne?"

Ah, so the woman did remain uppermost in Callum's mind. Anne would be pleased.

"She is fine, though gey worried about you. How do you feel?"

Callum looked surprised, as if he hadn't yet paused to consider his own welfare. Most likely he had not. "I am well enough. We ha' made good progress here, as you can see."

Bess looked where he indicated. She did not see Aleck Maxwell or Dexter, supposed to be minding the torches.

"Where is Dexter?"

"I think Maxwell took him up to the walls, after he burnt his hand."

"Dexter burnt his hand?"

"'Tis naught serious, and Maxwell wrapped it up." Callum focused on her fully and lowered his voice, even though in the continued commotion, no one would hear. "Let the lad ha' some time wi' his father. They are good together, surprisingly so. I hate to say so and never thought I would, but perhaps blood will out."

Breath gusted between Bess's lips. The same thing she'd been thinking, all this while.

She searched Callum's eyes. He alone, besides her, knew the truth of Dexter's birth. "But they have no idea—"

Callum grimaced. "It does no' seem to matter, does it? They've formed a bond. I'm no' the man to get between them."

Bess also lowered her voice. "They're so alike, sometimes I think everyone must see."

"Or that Maxwell will." Callum grunted. "If he does, if he asks me, I warn you, I will tell him the truth. Then, I do no' doubt, he will knock me down. But a man has a right to such knowledge, so I've come to believe."

Again a conclusion to which Bess had also come. But what would it mean for Dexter? Would Maxwell want to take the lad away with him, into his world of reiving and violence?

Who would Dexter then become? Bess had raised him from a newborn. Without him, her life—so far sacrificed—would be empty. Without Maxwell, doubly so.

"It is," Callum said, "a knotty decision, and no mistake. When I thought Maxwell naught but a deceitful bastard, I believed we protected the lad from him. Now that I've come to know him, fought beside him, I see something more."

"He forced Mary."

"Aye." Callum's eyes narrowed. "And I do no' doubt he regrets it."

Regret. Quite possibly Bess's most hated emotion. Did she regret having Aleck in her bed? Nay, not that. Never that.

With another glance at the gate, Callum made a decision. "I will go reassure Anne. I do believe William can carry on here."

Astonishing. Callum never abandoned a task in midstream. She lifted her brows. "Will you stay with her?"

"For a while."

Bess nodded at his filthy hands. "She will want to change your bandages."

"And I will let her." Emotion flickered in Callum's eyes. "Life is short, Bess. If we ha' learned one thing, it is that."

He called to William before walking away determinedly. Bess, torn, wondered if she should follow. She might offer her services here at the gates, but the crew seemed to have the job in hand.

Or she could climb to the parapets and make sure Dexter fared well. A burnt hand. At one time, he'd have run to her, eyes swimming with tears. Her wee lad had grown.

Which was, so she assured herself as she climbed the worn, stone steps to the battlements, how it should be. As Dexter had not stayed an infant in her arms, he would not stay a lad as high as her shoulder. He would leave her someday.

Maybe soon.

She found them at their favorite place, the southeast tower. The two of them held identical poses, leaning their elbows against the parapet, ostensibly on watch. Other lads kept watch in other places, interspersed with members of the guard. Bess nodded to them as she passed, and they spoke in return but did not withdraw their gazes from the dark of the countryside below.

Bless the dark, she thought as she joined Aleck and Dexter. She did not want to see what lay in Aleck Maxwell's eyes.

Instead, she swept Dexter with a comprehensive look. His right hand, it appeared, bore the injury. A filthy cloth, procured God only knew where, had been wrapped around it.

His face, too, looked smudged and dirty. But Bess saw the marks of no tears. Perhaps he'd outgrown those also.

"Are you all right?" she greeted him. "Callum said you've taken a burn."

He held up the offending hand. "I got too close to the end of the torch I was holding. 'Tis no great matter, so Master Aleck says."

Bess fought the desire to look at Aleck, and lost. He wore a grave expression, but emotions leaped in his eyes when they met hers.

Suddenly, she could feel it all again—the coarse hair of his chest beneath her fingers, the slow slide of his hand up her leg. The heat of him when she'd parted her legs and—

Nay, she would not relive that, even in her mind.

"Any sign of trouble?" she asked.

"Nay." Aleck shook his head. "Still, a close watch must be kept. These lads o' yours, mistress, are receiving a far better lesson in defense than ever Master MacFee could devise."

"So they are." She, too, leaned on the parapet, in order to avoid his gaze. Perhaps she'd taught Dexter all she could. Mayhap it proved time for him to move on.

To his father.

Dared she tell them? For the life of her, she did not know.

Chapter Thirty-Eight

Aleck's body ached with weariness from head to toe, and his head most of all. So tired was he that he found it difficult to think, and he struggled to figure out how long he'd gone without sleep.

He'd snatched a wink or two during his night with Bess. Not much, and not the kind of sleep he needed, deep and senseless.

Ah, well, what they'd shared had been far better than sleep.

Now he'd sent Dexter off to his rest and descended from the walls bound for his bed, only to wonder where that bed might lie. The keep, he felt assured, lay secure, the gates rebuilt and a careful watch still in place. Even the erstwhile MacFee had gone to his rest.

He'd wanted to tuck Dexter in. But one did not tuck in a young man, and that was what Dexter had so swiftly become.

A son the likes of whom any man would be proud. Aleck experienced a sharp twinge of longing. If only his son had lived, and grown to be such a young warrior.

He would change not a single thing, were Dexter his.

But he'd been denied his son—not by that bitch Mary, but by a cruel fate. Still, he felt privileged to know Dexter now. He had no son and Dex no father.

Perhaps, somehow, they could move on from their mutual lack.

But first he needed sleep. Or he needed Bess, one or the other. Both.

Upon that admittedly foggy thought, he reached her door and stood gazing at it stupidly. A fine line of light shone beneath the panel, showing she occupied the chamber.

If he knocked, would she open to him?

That thought spurred a wild tingle that moved through him with astonishing intensity. Would she open her mouth, her body, her heart to him?

Without his volition, his hand pressed the door. It swung open, and he found himself staring into a pair of stormy blue eyes.

For an instant, neither of them blinked or breathed. Then she spoke hurriedly.

"No," she said. Only that, but her body barred his way. She stood fully clothed, save for her boots, in her customary leathers. No provocative gown this night. Aleck didn't care.

"Where am I to sleep?" he asked simply, if plaintively, and the emotions in her eyes flared.

"Not here. Bunk below with the men. You have had all you will of me, Aleck Maxwell."

That raised a reaction from his tired flesh, mainly protest.

"I want your bed, lass, not ye." A lie. "I'll get no rest down below. Ha' ye no pity?"

"For you?" Her nostrils flared before her gaze unexpectedly softened. She stepped aside. "Aye, then, come in. You take the bed. I will sleep beside the fire."

Well, that made things clear and no mistake, even

to Aleck's foggy mind. But he nodded.

She'd already turned down the bed, so he saw, and it beckoned to him like a haven. Blindly, he walked to it, stripping off his clothing as he went. "Be sure and wake me, lass, at dawn, or sooner if there be a signal."

"Wait."

He froze with his shirt off and his trews half unfastened, and looked at her.

"You need a clean bandage on your head before you lie down."

"I need naught. I vow, I could sleep on my feet."

"Sit." She indicated the bench by the fire, and he fell into it, his eyes sinking nearly shut. Dimly, he heard her move about the chamber and felt her fingers unwind the tattered cloth on his head.

"You are lucky," she murmured, very close. "This head o' yours is made from solid rock."

"Eh?"

"Good border granite, I do not doubt. Is the keep safe?"

"Aye. For the night."

A damp cloth sponged his head. His eyes closed the rest of the way, on a wave of bliss. She touched him. He did not even care why or how. This he had needed all day long. Her company, her presence. Only this, to heal him.

"Good, then you can rest."

He could rest in her. Body, heart, spirit.

Once she finished tending him, he lacked the energy to rise. She helped him, draping his arm over her shoulders, and he tumbled onto the bed, asleep before his head hit the pillow.

"Stay wi' me," he murmured from the edge of

oblivion.

He dreamed of her. He dreamed they coupled together as they had the night before, first quick and hot, then with deliberate languor. In the dream he gave her all of himself, withholding nothing, and knew he had to tell her he loved her.

Still inside her, he lifted his head and cupped her face between his hands, the words trembling on his lips.

Yet he saw not Bess's face but Mary's, her eyes gleaming at him with spite. Mary, who had tricked him into lying with her again. Mary, with whom he remained linked.

Ah, God! "Ye lied to me, ye deceived me," he cried, glaring into those hard, blue eyes.

Her only reply was a smile.

****

The bed, so Bess decided, had room enough for two, even two who did not want to touch one another. And it proved far more comfortable than the bench in front of the fire. She figured she could lie all the way to one side, affording Aleck most of the space.

He sprawled on his back where he'd fallen, so deeply asleep she doubted if he knew where he lay. His breath came slow and regular, and his body gave off enough heat to warm a winter's night.

Eventually, she slept also, only to come awake when Aleck began to thrash. One of his arms slapped her shoulder; he made strangled sounds in his throat.

Aye, fever for sure.

Without bothering to light a candle, Bess laid hold of him. As soon as she did, he came awake, and stilled.

"Aleck? What is it?"

"Dream," he told her hoarsely.

Of what did such a man dream? Past battles? Old enemies?

He lay breathing raggedly.

"Have you fever?" she asked.

"Nay."

"Then what—?"

"I dreamed o' that bitch Mary Johnstone, once more lying to me. Telling lies o' me."

Bess recoiled. Before she could rise from the bed, he said, "Telling lies ye believe. That ye still believe, despite—"

Despite the consuming intimacy they'd shared, aye.

"That you forced her."

"I did no', Bess. She wanted everything that passed between us. She arranged it, set up our meetings. Why would I lie to ye?"

"Why would she?" Mary might fib. Aye, Bess had caught her in it. But the two of them had been close enough that Bess trusted her confidences.

"How do I ken? She—she liked playing wi' fire. I was that, to her."

"She would have told me."

He half turned in the bed. "So ye will no' believe wha' I tell ye now? Bess, I detest liars." His hand caressed her cheek. "I would no' lie to ye."

Ah, but she'd been busy lying to him all this while about his son.

She wanted to scramble from the bed then, wanted to move away from him. That single touch prevented it, melted the better part of her resistance.

Instead, she pressed forward into his arms.

So easy to do, there in the dark. She slept in her

clothing, he had removed enough of his that she could feel most of him, feel the skin of his chest, the heat lower down.

If he kissed her, could she forget the lies that lay between them?

Yearning, she stretched her body against his, and reached blindly for his mouth.

His lips a mere whisper from hers, he said, "Bess, Bess, I love ye."

She froze. There, up against his flesh with his hands cradling her face, her world abruptly froze in place.

"What?"

"I do, lass. I do. I tried to deny it. But ye're like no one else I ha' ever known. Ye've snared me, fair and proper. My heart, 'tis yours."

Bess's heart rose on a staggering wave of victory. For this man to love her—this one man—made the greatest gift life might offer. Then she crashed down again with sickening force. She should tell him she loved him in return. She should, she should. Because och, by all that was holy, she did.

But then, how could she tell him she'd lied to him for the past ten years, and that in fact Dexter was his? Even if she trusted him, he would never trust her again.

When she did not speak, he babbled on, his words fierce in the dark. "I ken fine I am no' the man ye might ha' chosen. Ye do no' trust me, never wanted me here in your life. But fate, aye? Fate has thrown us together, and her aim is true. I could no more live wi'out ye now than cut off my own hand."

Bess could not breathe. All the air had stopped in her lungs, and her heart beat desperate as a trapped bird, and with as little result.

She must say something. She could not leave such beautiful words hanging.

"Bess, lass, we can make this work, put aside our differences. I want a life wi' ye, and wi' Dexter. I love him almost as much as I love ye. Even though he's no', in truth, mine—"

The words hung in the air, begging for answering. It broke upon Bess, the generosity of this man's heart. He believed he'd lost his own son, yet he opened that heart to another man's orphaned lad. Och, how she'd underestimated him!

And had she also misjudged him? Could such a man have forced Mary? Yet she'd owned that truth these last ten years...

She did not know what to believe.

Desperate, she broke his hold on her. "Let me go."

"Bess?"

She wiggled off the bed and backed away from him, arms wrapped hard around her own body. She heard him sit up and follow her.

"Nay. Nay, Aleck."

"What is it, Bess? What ha' I—"

"Leave me be." Stumbling, bumping into furniture in the dark, she made her way to the door, praying he would not come after. He did not. Out in the corridor, she stood gasping, the door closed firmly behind her, and tears raining down her face.

He did not truly love her—or at least he would not, if he knew. For love could not exist upon lies.

Chapter Thirty-Nine

Up on the battlements, a strong wind once more blew. It streamed Aleck's hair across his face and fluttered the bandage on his head. Though he thought the clean air should make him feel better, it did not.

Instead, he would be hard put to say when he'd felt worse. As he stood surveying the upper walkways, his vision blurred so he saw two of the man on watch over the gate, and more than two of the figure that rested against one wall, gazing away into the morning.

MacFee. Mistress Anne, when Aleck questioned her, had said he'd be here. As for the whereabouts of Bess, the good lady had no suggestions.

Aleck's heart had persisted in hoping she'd be here. But he caught no glimpse of a honey-gold head.

Callum turned to regard him when he approached, and narrowed his eyes. "By the powers, man. You do no' look well."

Aleck did not feel well. After Bess fled her chamber in the night—and he had no other word for what she'd done—he'd cursed the impulse that had made him share his feelings with her. To be sure, though she might want him in her bed, she clearly did not welcome his suit. Her feelings for him had not changed.

He'd flailed and chastised his actions, and come to the conclusion he'd had to share those feelings with her, nonetheless. Anything else would be dishonest. Then he'd risen, donned his clothing, and gone looking for her.

He'd been looking ever since.

"Did that blow to the head damage you?"

Bess Mowatt had damaged him. He doubted he'd recover soon.

He shook the offending head, and regretted it. Perhaps that mug of ale he'd taken for breakfast—the only thing to pass his lips—had not been a good idea.

"Ye," he told Callum, "be the one who's walking wounded. Would ye so worry Mistress Anne?"

Callum smiled ruefully. "I just had to assure mysel' all is quiet. This place still feels like my responsibility, even though 'tis no longer."

"I am grateful for your assistance." Aleck meant it, somewhat to his surprise. "Have ye seen Mistress Bess?"

"Nay, not this morn. Is she no' wi' Dexter?"

"Nay."

Callum's eyes immediately filled with concern. "'Tis one of the first things she does every day, connects wi' him."

"Aye. The truth is, MacFee, no one has seen her, from the women in the kitchens to the men in the forecourt. I hoped she'd be up here."

Callum gave him a close examination from head to toe. "What ha' you done?"

"Me?"

"Do no' try and play the innocent, Maxwell. 'Tis no' possible for you. You maun ha' said something to her." Callum's hand hovered over the hilt of his knife. "Done something."

Aleck looked him in the eye. "I told her I loved her."

"Oh." Emotions chased one another through Callum's eyes. His anger swiftly deflated.

"'Twas the truth, what I shared wi' her. I have met no one like her—"

"There is no one like her."

"But she threw it back in my face and ran off. Ye do no' think she'd be so foolish as to leave the keep?"

"I do not."

"Yet no one has seen her. Not even the men keeping watch last night."

"She is, for all her courage, neither hasty nor foolish. And I do no' think she would leave Dexter without a word." With deliberation, Callum added, "She has lived her life for that lad, choosing always what is best for him."

"Aye, so, but she was gey upset. And, despite this quiet, I am no' convinced Danhal Thomson is gone."

"Nor I. 'Tis what brings me up here, again and again."

"So what's to be done?"

"You stay here. Keep watch. I will go speak wi' Anne and see whether she has any ideas. But Maxwell—"

"Aye?"

"Things may no' be always as they seem. People keep secrets, sometimes for good reasons."

"Secrets?"

"The question is, does love allow us to forgive?"

Surprisingly, Callum clasped Aleck on the shoulder before he moved off to descend from the walls.

Forgive? Aleck wondered. For what should he

need to forgive Bess?

****

"Coward," Bess thought bitterly, as she sat with her back against the curve of the tower room wall. The stone felt rough against her back, and the chamber—often a refuge in the past—did not seem like one, now. For she could not escape the battle in her own head.

Rarely, during the past years, had she questioned her courage. She'd stepped into a breach she'd never imagined filling—that of foster mother to an infant—thinking the measure would be temporary. She'd believed Mary wanted her to hide Dexter from Maxwell a little while, after which the mother would send for the child.

To be with him. To love and protect him, even as Bess had.

That had never happened. Instead, Mary had wed her first husband soon after Dexter's birth and sent word saying her husband would not welcome another man's brat. That if Maxwell found out the boy lived, it could cause trouble between them. Attacks, warring.

After that first husband's death, Bess thought again Mary would send for her child. By then, she half hoped not—she'd become attached to Dexter, though she still believed it best for him to live with his mother.

That had not happened either. Instead, Mary had traveled to France and come home with yet another husband. The years trickled by, and Bess faithfully kept her place and kept Dexter hidden. He'd turned into the lad she now loved so well, with the quick mind and flashing smile.

Maxwell's smile.

So she'd traded her life, her own chances at

marriage, and in some ways her conscience for him. Willingly, for the most part.

Until now.

Now, she did not know what to believe. Her heart wanted to trust the man she loved when he said he loved her and that he hadn't forced Mary.

She narrowed her eyes at the sunlight pouring through the slit window, sick inside. Even if she believed that, and God knew she more than half did, she did not see how Aleck would forgive her lying to him, when he found out Dexter was his son.

Tears filled her eyes. For all that, she needed to tell him, even if it destroyed what lay between them. He had the right to know, as did Dexter.

Dexter, above all else. She'd lived the last ten years for him. She would not stop now.

The door of the chamber creaked open, and Bess's heart leaped sickeningly. A dark head peeped in.

Not Maxwell, no—not him. Instead, as if her thoughts had summoned him, Dexter slipped into the chamber and shut the panel behind him.

"There you are! Bess, everyone has been looking for you, and gey worried." He searched her face. "Ha' you been weeping?"

"Nay." Another lie. Bess mopped at her cheeks, and Dexter hurried to her side, where he hunkered down, his concern palpable.

"Are you unwell, then?"

"Nay, Dexter."

"But you never weep. Has someone died?"

"Nay." She snaked an arm around his shoulders and drew him close. How often had they sat thus, with his head hard as a rock against her shoulder? When he'd been poorly, when he felt afraid, when the other lads called him names and made his life a misery.

When he longed for the one thing she could not supply—a father of his own.

Well, she could supply that now.

"Dexter, lad, I have somewhat to tell you."

He turned and looked into her face. "What is it?"

How best to speak the words? *I know you've always trusted me, but I've lied to you all your life.*

Her voice thick, she began, "Master Maxwell—"

"'Tis not him who's ill, is it? Not his poor head?"

"No."

"I am that glad to hear it, for I like him full well."

"I know you do."

He gazed at her with trusting, blue eyes, clear as a sky in May. "If I could ha' but one wish—besides you being well, that is—'twould be that he might be my Da."

Bess went breathless. She had to force the words through her throat when she said, "He is."

"I ken if I did ha' a Da, 'twould no' be so. He would likely turn out to be someone like Ronson's Da, who's harsh and expects much o' him, but—" Dexter's brain caught up with his hurrying mouth. "Wha' did ye say?"

"Alex Maxwell is your Da—your father, that is."

Dexter stared, uncomprehending. "I do no' understand."

"My darling lad, your mother did not want you to know. That is, she did not want him to know, for fear he might take you away from her, you see—"

Dexter shrugged Bess's arm from his shoulders and edged away a bit. "But—I am no' wi' my mother. I

289

never ha' been. I've been always wi' you."

"In my keeping, aye, on her behalf."

He began to shake his head. "Na, na—it canna' be so."

"My lad, it is." Bess tried to capture his hand, but he leaped to his feet. She followed, and found a stranger glaring at her from his blue eyes.

"You lied to me? For her? She means naught to me."

He knew Mary, of course—or more aptly, knew of her. She'd not been in his life, save as a figure elsewhere, one of whom Bess spoke, off doing other things besides raising him.

"I made her a promise," she told him. "I did, on the day you were born. She may mean little to you, Dexter, for you do not know her. But she was close to me, dear to me as a sister, and I could do naught but keep that promise."

"Why would she mak' you promise such a thing?"

"To protect you, as I say."

"But she does no' care for me. She never did."

"Of course she cares for you. You are her son." Bess, having uttered the lie, paused abruptly. Nay, it was she who loved Dexter, she who'd sought always to protect him at any cost.

"It's wrong!" he shouted, his voice echoing in the chamber. "You knew how I wanted a father. You knew how I admired him. I thought you cared for me."

"I do. Och, lad, you are all I have ever cared about."

"I do no' believe you. I trusted you!" It became a howl. "And you should ha' trusted him. Ha' you no' looked at him? Can you no' see how fine he is?"

"He's a reiver, and—" Again, Bess paused. Should she tell the lad his father, whom he so admired, had forced his mother and begat him in violence? Instead, lamely, she concluded, "He does not always tell the truth."

"Just like you," Dexter retorted scathingly, and fled the tower room.

Chapter Forty

Left alone in the tower, Bess distinctly felt her heart strangle and die in her chest. So great was the pain she doubled over and entertained the clear possibility she might well die of it.

A broken heart.

"Dexter." It came from her lips, a moan. "Where are you going?" He likely did not hear. He already flew down the twisting tower stairs. And anyway, she knew where he went.

To find his father.

Och, what had she done? Only blurted the secret she'd guarded so long, that Aleck had not known. A secret Dexter would now share, revealing to Aleck that she'd lied also to him.

I detest a woman who lies. Those words he'd uttered returned to her with a vengeance. Mary had lied to him, aye. Had she also lied about him? Had she met with Aleck, all those years ago, voluntarily and for her own pleasure?

Had Bess misjudged the man she loved, and denied both him and his son the past ten years together?

She placed her hand against the wall in an effort to keep upright. Her mind seemed to sputter in time with her frantic heartbeat.

Oh, aye, Dexter would run and find Aleck, tell him. Neither of them would ever forgive her. She might as well take herself to the window of this chamber and leap out. Dexter, her reason for living—gone. Aleck, her hope for a future—the same.

But she'd never truly had any hope for a future with him. She'd always known the day must come when he found out she'd lied to him. One could not live forever on a falsehood.

Tears filled her eyes and spilled over. Disregarding them, she followed Dexter down the stairs.

****

Aleck, stationed on the walkway overlooking the newly repaired gate, raised his head when Dexter pounded up the stone steps. He'd taken this station after searching the keep for Bess, hoping she'd come up to reassure herself, even as he had, that all lay safe. His eyes searched the clear distances even while his thoughts remained with the woman he loved.

The woman who trusted him not, who loved him not. No matter how he tried, he could not put the thoughts away from him. For though desire might thrive without trust, how could love?

If she didn't believe him when he told her he hadn't raped Mary, what hope was there for them?

His mind ceased chasing the impossible tangle when Dexter arrived, trembling and wracked with emotion. For the lad's blue eyes burned in a white face, wide with either anger or terror.

Bess? Had the lad come to tell him something had happened to her?

"Dex? Lad, what is amiss?"

The boy's lips thinned, and he fought to speak. Alex recognized the emotion then, just as if it were his own—aye, rage.

"By God, lad, spit it out."

"She lied to me!"

"What? Who—"

"Bess. Mistress Bess. All this time she knew, and did no' say. She lied to you too. To both o' us—"

Aleck seized Dexter by the shoulders even as he said, "Lad, get hold o' yoursel'. Wha' is this about Mistress Bess? Is she no' well?"

"I do no' ken. I do no' care!"

That took Aleck aback. From the first moment he'd set foot in this keep, he'd sensed the bond between Bess and her ward. He believed everything she did was for the lad's sake.

"To be sure, ye do care. Slow down. Tell me what's happened."

Over Dexter's head, Aleck caught movement. Bess, face stark white and eyes as stormy as the lad's, emerged from the stairwell.

Aleck swore softly. At least she was in one piece and moving under her own power.

He shook Dexter gently. "Ha' ye quarreled? If so, it can be made up."

Dexter's throat worked. "It canna'." Seeing Aleck glance behind him, he looked round and, at the sight of Bess, stiffened.

"Tell him," Bess bade the lad. "Go ahead."

"Tell me what?"

Dexter turned back and looked him square in the face, wearing an expression such as Aleck had never seen. "You be my father. She says it's true." And Dexter threw himself into Aleck's arms.

Aleck's world rocked. Quite distinctly did he feel the stones of the walkway move beneath his feet, and his body trembled like a tree when the axe is laid on.

A wave of emotion swamped him, so closely woven of strong feelings he could not tell them one from the other... Disbelief. Wonder. Doubt. Great and staggering joy.

Dexter clutched at him fiercely, as if he'd never let go. Even as Aleck hugged the lad back, part of him reveling in the fierceness of the embrace, he sought Bess's eyes.

She nodded. "'Tis true. He's Mary's son. And yours."

Mary's. His. Disbelief fled before what Aleck beheld in Bess's eyes, but that didn't make it any easier to comprehend.

"She told me he died. She said he died that day." Aleck spoke the words even as he strained the lad—this beloved lad—to him. "Ye knew—ye knew he was mine. And ye never told me differently."

"I ken. Mary made me promise, Aleck. I did it for her sake. And for his. Mary believed if you knew, you would take him. Poison him. Make him into what you...are."

Agony flooded her eyes at that, but Aleck dismissed it for the sake of his own pain. "So ye kept him fro' me, and me fro' him. Ten years. All this time I thought him dead. My son!"

Tears choked him then, filled his throat, and flooded his eyes. He never wept—him, a bold reiver, the wolf of the borders. But a lifetime's yearning—Dexter's lifetime—came bounding upon him. How many times had he wished his son had lived? That he might hear the lad's voice, share stories with him, instruct him at arms...love him? All opportunities kept from him by this woman.

Aye, he'd felt drawn to Dexter from the very beginning. Bess had seen the deep bond developing between them, and still she had not told him the truth.

Not even when she lay in his arms. Even that had been a lie.

"How did Mary manage it?" he demanded in a croak. "How did she manage to hide him so long?"

Dexter turned his head at that, seeking the answer.

Bleak resignation came into Bess's eyes. "I did it for her. With help from Robert Lithgow and Callum."

"Master Callum knew?" Dexter yelped the words.

And Aleck added, "Robert Lithgow knew?" Was that why Lithgow had given him the keep? Had it been his way of offering Aleck a chance to learn the truth about his son?

"They two, only," she confirmed. "Just we three were in on the secret. And Mary. Do not blame Callum. He was charged by my great-uncle Robert, even as I was by Mary."

Fiercely, Aleck cried, "Do ye ken wha' ye ha' denied us? What ye ha' cost us?"

"Aye." Her head fell like that of a child, scolded.

"Get out o' my sight." Aleck could scarcely believe the words came from his lips, directed at the woman he loved. He'd not meant to speak them. Instead, they came on their own, issuing from a place of deep hurt and pain.

Bess reacted like a horse struck with a whip. She stiffened, and her head came back up; Aleck had one glimpse of the storm in her eyes before she spun and ran back down the steps, away from him.

From them.

"Mistress Bess!" Dexter called after her, but she did not stop.

Dexter pried himself from Aleck's arms and reached a hand after the retreating woman. Pity the poor lad, Aleck thought, cursed with a mother like Mary, and with a father like him, for all that. And now he lost the person closest to him in all his world.

"Nay, Dex," he told his son. "Let her go."

"But—"

"I will make it up to ye, lad." When Dexter, his eyes wide, looked at Aleck, he went on, "I will mak' the last ten years up to ye. Ye be my son, and wi' me is where ye belong."

"But…" Though he fought a mighty battle over it, Dexter succumbed. His lip trembled, and tears trickled down his cheeks. "I love her."

So do I, Aleck thought. Or at least, he had loved her. He could not be at all certain how he felt, now.

He should have been aware from the outset that anyone who had been so close to Mary in youth would also share her deceitful tendencies. But Dexter bore a measure of Mary's blood, and the love Aleck felt for this child made nothing of it.

"Aye, lad, I ken. But now that we've found each other, from this moment forward ye belong wi' me. Understand?"

Dexter nodded, and a measure of peace came into his eyes. "I could no' ha' a better wish come true."

"Nor I, lad. Nor I."

Chapter Forty-One

"Callum, he knows. Aleck Maxwell knows the truth."

Both occupants of Anne's chamber turned and stared at Bess in surprise when she burst in. Callum, fully clothed, lay on top of the bed up against the pillows, where Anne had no doubt convinced him to rest. Anne stood beside the fire, preparing a basin and bandages.

Anne's face brightened. "You have told Maxwell how you feel for him? It is well."

"'Tis no' well." Callum examined Bess's desperate expression, and his lips tightened. "Come in, lass. Shut the door." He heaved up from the bed.

"Why shut the door now?" Bess agonized. "There will no' be anyone in the keep who does not ken, soon enough. Maxwell will put it 'round. Or Dexter will."

"Put what 'round?" asked Anne, looking baffled.

Callum tossed the words at her, "That Dexter is his son."

"What!"

"Bess, lass, how did he find out?"

"I told Dexter, who," Bess's lips twisted, "at once ran to him." Now they both hated her, the two she loved most in this world. She'd seen the hate, the disgust in Aleck's eyes. She could only guess what Dexter felt.

Ye be like a mother to him. Aleck had told her that,

and it was true. Her feelings for Dexter, deep and protective, were as sharp and vital as if she'd borne him. Yet, for all that, Dexter remained Mary's son.

And Aleck's.

Anne said, "I do not understand. How can Dexter be—"

Callum crossed the room and shut the door behind Bess. "Sit," he bade her. "Before you fall down. Tell me all o' it."

She did, her words stumbling woefully, even while he paced before the fire. As Anne listened, she paled and Callum's expression grew grim.

"All those years!" Anne exclaimed when Bess stumbled to a halt. "The man had a right to know. Dexter did. You've seen how that lad's yearned for a father."

Bess uttered, "'Twas no' my secret to tell."

"Nor mine," Callum agreed, still pacing.

"Well," Anne said, "'twas not a good secret to keep. Aleck Maxwell is a fine and decent man."

Callum turned on her. "He's a reiver, like those who killed your husband."

"No, she's right," Bess lamented. "I should have told them, as soon as I saw how attached they were growing to one another."

But Callum, always so fierce in his morals, shook his head fiercely. "Once charged wi' such a trust, a man—or woman—canna' betray it."

"And what now?" Anne tossed her hands in the air. "Will Maxwell turn us out? 'Tis his domain, after all."

A shiver passed through Bess from head to toe. "I will not wait for him to turn me out." From her home, the place she'd lived the last ten years while raising

Dexter. "I will leave."

"And go where?" Anne cried. "Where will we go?"

Bess made no answer to that, even though she had but one destination in mind. She wanted answers and knew just where to get them.

****

Aleck's anger died slowly, choked out of existence by the joy rising so steadily inside. His son—the one he'd believed dead at birth—had been miraculously restored to him. And such a son!

He remembered well that day he'd had word of Mary in labor and, throwing every other consideration to the winds, rode hard to her father's keep. He'd had to battle his way inside, with his men at his back. Aye, blood had been spilt. But he'd known by then just what Mary was. After their vicious falling out, he'd been sure she would try and keep the child from him, and he meant to have his daughter or his son.

Upon arriving at the keep, he'd heard it whispered, aye, the child was a boy. His heir, then, for he cared little for the bairn's legitimacy or the deceitfulness of its mother.

He should have remembered that deceitfulness when, lying there with the blood and sweat of childbirth still upon her, she told him the child had died. Well, he had asked to see the tiny corpse. She'd said those who tended her had taken it away. He should have insisted.

But he'd fancied he saw anguish in her eyes, and it had made him believe her. Shocked and grieving, he'd not demanded a viewing.

What an actress the woman was!

That did not shock or dismay him so much as Bess Mowatt's role in the thing. That injured him to the very root of his soul. The anger faded, aye. The hurt did not.

He glanced at the lad by his side. They sat together in the great hall with commotion all around them—bonded and isolated in their shared knowledge. So far, he'd told no one else.

He wanted to savor the magnitude of this gift for a wee while. To glory in the fact that, had he been given leave to choose any lad in the world for his own, it would be this one, with his ruffled dark hair and his crooked smile.

Ah, what a job Bess and Callum had done in raising him! He had to give Bess her due in that, if naught else.

Around them, the others still celebrated their victory over the Thomson clan. Battered and stung, they nevertheless bragged on their exploits, Anald the loudest among them.

Under cover of it all, Dexter turned to him and said, "Are you very angry wi' Master Callum? Bess said he knew."

"My anger fades, lad, in my gladness at finding ye."

Dexter brightened. "Fine, that. For Master Callum is dear to me, just as—" He broke off, no doubt at what he saw in Aleck's eyes.

"List to me, lad. I want to waste no more time in anger or revenge. But ye maun ken, from this moment things will change."

"Change…how?"

"Ye will no longer be raised by or answerable to Mistress Bess or MacFee. Ye belong to me, understand? I will finish your raising and your training."

Dexter's expression flickered between joy and doubt. "I like that fine, but—will we stay here? I ha' lived here, you ken, all my life."

Home. Aleck understood the concept, though he'd never been fully invested in it. He'd been born in his father's house near Galashiels, spent some years with his grandfather, and been fostered out for training with his mother's brother. He supposed he could take Dexter back to his father's house now.

Yet this place for which he'd battled so hard was his. Had Lithgow, that wily old fox, intended him to stay?

What would be best for Dexter?

"I ha' property elsewhere. All will be yours after me, lad."

"If we stay here, will Master Callum and Mistress Bess stay also?"

Aleck's very spirit shied at that. "Nay."

"Then what will happen to the other lads? The school?"

"Ye are full o' questions, are ye no'?"

Dexter looked abashed. "Och, I am that sorry. Mistress Bess told me always to ask."

"Mistress Bess was right." Curse her. "Ye may say and ask aught ye wish to me. We ha' been apart too long to keep from speaking our minds now."

Dexter's eyes filled with wonder. "Will we tell the others? All the lads?"

"We will mak' o' it a grand announcement." Just as soon as Aleck decided what he wanted to do. "Perhaps Master Callum can relocate his school elsewhere." The man had lied to him, aye, at least by omission. But after fighting beside him, Aleck still held

Callum in some respect.

As for Bess—again, his mind shied from the thought of her. Her lips, sliding over his skin. Her body wooing his, the taste of her, ripe and sweet.

Did he love her still? Ah, what kind of fool would that make him?

"Perhaps," Dexter agreed. "And mayhap Mistress Bess can stay here with us."

"Dexter, lad—"

"I ken you are angry wi' her. But she is dearest in all the world to me." Dexter looked stricken. "Apart from you, that is."

Anald strode up then. "Why are the two o' ye sitting here whispering? This is a celebration. And ye, Aleck, be the hero o' the hour."

"Ye be right." Aleck scraped back the bench and got to his feet. "And I ha' an announcement to make."

Chapter Forty-Two

"Where is she? I ha' words I mean to say to her."

Aleck had been thinking about those words all afternoon long, while the celebration over the announcement he'd made continued and his men congratulated him, even while he watched the other lads eye Dexter with a new air of wariness and respect.

Now Callum entered the hall, with Mistress Anne at his side. The man looked grim and steady, ready to face Aleck.

So far, though, Bess had made no appearance. Aleck fancied she must be hiding in her chamber, or elsewhere in the keep, unwilling to face him.

A pity, that. He wanted to vent his spleen on her. He wanted to sting her, even as she'd stung him. He wanted an apology from her lips.

He was not sure, for all that, he could deny Dexter—his son—her company.

Even now, Dexter looked to Callum with concern.

"Aye, Master Callum," the lad added his inquiry to Aleck's. "Where is Mistress Bess?"

Callum focused on Dexter, and not Aleck. His gaze softened. "Gone. I am that sorry, lad—"

"Gone?" Aleck interrupted. "Whatever do ye mean? Into hiding, ye say?"

"Nay." Callum shook his head. "Gone. She's left the keep."

Aleck distinctly felt the blood drain away from his head. "Impossible. I ha' men keeping watch from the walls. Someone would ha' told me."

Caution flickered in Callum's eyes. "We, too, ha' men keeping watch."

"But—'tis no' safe out there. Thomson may ha' withdrawn, aye. We do no' ken how far. Why in hell did ye let her go, man?"

"She is no' mine—nor yours—to hold here."

"She could be attacked, captured. Slain." Aleck, feeling the lad beside him stiffen, stopped speaking abruptly. Ah, but Dexter must understand the realities of this life they shared.

"Mistress Bess," Dexter bleated.

"How long ago did she leave?" Aleck demanded. He'd go after her. Scold her—possibly kiss her—and bring her back.

Mistress Anne pushed past Callum and said, "Hours ago. I fear you are too late."

"Hours?" Already, Aleck knew, it grew dark outside. Even with Thomson out of consideration, the countryside lay full of peril.

To be sure, Bess could take care of herself. And she no longer concerned him. Did she?

"Ye must know where she's gone."

"Aye," Dexter whispered.

Again, Callum focused on the lad. "I am no' certain. She was quite careful not to say. But if I had to venture a guess—"

"She's gone to see your mother, lad," Anne broke in, "to try and learn the truth."

****

It paid, Bess thought with a measure of self-congratulation, to have friends in critical places. An old friend on watch—namely William—had been instrumental in securing her mount and getting both it and her out of the keep.

As soon as she'd poured her story into old William's ears, he'd proven willing to help. He'd laid about a story that the pony—one of Callum's—showed lame, and needed to be put through its paces, and tended. He'd pretended to consult with Bess over the treatment. Several pairs of eyes had seen her step out of the keep, her belongings disguised in a feedbag, and watched her walk down to meet William, ostensibly riding back.

When she in turn rode off, no doubt they thought William had asked her opinion on the horse's condition.

In the ensuing confusion, and the exciting news coming from the hall—that the lad, Dexter, was Maxwell's son!—they did not notice she failed to return.

William, as Bess knew, would take word of her leaving to Callum. William could keep naught from his master for long. But she'd already told Callum and Anne she meant to go.

Aleck, she did not doubt, would be pleased with her absence. Back at the keep, he'd scarcely been able to look at her. A sharp pain stabbed her heart when she remembered that, but she set her lips in a grim line and rode on. She'd kept a promise given, whatever it might cost her now. What was done could not be altered.

She gave more thought to Dexter, who would fret over her departure and the fact that she'd failed to say farewell. She wished she might have spoken with the lad before she left. But he now had what he'd always wanted—a father. She, Bess, made but a poor substitute.

She had only two concerns now. Avoiding Thomson's men, if they still lingered in the countryside, and deciding where Mary might be found.

She struggled over that last point, even as she picked her way cautiously through the woodland, trying to remember the details of Mary's life. Three times married, and with a number of other children, she could be traveling between them—as they had different fathers—or held up anywhere. Her latest husband, a wealthy landowner called Falon—lived well south of the borders. A long way to ride, if Bess did not find her quarry at the end of it.

Better, perhaps, to ride to the holding of Mary's father, not so very far from here, and the very place where Dexter had been born, in order to learn where she might be found.

Still a good day's travel and over dangerous ground. Danhal Thomson would love to take her hostage, and the devil only knew what her fate would be at his hands.

Do not think about it, she instructed herself. And do not think about Aleck, or how much you love him. Do not think about your life lying in ruins, or you will not be able to go on.

Time blurred, even as her vigilance flagged. Riding eastward, she came upon the bulk of Thomson's troops. Not retreating—nay, and not showing any signs of doing so, either. Instead, they had stopped some distance from the keep and formed a camp.

Bess, seeing and hearing them through the trees, ducked out of sight before their outposts spied her. By then, dark had fallen. She made a camp of her own, cold without a fire, in a patch of woodland. She thought about what must be happening back home, and lay aching until dawn.

Late the next day she arrived at Lithgow House, close enough to the holding where she'd grown up that she might have tossed a stone and hit it. It occurred to her, then, that when all this ended—when she either had the truth from Mary or did not—she might return home. Her father, she supposed, would have to take her in, though he would not be pleased about it. A spinster long past her prime at nearly a score and eight years, a warrior rather than a maiden, and her reputation quite ruined…what would he do with her?

She'd not been home for many years, save for brief visits when her mother sickened and died. Och, what a fate.

Perhaps, rather, if Callum and Anne wed and set up a household somewhere, they would welcome her in. She squinted her eyes, trying to see a future she could not imagine, and rode in through the gates.

They knew her here, of course, despite the passage of time. As girls, she and Mary had been inseparable; she'd slept here as often as at home.

One of the guards sent for Mary's father, who came down to greet her just inside the gate.

"Bess, lass!" A big, bluff man with fierce blue eyes—not unlike Dexter's—and a balding head, he now looked concerned. "I am that surprised to see you. We had word that Kellsbrough Keep came under attack. Has it fallen, then?"

"Nay." Bess gave him a quick embrace. "We were able to defend it, and all within."

A new expression invaded his eyes. "Ah, then, you must ha' heard."

"Heard?"

"About Mary. I should ha' known you would come to her, in her time o' need."

"I am looking for her, aye, and hoped you might know where she could be found."

"I do, aye. Mary's here, and she's dying."

Chapter Forty-Three

"I came home, in the end," Mary said bleakly from her pillow. "Just like a wounded bird, returning to its nest." She gave a wan smile. "The truth is, no one else would have me."

Bess, striving mightily to hide her shock at the sight of her friend, sank into the chair beside the bed. Had she not been prepared by Mary's father, she might not have recognized the woman propped against those pillows. Mary, always so beautiful, so full of life, and with a wicked spark in her eyes, now looked frail and as pale as the linen. The hand she extended to Bess appeared skeletal.

Bess clasped it nonetheless. This was the friend of her childhood, once her sister in spirit. Dexter's mother.

"What has happened to you?" she asked, and Mary's lips twisted in a grimace.

"'Tis a long story. Not a pretty one. Some might say the fruits of my sins have come back upon me. That is, in fact, what the priest says."

"But—"

"My husband, Henry Falon, has tossed me out."

"Not—not because you are ill?"

"He says not, though I believe that had somewhat to do with it. He wanted a vixen in his bed." Mary's eyes met Bess's in a rueful look. "He did not want that vixen straying to someone else's bed. 'Tis an old story.

I came up carrying a child—not his, for an injury keeps him from fathering any more children. I lost the bairn early. A blessing, some might say."

"I would not say it."

"But when the physicians came to tend me, they found out why I could not carry the wean." She splayed her free hand across her belly. "There is a sickness inside. Here, where I so often sinned."

Bess turned sick to her stomach, and protest rose. "You can mend though, aye? You are strong." Though, at the moment, Mary did not look it.

Another bitter smile curved Mary's lips. She shook her head. "Not this time."

"Och, Mary—" Bess's eyes flooded with tears.

"Nay, do not weep, or you will get me started. How did you know to come? How did you know I was ill?"

"I did not. I came here seeking you for another reason."

"You always have been there for me, Bess. I have always been able to rely on you."

Aye, and only look what it had cost. Ten years of Bess's life. The ease of her conscience.

"But look at you!" Mary's fingers tightened. "Dressed all in leathers instead of a gown. You look more the warrior than a maid."

"I am."

"We heard the keep came under attack."

"By Danhal Thomson, aye. We repelled him and his men."

"When first I heard of it, I wanted to come. I wanted to see you, by any road, before—And my son. I wanted to see Dexter. But the illness progresses too swiftly. I was marooned here and could not travel."

"Aye, I see."

"How is he, my son Dexter?"

"He is well, very well. You would be proud."

"Do you remember that day I placed him in your arms? He was born in this very chamber. And you promised, promised me you'd keep him away from his father. But he is there now, is he not? Aleck Maxwell—Uncle Robert deeded the keep to him."

"Aye, Mary. He and Dexter have met, and formed a bond. I had to tell them. I had to tell them they are father and son."

The fierce light faded from Mary's eyes. Abruptly, she closed them. "Ah, it does not matter now."

Not matter? Bess had lied and wrangled, protected this woman's secret at the cost of her own happiness, and she said it did not matter...

Very carefully, she asked, "I thought you did not want Dexter in Maxwell's hands."

Eyes still closed, Mary said, "So I did not. I was angry with him, sure. He broke off with me." Her eyes came open, once more filled with fierce light. "Me! No one spurns me and goes unpunished. Should I let him have his son, after that?"

"He—but you told me—"

"He'd grown weary of me, of my lies and selfishness, so he said. And him a bloody reiver, no better than he should be. How dare he preach at me? He wanted to cease our meetings, no longer would have aught to do with me."

"Meetings? But you said—"

"We would meet in the woodland. The first time was by chance. I thought he might harm me, then, but nay—he would have let me ride on. But how often does a lass have a chance to taste a man like that?"

Shock kept Bess silent.

"I threw myself at him, aye, but no man could resist me, then. It was wild and—and satisfying. Doubly so because no one knew. But he wearied of me. Can you warrant it? And one day he did not keep the tryst…I grew angry then, right enough. Not a fortnight later, it became clear I carried his child. I'd been with no one else."

Horror nearly stopped Bess's throat. "But you told me he forced you. You confided so, in this very room. You wept over it."

"Aye, I know. I had to tell you something, to secure your help. Besides, I did not want my father to know I'd been shameless, and meeting with one of his sworn enemies. Folk were ready to believe such a thing of Maxwell, given his reputation."

She, Bess, had believed it without hesitation. Even when he told her she was wrong.

"Mary, do you know what you've done? Denied Maxwell the knowledge of his son. Denied Dexter the past ten years with his father. Dexter has felt that, Mary. He's suffered for it."

"Just another sin to lay at my feet. I told the truth, in the end."

"Eh?"

"I told Uncle Robert, when he came to see me. I was dying, and so was he."

"So that is why Robert granted the keep to Maxwell, so he and Dexter might have a chance to find one another."

"Aye, so. I begged Uncle Robert not to betray me. Though I quite see, now, it does not mean aught, as I will never see either of them again. I wish them well of each other."

Her eyes sank shut before opening wide again. "The pain is very bad, Bess. Mine will not be a good end."

And what sort of end did Mary deserve? Bess could not keep from wondering. Out of pure spite Mary had told Aleck his son died. She'd elicited a long and merciless sacrifice from Bess over the last ten years. Though Bess would not have traded even one of those days spent raising Dexter, not for all the world.

"Mary," she said softly, "I love him. Aleck Maxwell, I mean."

"You cannot love a reiver, lass. That much I do know."

"I do love him, and there is no changing it. But he hates me now, for deceiving him over Dexter. I do not think he will ever forgive me."

Mary gazed straight into Bess's eyes. Almost dreamily, she said, "Have faith, lass, in the ties that bind us to one another. Did they not keep you tethered all this while to me? Now, tell me about my son. 'Tis all I want to hear."

Aye, for Mary's lies and foolishness had cost her, also—cost her the joy of watching Dexter grow and flourish. With pity in her heart, Bess spoke softly, describing the lad she loved so well, until Mary's eyes drifted shut.

They did not open again.

****

"Where has she gone? Ye must ha' some idea." Desperation turned Aleck's voice harsh. Mistress Anne, whom he addressed, already looked upset and worried.

No more worried than Aleck felt.

He should be angry with Bess Mowatt—enraged. And he was. She'd refused to believe him when he told her the truth about his relationship with Mary. And she'd kept the truth about Dexter from him, a truth both he and the lad had a right to know.

He'd pondered both those facts all night, in lieu of sleep. The fact that the first point had, no doubt, prompted the second changed nothing. She'd lain in his arms, close as a man and woman could get, and lied to him.

Get out o' my sight.

Aye, he'd spoken those words. He might even have meant them at the time. He meant them no more. He'd risen this morning knowing he had to find her and bring her back to the keep—nothing more. His words, and his anger, had driven her into a dangerous world. Were she taken hostage by Thomson, he would not give two figs for her chances.

Anne bit her lip and looked at him uncertainly. "Why do you want to know?" Before he could answer, she pressed on, "There are reasons, and reasons. Do you wish to pursue and punish her?"

"Nay." Aleck glared at Callum, who stood silent beside his lady, arms crossed on his chest. "I want her safe."

"Why?" Anne asked again, a challenge this time.

"Dexter worries for her. She is the closest thing he has to a decent mother."

Indeed, Dex had come to him soon after dawn, full of entreaties. But that alone did not drive Aleck now.

"A good reason," Anne granted, "but not good enough."

Callum spoke. "Bess is a grown woman and has a right to go where she will."

"And get hersel' captured?" Aleck ran a hand through his hair, distracted. "Get raped, or killed?"

"Have more faith in her than that. Bess is a clever and canny woman, a warrior." Callum's eyes flashed. "She survived a long while before you came along."

"Aye, I ken."

Callum shook his head. "No matter—William helped her, and even he canna' tell you where she's gone. She took one o' my horses and rode out early. No one made aught o' it."

Frustration clawed at Aleck's throat. What was he to tell Dexter? What could he promise his own heart?

"No one may have marked her departure," Anne agreed, "but I can guess where she went."

Aleck focused on her. "Aye?"

Anne leaned forward and touched his hand. "But first you must tell me—do you love her?"

Aye, there lay the question, right enough. Could he still love a woman who'd lied to and deceived him, all while accusing him of lying? Long ago, when he broke things off with Mary, he'd sworn never to have aught to do with any woman who lied to him. And upon meeting Bess, he'd believed her to be an honest woman, the sort who looked you in the eye and said what she meant.

Now his heart whispered, *She lied to protect another*. Not that baggage Mary, but Dexter. She'd lied to protect someone she loved.

Would he not do the same?

He knew right down to his bones he'd do whatever he must to protect Dexter. Fight to the death, cheat, deceive. The love he felt for the lad was deep and inexpressibly wide.

And what of the love he felt for Bess? Would it allow him to forgive her?

He returned Anne's stare. "I love her, aye," he said honestly. "And I want her back here wi' me."

Anne gave a small, satisfied nod. "This is where I think she has gone…"

Chapter Forty-Four

Mary's father begged Bess to stay for her burial. "She would want you here," he insisted, "helping prepare her for her final journey."

Unable to refuse, Bess agreed to sleep there the night, though in truth she found precious little rest. She helped Mary's kin wash and dress her in clothing that no longer fit, so wasted had her body become. Directly after the funeral rite the next morning, she set out beneath gray skies for home.

But she no longer had a home, did she? Kellsbrough Keep belonged to another, one who did not want her there. She must instead return to her father's house and try to take up some sort of a life, though she could scarcely imagine it.

Her father, being her father, had to take her in, as Aleck Maxwell did not.

But she wanted to see Dexter first. She needed to tell him of his mother's death, and she owed Aleck Maxwell an apology.

Was she woman enough to deliver it?

That question haunted her as she rode west. The rain started not long after, adding considerably to the depth of her misery. If she rode hard, she might make the keep by nightfall. But she did not want to ruin Callum's good mount, and she questioned her welcome when she arrived. Would Aleck even let her in?

Get out o' my sight.

She heard again the loathing in his voice when he spoke the words that now fair possessed her mind.

She realized, later, those words had distracted her. In truth, her thoughts and her weariness made her incautious. Half blinded by rain, and soaked to the skin, she rounded a curve in the track through the woodland.

And rode straight into a troop of Thomson men.

Instinct made her haul hard on her reins. But they'd seen her; she barely had time to turn her mount before they hollered and gave chase.

Her horse, already tired, had not enough left in him to make good an escape. All too soon were they run down and caught. Thomson's men surrounded them.

A hand came out and seized her bridle. With a sinking heart, she looked into Danhal Thomson's eyes.

In truth, she barely recognized him. As drenched as she, he wore a bandage wrapped around his forehead, and his face, beneath its wild beard, bore bruises that darkened most of the visible skin. But he bared his teeth at her in a fierce grimace.

"'Tis a woman!" he exclaimed in surprise, as he searched Bess's face. "And one I know, by God. You're the wench who faced me back on the gate at Kellsbrough. Ally to Aleck Maxwell."

And belonged to him. Heart and soul.

****

"I want to go wi' ye."

Dexter stood foursquare in the courtyard, blocking Aleck's way. Clad all for riding, he wore his knife through his belt and a determined look on his face. He might have—almost—been laughable, but Aleck had no heart to disparage him.

Instead, he snapped, "Out o' the question."

"But why?"

"Ye will slow me down." Aleck had been certain, when he rose at dawn, he needed to ride out and find Bess. What might take place between them when he did, he could not say. But it did not require Dexter for a witness.

"I will no'. I can ride very well. Bess taught me."

Something in the lad's eyes made Aleck's heart soften. "She taught ye many things, and well. But, Dex, I do no' ken what may be out there, or what I will find."

"All the more reason to tak' me."

"I will tak' some o' my men." Anald, and his cousin Dunston. Callum would stay here to guard the keep, and Dexter.

"But she's most important to me. And if she be in danger, I am the one who maun fight for her."

Aleck's heart swelled. Had anyone ever possessed such a son? He smiled reluctantly. "While I admire your spirit, she is quite likely no' in danger at all." Just at the home of Mary's father, the last place Aleck wanted to be. Was Mary there? Would Aleck be forced to encounter her?

If he took Dexter, might the lad see her also?

"List to me, lad. Wait here—"

"I will no'!" Dexter set his body determinedly and drew a breath. "Da—"

Da. A word Aleck never expected to hear on this lad's lips, one that fair twisted his heart. "I ha' a feeling she's in danger, that she needs me."

"Do ye?" Aye, Aleck had the same feeling. Akin to instinct, it rode his blood and made him desperate to get away. "Right, then, I suppose ye'd better come along wi' me after all."

****

The rain stopped sometime after sunset, but Bess, already wet to the skin, found little relief. Thomsons had made camp in the trees where Danhal ordered her tied her up, hands and feet. A good fire burned but, though he'd placed Bess where he could see her, she was situated too far from the flames to derive any benefit out of them.

Thomson's party consisted of seven men, including the reiver himself. Where the balance of his force may have gone, Bess could not say. Perhaps he'd left them concealed nearby, to await a further attack on the keep.

And perhaps this group headed back to home turf for doctoring, for all of the troop bore significant wounds, not the least Danhal. In addition to the bruises and the white bandage that swathed his red head, he wore bandaging at his left shoulder, and cradled that arm close to his side.

But aye, he remained agile with the right hand, and had belted Bess soundly when she fought her capture. She'd aimed her blows for his wounded side, and hurt him too before he and his men managed to subdue her. As a consequence, she now had a swollen lip and heavy bruising of her own. At least the blood inside her mouth had stopped flowing.

Even as she wondered what would happen to her next, Thomson came and hunkered down in front of her.

He had an ugly face, broad and freckled, with ears that stuck out like toadstools and eyes of reddish-brown that echoed the hue of his hair.

He gazed at Bess thoughtfully before he asked,

"Are you MacFee's bitch, then?"

Lifting her head, Bess retorted, "I am not."

"But you be the woman who helps him train those lads, aye? There have long been rumors about the two o' you, you see. Living all cozy in that keep this long while."

"Are you the sort o' man who listens to rumors?"

"Nay. 'Tis why I am asking you, just. You fought beside him. Him, and Maxwell." He sneered over that name. "And fought well, for a woman."

Bess wanted to spit. Her mouth felt too sore.

"I intend to go back and kill them both," Thomson said almost pleasantly, "just as soon as I be healed up enough. But now—" He inspected her again, this time with a hint of a leer. "I have a hostage. You must mean something to one o' them."

Bess's blood ran cold, and her thoughts scrambled. Claiming importance might provide her a measure of protection—Thomson likely wouldn't savage goods he wanted to trade. But negotiating for her return might put Callum—and others at the keep—in danger.

"I mean naught to them."

"Now, that I do not believe, at all."

"They turned me away. 'Tis why I am here."

"You are bound back to the Kellsbrough from somewhere else, are you not? 'Tis my guess they sent you with a message for someone. Summoning more help, maybe. No matter. If Maxwell will no' negotiate for you, he might for that horse. 'Tis a fine animal."

Again, he inspected Bess. "I and my men will have other uses for you. You may be clad like a man, but you be a woman under it all."

Bess gritted her teeth and said nothing. Could she

endure? For Dexter's sake, perhaps she could.

For Aleck's sake.

She closed her eyes for an instant, and an image of his face bounded upon her—not fierce and warlike, not the reiver wolf, but softened by tenderness.

She would never see that emotion on his face again.

"Do what you will," she told Thomson. "You failed to take the keep before. You will not take it now."

His ruddy eyes glowed, and he reached out a large, filthy hand to caress her cheek. Bess jerked away.

"Oh, lass, I vow it on my life. I will."

Chapter Forty-Five

Aleck smelled the camp fire before he caught any glimpse of Thomson's bivouac—a scent of scorched wood on the damp air, of heavy smoke struggling to rise. Dark had recently fallen, and though that might afford a measure of concealment, he schooled himself to caution. A misstep now could cost not only his life and those of his men, but Dexter's.

That he would not risk.

He gestured to the men behind him and spoke in a harsh whisper to the lad at his side. "Ye fall back now. If the rest o' us go down, I want ye to ride hell for leather back to the keep, and tak' refuge wi' Callum."

MacFee would look after the boy. Aleck had that comfort.

"Nay," Dexter protested.

Aleck bent a glare on him. "Aye. Will ye show me defiance?"

He saw the lad's throat work. "I do no' wish to. But if Bess be in danger—she is like a mother to me."

Aleck thought of the lad's real mother, a lying, deceiving vixen in perpetual heat. "Aye," he said more softly. "But those are Thomson's men ahead. We do no' ken if Bess be there, or even if she came this way."

"I can feel her," Dexter announced stubbornly. "Can you no'?"

Aleck could, just as if some secret knowing

whispered it to him, as if, over the reek of the struggling campfire, he could catch Bess's scent.

Anald edged his horse closer to Aleck's. "Wha's for it, man?"

Aleck bade him, "Go ahead and scout. Careful, mind."

Anald grinned, dismounted swiftly, and went.

Aleck seized hold of Dexter's bridle, just in case the lad decided to take matters into his own hands.

Soft as a breath, Dexter asked, "Do you think she is all right?"

Aleck's heart thudded in his chest. Could he live in a world without Bess Mowatt? Mayhap, but he would never recover from the loss of her. Naught in his world would be the same.

"Lad, did Mistress Bess teach ye your prayers?"

"Nay. But Mistress Anne did. At least, she tried."

"Then I bid ye pray."

Moments trickled by like years before Anald returned, silent on his feet for so big a man. Aleck dismounted, and Anald stepped close.

"They have her. Tied up on the far side o' their fire—"

He got no farther before Dexter moved. Swift as a thought, the lad slipped from the back of his pony and disappeared into the trees.

For an instant, so great was Aleck's dismay he struggled to breathe. Bad enough finding Bess in peril. But both of them!

Ah, so this was how it felt, to love.

Swearing bitterly and with but one look for Anald, he drew his sword and followed the lad.

Only he could not see Dexter anywhere ahead of

him. The lad's slim form made not so much as a flicker among the trees and cast no shadow. Caution stirred in Aleck's mind. It was madness to go stumbling toward an enemy's camp. But where his son went, he would follow.

The fire, poor as it was, lit the scene garishly. Six men took their ease, with their horses tethered just beyond. And there—on the far side just as Anald said, situated up against the bole of a fallen tree—Bess sat with her head bowed.

His heart quivered within him. He should be angry with her, aye, but he felt no rage, no indignation—only love and concern.

Damn that lad, where had he gone? Aleck still couldn't see him and figured he must have circled round through the trees in an effort to get behind Bess.

Had Thomson not posted a guard? Did the man feel so confident, in possession of a hostage, he supposed he did not need one?

Aleck could see Danhal Thomson right enough, at the center of the camp, and sporting a large, filthy bandage on his head. He appeared to be arguing over something with one of his men. The others focused on the confrontation.

A flicker of movement caught Aleck's eye. There—deep in the shadows behind Bess—he saw his son, and his heart leaped into his mouth.

Ah, God, do no' let me have found him only to lose him now.

He saw Bess stiffen, saw her head come up. She strained to peer over her shoulder, and he stiffened also, for via the unlikely bond that connected them he felt her dismay, her alarm.

****

A hand touched Bess's wrists, bound behind her. A jolt of alarm speared through her body, and her head jerked around. A voice said, "Whisht, it is only me."

Bess knew that voice. Dearly loved, it was. But she did not want it in her ears here and now.

"What—" she began.

"Hush. While they be arguing."

Bess bit her lip so hard she tasted blood. How had Dexter come here? By God, if he got himself captured, Thomson would have a weapon that truly mattered to Aleck.

She could think of nothing Aleck Maxwell would not do to ransom his son. She could think of nothing she would not do. Craning her neck, she caught a glimpse of Dexter, dark head pressed close to hers.

"Get away," she bade him. "Get—"

He ignored her, working furiously on her bonds. The knife he wielded nicked her hand; she did not even flinch. "Go."

"Nay, I—"

Danhal Thomson turned. In that terrible moment, everything seemed to happen at once too quickly and too slowly. His reddish eyes flickered in the light of the fire and fixed upon them.

"Ah, God!" Bess groaned at Dexter. "Run!"

But he'd not succeeded in freeing her hands, and even as she uttered the words, she knew this boy she'd raised, this lad with the determined mind and the heart of a wolf, would not abandon her.

Instead, Dexter stepped over the tree and faced Danhal Thomson, his knife raised.

Curiously, he did not look small standing there,

facing the strapping man. Instead, his valor lent him stature, and for an instant Bess's heart quivered with hope.

Then Danhal Thomson grinned. He pulled his sword in an ugly gesture. "Who, by the blessed lady, are you?"

Bess realized Thomson did not know the prize he'd caught. To him, Dexter was just a lad who had unaccountably turned up. What reason would he have to seize the boy?

She willed Dexter to silence. *Do not tell. Please do not—*

"I am her ward," Dexter said, clear as a bell. Bess heard no fear in him. Och, he was made of stern stuff, this lad of hers. "Let her go."

"Ah?" Thomson quirked an eyebrow. "One o' they students fra' MacFee's school, are ye?"

"Aye."

"Begone, lad. I ha' no quarrel wi' you."

Aye, go! Bess begged it silently.

But Dexter said, "Only if Mistress Bess comes wi' me."

The men laughed, all of them. Thomson waved his sword. "She is going nowhere. I ha' uses for her, see."

For the first time, Dexter appeared uncertain.

With amusement in his voice, Thomson asked, "Will ye mak' combat for her, then?"

Dexter considered it. Bess fairly felt his thoughts move. Despite his bandaged head and hampered arm, Thomson looked formidable—as he was, in truth. Bess had seen him fight, on the walls. And he stood armed with a sword, against Dexter's knife.

Yet the lad answered, "I will."

"No. No!" Bess shouted the words. Desperate to free her hands, she struggled wildly. If anyone must face Danhal Thomson, it should be her. But Dexter had succeeded in cutting only part way through her bonds.

Thomson cast a look at her. "Ah, mistress, I think you should let your young charge fight. Would you throw his act o' chivalry back upon him?"

"Such a combat is not fair!" Bess roared, and fought her way to her feet. "What manner of man are you? Fight me, instead."

"Nay!" Another voice shattered the night. "Fight me."

****

Bess knew that voice also, and hearing it now nearly took her to her knees. Dearly loved, deeply cherished—but how could Aleck Maxwell be here?

She could not guess. Yet, having come here, could he do aught but step forward to defend his son? She thought not.

That he acted to protect Dexter, and not her, Bess did not doubt. The last time they'd spoken together, he'd ordered her out of his sight.

Now, though, he did flick one look at her as he stepped clear into the firelight, his sword raised.

He shot a second look at Dexter. As if they communicated silently, Dexter nodded and stepped back to Bess, where he resumed work on her bonds.

To Danhal Thomson, Aleck said, "This has been a long time coming."

"You," Thomson sneered, already beginning to circle, his paces measured and deadly, "setting yoursel' up as master o' Kellsbrough Keep."

"Nae more than I am. Robert Lithgow granted the

place to me."

"I do no' believe you. Why should the old man do that? Keep back," Thomson grated to his men. "This is between me and yon reiver wolf."

"Then let us finish it," Aleck said.

Chapter Forty-Six

The leather thongs that bound Bess's hands parted at last, at the insistence of Dexter's blade, which bestowed another nick in passing. Just as well they came apart when they did, for the instant Aleck's sword met Danhal Thomson's, Dexter forgot all else and stood as one enrapt.

Only then did Bess realize Dexter had never seen his father engaged in actual combat. She had fought beside Aleck at the gates, but though he and Dexter had sparred in play, this fight proved deadly and earnest.

Both men bore injuries. Indeed, a hysterical laugh rose to the back of Bess's throat as she watched them pace one another, nearly matched bandages on their heads. Yet there was naught humorous in any of this.

She seized Dexter's shoulders, half afraid he might dart forward, but he continued to stand where he was, arrested. On the far side of the camp, Thomson's men also seemed caught by the spectacle.

She took advantage of the distraction to pry the knife from Dexter's fingers and cut through the bonds on her ankles. Then, balancing lightly on the balls of her feet, she watched.

Aye, she thought, what had begun on the walls at Kellsbrough would finish here. A fight to the death? Nay, she prayed not.

The clang when the two broadswords met sounded

overly loud. Danhal Thomson grunted as he threw Aleck off. A sound of pain?

"His side. Go for his side!" Dexter muttered.

As if Aleck heard him, he feinted right and, when Thomson spun, darted in quick under the reiver's guard. The two men parted, only to come together again. This time they did so in a blinding flurry of movement, almost too swift for the eye to follow. When they once more parted, a thin line of blood appeared at Aleck's shoulder.

Dexter caught his breath. Thomson followed up his advantage with another series of crashing blows. Aleck stepped back, and back.

"His arm, Da!" Dexter cried. "Go for his injured arm."

Thomson paused, and an ugly grin spread across his face. He cocked an eye at Aleck. "Da? Ne'er tell me the whelp is your cub?"

"Harm one hair o' him," Aleck growled, "and ye'll do naught more."

From that moment forward, the outcome seemed assured. Aleck drove Thomson back in turn, a fierce assault. Though the crooked grin remained fixed to Danhal's face, his steps became ever more desperate. When, driving his sword up under Thomson's guard, Aleck laid open the man's injured shoulder, Danhal swayed on his feet. A renewed onslaught took him over onto the ground, a cry tearing from his throat as his broken arm made contact with the stony soil.

No one breathed as Aleck leveled the point of his blade at Thomson's throat. Ruthless border reiver as he was, Bess expected him to ram it home.

But the moments crawled past until, with an almost

angry movement, Aleck sheathed his weapon. To Dexter, quite deliberately he said, "Ye can see, lad, there is no honor in slaughtering a defeated man."

But, Bess thought, had not Aleck, also injured, earned his victory? The contest had been fair enough. Not that she wished Dexter to witness his father slaying an opponent.

"Get up," Aleck told Thomson. "In future, stay awa' from me and mine. Kellsbrough Keep belongs to Aleck Maxwell, understand? To Aleck Maxwell and his heirs."

Danhal Thomson said nothing. His men hurried forward and helped him up. To Bess's astonishment, Anald Robertson and others of Aleck's crew materialized from the trees.

Anald asked Bess, "Lass, are ye harmed?"

She shook her head, but spared him no words. Her attention still centered on Aleck, who walked toward them with that characteristic slight swagger—or rather, walked toward his son.

"That was a damn foolish thing to do," he bawled at Dexter. "It was gey dangerous—and unco' brave." He flashed his grin, the one so much like Dexter's own. "I am that proud o' ye."

Dexter trembled where he stood. Bess sensed he wanted to throw himself into his father's arms but hesitated to indulge in so childish a display.

Instead he nodded, man to man.

"Ye," Aleck pronounced, "be going to make a damn fine reiver."

****

Bess stood in the window of the tower room, all alone. Beyond the casement stretched the familiar, beautiful swell of the Scottish marches, beloved as a cherished face. For ten years had she lived here. She'd fought to defend the place. Now, she tried to gather the strength she would need to leave.

Following the combat between Aleck and Danhal Thomson, they'd all returned here, arriving early the next morning. Aleck and Dexter, the bond between them nearly visible, rode side by side, Dexter chatting earnestly, and Aleck listening with new respect.

Aleck said no word to her, Bess. Neither did he look at her, save once at Thomson's camp site when he asked if she'd been hurt.

She'd known, then, her only remaining reason for returning to the keep lay with Dexter. She would speak her farewells to Anne and Callum, try to make a fair parting from Dexter also. But staring out into the beautiful afternoon, she did not know how.

Dexter did not need her anymore, not the way he had, once. Oh, he would always love her, she knew. And she would love him until the day she died. In all the ways that mattered, he was her son.

Yet he needed his father now, needed to grow the precious relationship that had been birthed between the two of them, one of liking and trust. Dexter needed the guidance of a man so he might, in turn, become the man he was meant to be. He'd shown his spirit back beside that camp fire. Bess needed to leave and let him get on with it.

Where would she go? Back to her father's house, of course. She sighed as pain blossomed in her breast. How to make a life without Dexter? How, without Aleck? She couldn't begin to imagine.

A soft sound behind her—the scrape of a boot on

stone—spun her away from the window. Aleck stood in the doorway of the chamber, just as if she'd conjured him into existence.

"I thought I'd find ye here," he said, and the breath caught in Bess's throat. "Your wee hidey-hole, is it?"

Giving in to irresistible temptation, Bess examined him from the thick, dark hair on his head, now well-ruffled and so like Dexter's—to the worn, hide boots. He wore his sword. A man like Aleck Maxwell always would.

She found it difficult to meet his eyes—that feral wolf's gaze—but forced herself to. She owed him that, at least.

"I'll be leaving," she told him in a voice that sounded strange to her own ears. "I want you to know that."

"Aye?" He tipped his head.

"Just as soon as I can find a way to say farewell to Dexter."

"I canna' think he'll like that much."

"He'll get used to it. He has you now. But before I go, there are things that must be said."

"Aye, so there are." He advanced several steps into the room.

Bess squared her shoulders. "I owe you an apology."

"D'ye say so?"

She nodded. "Mary Johnstone is dead. I was there, at her father's house, when she passed—in the same bed where Dexter was born. I was there that day, also. I took him—took him in my arms, at her bidding. To hide him from you."

In many ways, she'd never let go of Dexter since.

She never would, at least not in her heart.

"You must understand," she went on doggedly. "Mary said I needed to protect him from you, at all cost. That you'd forced her, raped her, and could not be permitted to get your hands on him, to poison him."

Aleck said nothing.

"I believed her. That is why I kept him from you. For his sake. I understand that does not make it right."

"Does it no'?"

Bess shook her head violently. "I am that sorry I didn't believe you when you told me the truth. I should have done. There was that between us that should have allowed me to believe you over Mary.

"She did tell me the truth before she died—how you met at her insistence, in secret. She would not admit it, lest her father might blame her. To my very heart, Aleck, I am sorry."

Still he said no word, though he advanced a few more steps into the room.

"My initial lie cost you nearly ten years with your son. My refusal to believe you, when you told me the truth, cost you still more precious days. I do not expect you to forgive me, but I hope you will forgive Callum. He acted only for Dexter's sake."

Aleck spoke at last. "MacFee's a good man, an honorable one. Indeed, I ha' just been speaking wi' him. He and Anne mean to wed. I can use a captain o' the guard here. They will stay on."

"Good. That is good. It is very generous of you to forgive him."

Aleck raised an eyebrow. "I am a font o' good qualities now, am I?"

"I would not go that far." He was a reiver to the

bone, and always would be. Bess faltered, then met his gaze once more. "Dare I hope you might find it in your heart to forgive me?"

He took another step. "'Twould be a lot to ask."

"It would."

"Ye lay in my arms, Bess Mowatt. Ye gave me your kisses, and trusted me to share your body as I would. Yet ye did no' trust the words that came from my lips."

To Bess's dismay, tears flooded her eyes. "I know."

"It might be said, ye did wha' ye did for Dexter's sake, just like Callum. And I can no' quarrel wi' that. I would, mysel', move heaven and earth to protect that lad."

"Aye."

"But I will no' be able to protect him going forward. I'll need to let him stand on his own two feet, mayhap mak' mistakes the way I did, when I became entangled wi' Mary Johnstone. Allow him tae be a man, wi' all the consequences."

"Aye. Though 'tis hard to think o' Dexter as a mistake."

Aleck's eyes glowed. "So it is. My point is, Bess, we mak' mistakes. As men and women, we pick ourselves up and go on from them."

Two tears rolled down Bess's face. "I made a terrible mistake when I failed to believe you over Mary. I knew who you were, by then. I'd touched you, tasted you…held you close to my heart."

He took a final step that brought him right up against her. He reached out and soothed away her tears, using the pads of his thumbs. "'Tis all about the heart, is it no'?"

Gazing into his eyes, Bess went breathless. Dared she hope?

He captured one of her hands and raised it to his lips in a gesture so beautiful, it made her tremble. "My heart, Bess Mowatt, belongs to ye. 'Tis the heart o' a reiver, and I am no' sure ye want to accept it. But whether ye will or whether ye will no', 'tis yours till the end o' time."

"Oh, Aleck! Oh, does this mean you can forgive me?"

"To be sure, lass. I love ye, and love forgives all things."

She melted into his arms, the one place she wanted to be. His strength enfolded and uplifted her, like a healing balm.

"Marry me," he whispered in her ear. "And then sleep wi' me ten thousand nights, on into the end o' our lives. Stay here wi' me and the lad. 'Tis what we both need."

"Aye. Aye," she vowed. Laughing and crying, she pressed her lips to his, knowing this man with the wild streak, which somehow made answer to her own, fulfilled her every need, and her every dream.

She broke their kiss only so she might gaze into his eyes and say, "Someone must look after you, Aleck Maxwell. You and that bold young reiver's cub."

A word about the author…

Multi-award-winning author Laura Strickland delights in time traveling to the past and searching out settings for her books, be they Historical Romance, Steampunk, or something in between. Her first Scottish Historical hero, *Devil Black*, battled his way onto the publishing scene in 2013, and the author has never looked back.

Nor has she tapped the limits of her imagination. Venturing beyond Historical and Contemporary Romance, she created a new world with her ground-breaking Buffalo Steampunk Adventure series set in her native city in Western New York.

Married and the parent of one grown daughter, Laura has also been privileged to mother a number of very special rescue dogs, and is intensely interested in animal welfare. These days while she's writing, you can always find her latest rescue, Lacy, nearby.

Her love of dogs and her lifelong interest in Celtic history, magic, and music are all reflected in her writing. Laura's mantra is Lore, Legend, Love, and she wouldn't have it any other way.

Thank you for purchasing
this publication of The Wild Rose Press, Inc.

For questions or more information
contact us at
info@thewildrosepress.com.

The Wild Rose Press, Inc.
www.thewildrosepress.com